A low rumble s

An earsplitting sou
penetrated the air. 'I
spitting gravel. Ston
shattering the windshield.

"What in—" Gage began, but before he could finish, another curtain of rocks fell on them.

"Rock slide!" Alex called out.

"Rock slide?" he echoed. "Nobody said anything about rock slides. I get claustrophobic!"

"Claustrophobic?" she asked. "You'll be lucky if you're not dead when this is over."

Dust and dirt lifted off the ground like a thick fog. Gage cast a hasty glance around the headrest, through the rear of the auto. There was blockage behind them, and he didn't know what lay ahead.

"I can't see," Alex said in a controlled voice.

From the edge of the dirt road to the valley below, it was almost straight down....

ABOUT THE AUTHOR

Laraine McDaniel has been inventing mysteries since childhood. So, in adulthood, it was no surprise that she found herself working for a county judge in a sagging old building that housed a sheriff's department. That job lasted eight years. Now, Laraine is making use of her experiences in her first Harlequin Intrigue novel, *Against All Hope*. The story takes place in Wickenburg, Arizona, where, in real life, the author resides with her family.

Against All Hope

Laraine McDaniel

Harlequin Books

TORONTO • NEW YORK • LONDON
AMSTERDAM • PARIS • SYDNEY • HAMBURG
STOCKHOLM • ATHENS • TOKYO • MILAN

For Rosemary Sneeringer,
who gave faith and support...
For John,
who gave love and labor...
For Deputy Sheriff Vern Marconnett,
who gave his life...

Harlequin Intrigue edition published August 1991

ISBN 0-373-22168-1

AGAINST ALL HOPE

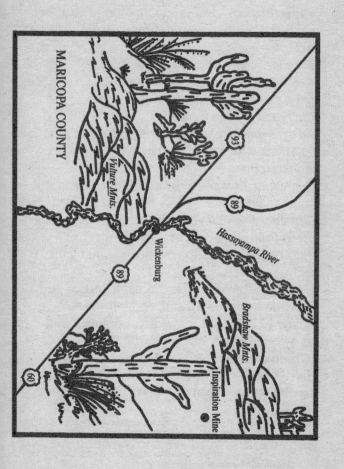

CAST OF CHARACTERS

Alexis Sinclair—Her determination to clear her murdered partner's reputation took a sinister turn.

Gage Morgan—The Internal Affairs investigator was convinced that Alexis's partner had a part in his own undoing.

Ken Forney—Did he die in the line of duty?

Sheriff Wainwright—The crime provided the candidate with a miracle that could help him win reelection.

Lieutenant Tucker—Why didn't the substation commander retire?

Skip Tucker—The young man had good reason not to follow in his father's footsteps.

Wes Davenport—A loner who worked by his own set of rules.

Marvin Dickerson—The mechanic turned police informant showed up at the oddest times.

Howard LaRue—The sheriff's opponent had his own reasons for helping with the investigation.

Hector Martinez—Had the townfolk looked, they might have seen that his main concern was his own ranch.

Skinner—Some thought he performed his gruesome tasks by rote, but everyone agreed that he missed nothing.

Digger—The desert dweller was crazy like a fox.

Chapter One

It was a little before ten in the morning when Alexis Sinclair arrived at the Maricopa County Sheriff's Department substation in Wickenburg. When she emerged from her Bronco, the Arizona heat closed around her like a blanket. With a stiff, almost military stride, Alex crossed the parking lot and headed toward the rear entrance of the substation. Sheriff Striker Wainwright was making her his honored guest at an eleven o'clock meeting. How lucky could a deputy get? A light-headed moment stayed her steps at the door and she tried to wrench self-confidence from some hidden inner place.

The knob yielded to the pressure of her unsteady hand. Inside, the substation's corridor was as still as death. She'd been off work for a few days. She wondered if she was ready to come back. A chill bloomed at the base of her spine. Alex paused and bit at her lower lip. The dread she felt was so huge, it threatened to engulf her. And she was already sick from her own inner struggle. She'd missed work and her partner was dead.

Worse—he was suspected of having had a part in his own undoing. There wasn't much information yet, but enough to create a great deal of speculation that perhaps Ken Forney's apparent neglect to exercise department procedure contributed to his demise. For Alex, that was the most frustrating aspect to emerge from the case. Alex herself refused to yield to such speculation. Her decision rested on a very fragile strand of evidence, Ken Forney's integrity. Nonetheless, the few clues had just brought more questions, not answers. Alex had lain awake at night juggling the components of the crime, but no pragmatic solutions were jumping out of the woodwork. She'd played the who-and-why game over and over until her head ached, and now her brain was overloading.

The scarce evidence taken from the crime scene had turned the murder into a mass of contradictions. Homicide scavengers had kicked dust and metal for evidence to no avail. What had emerged was a bizarre puzzle. No real clues. No suspects. No struggle. And this last twist wasn't helping matters one bit.

Alex leaned against the corridor wall, pressed her fingers to her temples, and rubbed absently in small, tight circles. She would survive Sheriff Wainwright's interview, just as she had the departmental meeting. The department's questions had mostly concerned Ken's character. Was he the kind of deputy who would pull onto an abandoned mine road for a snooze? *No*, she'd said. Would he have radioed a sighting of suspicious activity? *Of course.* Then why hadn't he maintained radio contact? *I don't know,* she'd said. What kind of partner was he? *Instinctive.* Then why hadn't he called for backup?

How they'd led up to that last question was tricky, Alex thought now. Still, she realized the purpose of the question. After all, her partner had spent at least forty-five minutes at the murder sight before the shooting. There had been plenty of time for him to call for backup. The logical solution was that Ken *had* been asleep. But why would anyone kill a sleeping deputy? she asked herself. There was no need to, unless the intruder had awakened Ken and then realized he had to eliminate an eyewitness. Eyewitness to what?

Behind Alex, the door creaked in protest as it swung open. The welcome diversion she'd hoped for was short lived. She listened to the familiar shuffle of boots, then she looked over her shoulder and shot Wes Davenport a withering glance. He was only momentarily wounded. As the lanky deputy came toward her, Alex found herself wishing that he would pick up his feet when he walked. His mouth was working a perpetual toothpick, and the intense Arizona sun exaggerated the freckles covering his face. A stray curl escaped the confines of his Stetson, his forehead was sweating, and his boots lacked spit and polish. Wes, Alex decided, had no equal in a setting like Wickenburg, one of the last Western towns for one of the last redneck cowboys.

"Alex?" Wes said with a note of urgency in his husky, West Texas drawl. "You okay?"

Alex continued to lean against the corridor wall. "Hello, Wes," she said. "I'm fine." Since Ken's murder, a low-key demeanor had replaced the typical good-ole-boy, down-home charm of Wes Davenport. He'd even managed to express the appropriate amount of shock and grief. But always self-serving, she knew eventually he would turn the loss to his advantage. "Thought you were on graveyard. You pulling a double shift?"

"Overtime," Wes said. He sucked in a gush of air and puffed with importance, as if he thought that everyone was envious of him. "Didn't you hear about the collars I bagged?"

Alex nodded. She had heard that he'd made some heavy arrests. It was about time. Wes had bagged his share of criminals, but never any big poachers. "I heard from the lieutenant that one's an illegal-alien guide," she said.

"I spotted him for a coyote right off. That fast." Wes snapped his fingers and smiled. "Can't smuggle undocumented aliens across the border, not while Wes Davenport's around," he continued.

Alex nodded, preferring not to comment on Wes's egotistic attitude. Considering he'd never cared about anybody besides himself, Alex had learned not to take Wes too seriously. She didn't take his ideas about Ken's shooter seriously, either. Wes had his own theory. But didn't everyone? The long-nurtured vengeance, reprisal from a felon, was every cop's worst nightmare. Maybe Wes was right. Maybe they should be checking out the obvious. "You've got a report to write," Alex finally said. "Don't let me keep you." She moved from where she'd been leaning against the wall and headed down the corridor.

"Wait a minute. I've been trying to call you." Wes's tone sounded too soft and parochial, yet persistent. "I figured you'd be needing someone. And I thought we might have dinner or something."

"This isn't a good time for me," Alex said, keeping her anger to herself. Did he really think that all it took to see her again was her partner's murder? Five years ago, they'd dated briefly when he'd moved to Wickenburg from Dallas. Then, as now, Wes had refused to view her as a professional. But he was always willing, in his condescending way, to allow her to prove herself as a deputy sheriff. He'd always camouflaged his protective attitude by putting walls around her. Claustrophobic walls. What Alex needed was space—space in which she could make her own mistakes. Wes wasn't a bad sort. Just insensitive. Still, Alex felt no real kinship with him.

"Now look, if you need anything, call me," Wes said. A smile wreathed his lean face as he sauntered ahead of her and down the hallway. "Day or night. Buck up. You'll get through this. I'll get back to you about dinner."

"Sure," she said, realizing it was pointless to protest. Wes had a propensity for pursuing unrealistic goals. It had been over between them a long time ago, and Alex didn't know how much longer her tolerance for his foolishness would endure. A sharp intake of breath steadied her. She straightened her shoulders and lifting one foot in front of the other, she moved down the corridor behind Wes while the gears in her brain continued grinding out thoughts of both Wes Davenport and her murdered partner.

Through a window, she could see that the crowded radio room hummed with tension. Three or four deputies in light brown shirts, with black-striped badges and black ties quietly lined the grimy walls. They watched the clock while they waited for their court appearances. At the far end of the corridor, closer to the courtroom, a churning mass filled the lobby.

Alex wasn't in the mood for any more light conversation. She slipped into a conference room for a cup of coffee. It looked stout. She filled a mug anyway and sucked down a sip. One powdery donut remained on the tray. Deciding that a sugar fix would go a long way today, Alex bit into it. A shower of white flakes dusted her shirt.

She plucked a newspaper from the conference table while she munched. The print jumped out at her, and she stared at the black letters until they started to squirm.

At 12:04 a.m. on Friday, August 9, Deputy Ken Forney was briefed for duty. At 12:17 a.m., he rolled out of the Wickenburg Sheriff's Department substation and drove north on U.S. Highway 89. At approximately twelve-forty-five, he made a radio transmission, his last. Four hours after the breaking of radio contact, authorities discovered his body in his patrol car in a remote area of the desert. The bizarre murder has experts working round the clock.

Alex slapped the newspaper back onto the conference table and crammed the last bit of donut into her mouth. Even though she knew the facts, the words still echoed in her mind and goose bumps erupted on her arms.

"Donuts any good?" The voice was deep and guileless.

The bite in Alex's mouth turned into a doughy glob. Her attention focused on the man who'd just entered the conference room. A benevolent smile reached all the way to his penetrating dark gray eyes. He was in his late thirties, lean and towering in height. He had to be law enforcement. He wore street clothes, but he had that look about him, like a cop.

"I hope you're not hungry," Alex managed to say after swallowing. "I just ate the last one." She caught the scrutiny in his gaze. He seemed to evaluate her according to some secret criteria. She gave him a long, steady look and summed him up as a detective. His detachment was a dead giveaway.

"Cup of coffee will do," he said, his dark eyes never leaving hers.

"Right over there," Alex said, pointing to the pot. "You're from the press?" she asked, tearing her gaze from his and hating her transparency.

"I'm Gage Morgan," he said. "Lieutenant Gage Morgan. From Internal Affairs." He extended his hand.

Alex paused, looked at his hand, then shook it. "Internal Affairs?" she repeated, relaxing her grip.

"That's right," he replied.

"I'm Alex Sinclair. Deputy Sinclair. And you'll have to excuse me. I'm expected at a meeting—"

"If you're smart, Deputy," he interrupted, "you'll take care of yourself in there. But you already know that, don't you? Just tell them to go to hell."

"And what do I tell you, Lieutenant Morgan?"

"Before this is over, you'll probably tell me the same thing."

GAGE WATCHED the attractive brunette disappear into the corridor. The moment Alex Sinclair had learned he was from Internal Affairs, her attitude had changed. The climate of cooperation had become strained. He blew out a breath and looked at the coffeepot. The coffee was too stout.

Gage felt nervous and stressed out for reasons he couldn't readily discern, and he needed a cigarette. He reached into his breast pocket. The cigarettes, of course, were gone, but the habit lingered. Maybe he just needed some fresh air. He headed down the corridor. When he reached a massive steel door, he pushed it open with all his might, letting the metallic thud reverberate through the old building.

Alex, he thought. She called herself Alex, not Alexis. Okay. This didn't have to be a big deal. He would simply walk back in there and schedule an appointment with her. But something told him this wasn't the time, that he should let her work through her problems in her own way right now. Nonetheless, the thought of Sheriff Wainwright confronting her made him feel compelled to rush back inside and...do what? She wasn't about to drop her defenses to an IA man. He was well acquainted with the stigma attached to Internal Affairs investigators.

Gage wondered about her relationship with Ken Forney. Had she been in love with him? He could understand why Forney might have fallen for her. Then Gage remembered that Forney had been married for some years. Well, Forney must have liked her. Gage knew even he was going to like her. He didn't know why, but he knew he was. Maybe because he'd traveled through the same private hell she was going through right now. Gage thought of his wife, Laura, then pushed the thought away. This time, it was his job to see that Alex relived the night of her partner's death all over again. It was his investigation. So what if he thought that Internal Affairs's procedure stank? His tolerance for death, despair and his job was wearing thin.

He wasn't buying the sheriff's explanation about a deputy sleeping on the job. The sheriff had made it increasingly clear that Ken Forney was under indictment for dereliction of duty. There was no doubt about it. Striker Wainwright considered the case a ringer, one without a motive. But then, he thought every case a moot subject. He was the kind of man who just seemed to want fast answers. Gage had his own set of criteria for what made a derelict cop. His idea about this thing ran along more sordid lines. He hadn't ruled out the possibility of a corrupt officer, jaded by organized crime and grabbing a little on the side. If the murder had been a revenge killing, good. Revenge was a motive Gage understood. On the other hand, the deputy might have been legitimate. Whatever the case, Gage was going to find out. His own investigative talent wasn't something he'd consciously nurtured. As much as he hated procedure, the work itself interested him, so it came easily. Too easily, he decided. At least most of the time.

In this particular investigation, Gage was missing something. What had gone so deadly wrong for Ken that he'd abandoned radio contact? That wrinkle disconcerted him. Ken Forney hadn't been the type to take chances. His twenty-year tenure of active duty vouched for that. True, not everyone could pull the graveyard shift without a hitch, but a veteran like Ken Forney could have pulled it off in a coma. Sleeping on the job? It was true that such a simple explanation took care of the persisting questions, but it was too easy.

The chances of proving a sighting theory hung as frail as a strand of a spider's web, too. If Ken had spotted something, what had transpired during the forty-five minutes between his radio contact and his slaying? Gage shrugged. He went back inside and strode down the hall toward Lieutenant Tucker's office. Perhaps, he'd sit in on the meeting with Alex Sinclair after all, rather than schedule an appointment with her for later. Far too much of his time had been lost due to the strange facts in this murder. Still, Gage wasn't going to start jumping to conclusions.

ALEX FINALLY KNEW what the sheriff was up to. Internal Affairs had a way of preventing the pluses from outweighing the minuses. The purpose for today's meeting with Striker Wainwright was to nail shut Ken Forney's coffin, and to do that, the sheriff needed an IA man. It was politically expedient for Striker Wainwright to wrap up this case and clear his office of any malfeasance. Apparently, Gage Morgan was here to lend Wainwright a helping hand.

With time to spare, Alex ventured down the hall toward Lieutenant Tucker's office. She'd always thought that the substation commander brought a complimentary air of dignity to the building that had stood there for more than a half century. The substation was as full of history, tradition and tacky old furniture as any of the old buildings along main-street Wickenburg.

Tucker had been the closest thing to a father she'd ever known. And while other sixteen-year-olds had been memorizing cheerleading calls, she'd been at the substation memorizing radio codes with Tuck. He had always been there when she needed him. She hoped nothing had changed today. The feeling that Ken wasn't the only one under suspicion was nagging at her. The sheriff had been forced to hire her due to affirmative action, and he'd been trying to justify his hostility ever since.

It still surprised Alex that Sheriff Wainwright would take time out of his reelection campaign to travel fifty miles to Wickenburg for a meeting with her. Aligning himself with political personages, shaking hands in heavyweight crowds, and kissing babies took priority these days. She knew his driving force was his outright determination to win the primary election, which was only a few weeks away. He clearly viewed himself as destined for the sheriff's position again.

Because of the sheriff's soft stance on poaching, his environmentalist opponent, Howard LaRue, had accused him of neglecting the issue and LaRue was capitalizing on it with exaggerated vehemence. Alex knew the sheriff was a man who suspected everyone and everything while his own purity of purpose remained questionable at best.

She paused short of Tucker's office, pressed her body to the wall and tried to relax. Loud, beefy laughter penetrated the hallway. The county building seemed to let out a groan, as if effort were required for it to stand upright on its sinking foundation. Alex closed her eyes and took a deep, unsteady breath. The tile floor smelled of pine cleaner.

Tense and alert now, she raised herself on tiptoe and looked through the window of Tucker's office door. She spotted the sheriff. He was seated at Tucker's desk. The phone receiver was pressed to his ear. He looked bright eyed, keen and decisive. He definitely had an ample share of intelligence and cunning. But it was her old friend, her mentor, Tucker, whom she sought out.

The reticent Lieutenant Tucker sat next to the window, unobtrusively pushing a pencil. He'd amused her more than once with his comic drawings. She knew that his sketching was something he reserved for tense situations. His square, puffy face bore kind lines, a testament to many years of dealing with problems, and what was left of his gray hair had been pushed back by one of his thick, firm hands. The increasingly grim mood Tucker exhibited these days was taking some getting used to. The usual hearty lieutenant appeared depressed, uncertain of what was going to happen and not very hopeful that much good was going to come. Clearly, this deeply worried man felt constrained by a great deal of pressure. Because Ken had worked for Tuck, Tuck's career hung in the balance, too.

GAGE STRODE INTO Lieutenant Tucker's office at eleven o'clock sharp. The moment he did, the sheriff waved, indicating that he could take a seat. Gage glanced over at Tuck, whose roundish eyes seemed hooded from the window's glare by his bushy eyebrows. Gage thought Tuck looked a little like a hawk. Aside from his thick, veal colored lips, the lieutenant's most arresting feature was the marks left behind by adolescent acne.

"Well, hello, Gage," said Tucker. He glanced at the sheriff as if seeking approval.

A submissive subordinate? Gage wondered. Maybe. It was more likely that Tucker was subtle, unwilling to make waves. Politics was the adhesive that bound the sheriff's department together. If Striker's opponent beached him in the primary, Tuck's head would be buried in the sand, too. This meeting would test his loyalty, not only to the sheriff, but to Alex. Gage sensed a gentleness about the lieutenant and he wondered if the man would cave in to the forces here today and side with Wainwright against Alex.

"I was wondering if you'd make it," the sheriff grumbled.

Slow to answer, Gage studied the sheriff. Tall and thin, he was all lines and angles. His beady black eyes gave him the appearance of an insect, Gage thought. And he had a drooping eyelid that twitched against the morning sunlight that streamed into the room. It made him look cynical.

"I decided to come after all, rather than just make an appointment with Alex, and you said eleven," Gage replied. He eased into a stiff, old vinyl chair. "Lead on, Sheriff."

"In a minute," Striker snapped. "In a minute." Then the sheriff leaned forward and opened his attaché case. He scanned the topmost file, pulled it out, then closed the case and spun the combination lock securing it.

While the sheriff studied the file, Gage surveyed Lieutenant Tucker's office. It was small and crowded with trophies, stacks of books, furniture and Alex. She was still standing, her attention fixed on the sheriff. Gage imagined that she was fragile and broken from the loss of her partner. That observation caused an uncomfortable ache inside him. In his gut. Where memories came in pangs instead of images. He shuddered. Grief over his wife's death had made an ordeal of the simplest things in life. Because of that Alex's pain was real to him. It was like déjà vu, and it tugged on tender scars.

The air between Alex and the sheriff was so emotion filled that it seemed to hang between them like a veil. There was one sure thing about a meeting with Striker Wainwright: there were no surprises. This was Ken Forney's wake, and everyone knew what the outcome was going to be. Gage drummed his fingers on the arm of his chair and waited.

The sheriff placed the file aside and rocked back in Tucker's desk chair. He began his attack obliquely and cleverly. "We're concerned about you, young lady," he said.

"Please, don't call me 'young lady,'" Alex said in clipped tones. "I'm a deputy sheriff."

He had figured Alex wrong, Gage decided. She definitely exposed a more aggressive side when she stood up to the sheriff. Gage's wife, too, had been willful and filled with resolve. He still admired that innate strength.

The sheriff eyed Alex with a succinct expression.

Alex's face flushed, but she returned the stare without flinching. She tossed her thick, dark hair from her shoulder in a gesture of defiance.

"I realize what you're going through," the sheriff drawled with distinct mockery.

Gage knew what he was getting at. Some part of Alex appeared to know, too. The sheriff meant to imply that Alex was incompetent, but he said it incompletely, as if there were another meaning that rode tandem with it. Gage watched Alex stiffen as her temper rose in response.

"Why did you want to see me?" Alex asked in a tone that demanded he get to the point.

The sheriff maintained his usual demeanor, but dropped his gratuitous concern. "I'm forced to ask you to relive the night of Ken Forney's murder and, with that, all the pain you experienced," he said. "I know how hard this is for you."

"I'm a five-year veteran of law enforcement," Alex said. "I can handle it. Ask me whatever you like," she assured him. "I'll be glad to answer your questions."

Was Alex's show of courage just a brave facade? Gage removed a small tape recorder from his brief case and pressed the On switch. Alex clearly conveyed keen intelligence and driving energy. There was no naïveté on her part. Alexis Sinclair was a professional. Still, Gage hoped she was prepared for the pounding the sheriff was about to give her.

"Odd coincidence, isn't it," the sheriff began, his voice inappropriately cheery, "that you miss your first day of work in three years and your partner rolls out solo to his own murder?"

Wainwright's sarcasm was uncalled for. And Gage sensed that Alex had not been prepared for the remark the sheriff had just let loose on her. Why didn't he hit *Tucker* with that A-bomb? Was it really necessary to be so blunt with Alex herself?

"That it might be a coincidence has crossed my mind," Alex replied.

"There's something fishy about it," the sheriff continued, shaking his head with real disgust. "I'm glad you see that for yourself."

One of the many questions in the investigation had been why Ken Forney had rolled out solo on the night he was murdered. The final responsibility for answering it rested squarely upon the sheriff's shoulders. And it was eating him up. Gage wondered why Tucker hadn't assigned another deputy to ride with Forney.

"I'd say Ken was probably the best law-enforcement officer in this precinct," Alex said. When the sheriff made a sound indicating he was bored, Alex went for the kill. "I didn't have a *motive* to murder my partner," she said. She spoke with deceptive calm, but seemed perched and ready to jump on Striker like a vulture on a corpse.

"I hope you're joking," the sheriff retorted. "You act as if I'm directly implicating you in his death."

"I wouldn't joke about murder," Alex answered quietly.

The sheriff's eyes narrowed. His face flushed. He was struggling not to raise his voice. "The media is harping on the fact that Ken was riding alone that night," he said. "I want you to stay clear of the reporters. Keep a low profile."

Gage could tell that the sheriff couldn't come to terms with this investigation. He'd expected Wainwright to question Alex more fully. What was he thinking? That the murder would just go away, or recede from the ranks of importance, if he kept Alex away from the clutches of the media?

"It was Ken's suggestion that I take the night off," Alex said in her own defense.

Gage listened. That was his job, to hang on every word in a desperate search for clues. Her remark made no visible impression on the sheriff.

"No one would have believed he could have been murdered that night," Alex said. She paused for a moment. "Aren't you overlooking the fact that I had a plausible excuse for my absence?"

"You follow your conscience concerning that and I'll follow mine," the sheriff replied. His voice was carefully colored in neutral shades.

"I was sick," Alex said in clipped tones.

"We all do what we have to do. We'll leave it at that." His tone was dismissive. "You look beat. This is going to be a long investigation, and it won't be pleasant. Until it's over, I want you to hang around the office and try to relax."

Long investigation? Gage thought the remark odd. He knew every crime that didn't result in arrest in the first forty-eight hours usually went unsolved. Well, he didn't understand Wainwright's remark, but there was a lot he didn't understand. For one thing, he had expected Lieutenant Tucker to defend Alex. This was home ground, but other forces were apparently at work.

"Hang around the office?" she echoed. "I don't come to work to relax."

Alex glanced at Tucker, as if for a sign of objection. The lieutenant sat mute. Gage knew that Tuck was only two years shy of retirement. Perhaps that was why he was play-ing it safe. Alex stood vulnerable, helpless and orphaned. Gage felt equally helpless. There wasn't a damn thing he could do to help her.

"You're stressed out, Sinclair," the sheriff continued, giving her one of his inscrutable smiles. "Your condition could make you too tolerant to do your job."

"Tolerance doesn't necessarily mean an absence of stan-dards," Tucker protested finally, giving vent to his resent-ment.

"I beg to differ on that," the sheriff said. He shrugged. "You can take me to task for being the cynic." His florid, self-satisfied face mocked Alex. "You're the expert, Gage. What do you think about Deputy Sinclair's condition? We don't want her ending up like the deceased."

Deceased. Gage watched Alex cringe. He slapped his hand to his breast pocket. Damn habit. He was developing a real distaste for the sheriff. And just being in a room with someone he disliked gave him claustrophobia.

"The woman is a deputy sheriff," Gage said in a coolly disapproving tone. "And I don't work this way." His con-cern for Alex surprised even himself. "I didn't come here to be a spy waiting for the slightest glimpse of impropriety. Besides, any evaluation of Alex's performance is Lieuten-ant Tucker's responsibility."

Alex's face flushed from the rush of fury that heated it. Gage watched her embrace her anger, knowing she could only watch and listen. If the exchange had challenged her control, she was still masking her inner turmoil with a de-ceptive calm. The overcompensating—he recognized it well. He, too, was guilty of it. Alexis Sinclair deserved an Oscar for her performance this morning, he thought.

"All right, all right," the sheriff capitulated. He picked up a cigar and lit it. The finest smoke Cuba could offer spread through his fingers, and the cigar's end glistened a slick black color from his saliva. He tilted his head to one side. "I'll spell it out for you, Sinclair."

A speller, Gage thought. The only thing worse was a repeater.

"When the furor over Forney's death abates a bit, things will fall back in place and you can resume your normal routine in the field. Understand?"

Alex glanced at Tucker, but Tucker only nodded as if in agreement with the sheriff. "When hell freezes over," she muttered.

"What?" the sheriff asked.

"Perfectly," she said. "I understand perfectly."

"Glad we had this little chat." The sheriff turned his attention to Lieutenant Tucker. "The vultures need something solid to sink their teeth into. What kind of leads do you have, Tuck?"

"Short of a clairvoyant, we're grasping at straws. I've never seen a case this clean, but we're turning every stone. My hope is to bag enough evidence to make a comfortable guess."

"Just illuminate me with a motive."

"I need time," Tucker insisted.

"Forney's unexplained radio silence might carry sufficient weight to close the case," the sheriff said. He settled back in Tucker's swivel chair and laced his hands across his chest.

"It's not unheard of for a rookie on a graveyard shift to get sleepy," Tucker retaliated, "but Ken Forney was a seasoned officer, and a damn good one."

"Anybody can get sleepy," the sheriff insisted as he rose.

Gage felt even more frustrated. At last, the bitter little notion in Wainwright's brain had found expression. The sheriff continued, "How else would you explain a seasoned deputy losing his life at the wrong end of a gun? That nap cost Ken Forney his life.'' Smiling as he always did when dealing with something others found unpleasant, he closed the distance to the office door.

''Where were you when Ken was murdered?'' Alex called after him, but the sheriff was already gone.

Chapter Two

Outside, triple-digit temperatures registered real heat. The wind kicked up and plastered Alex's shoulder-length hair to her head. Fortunately, their leave-taking was mercifully brief. Gage had disappeared into the records room. The Internal Affairs investigator's distaste for the sheriff was significant, Alex decided. But she wasn't going to be stupid about his attentiveness toward her. There was a big *but* sliding around in what he hadn't said. After all, he was here to investigate the circumstances of Ken's death. And that included the fact that Ken had been riding solo.

She dug inside her purse for a snack. Nothing. Not even a piece of gum. She'd neglected to replenish her munchie supply last night. And the effects of the donut had worn off. Her stomach growled as she walked toward her Bronco.

"Alex!" Tucker called out, signaling for her to wait for him.

She stopped and slowly turned. She sucked in air and held it for a moment before blowing it out in a steady rush. Tucker caught her by the elbow abruptly and firmly escorted her to her Bronco.

"I can't believe what happened in there," she said. "What's going on?"

The scenario was the same as it had been since she was sixteen: she and Tucker, one on one, whenever her world turned upside down. But the rock of a man she was used to only shrugged helplessly now. She couldn't miss it. The hint of uncertainty was there—in Tuck.

"Alex, listen," he said insistently. "I do understand how you feel."

"Good. Then we're in agreement about the sheriff's attitude?" she said sarcastically. "The last thing I need now is to be put on desk duty. And whether that happens or not is really up to you."

"You've got to understand his position."

"Not you, too! If you're going to give me a sanctimonious sermon about him—save it."

"I don't have to be sanctimonious about this. It's what I believe."

"So I gather." Alex couldn't help feeling that Tucker had let her down during the meeting. "You actually think you're defending a champion. You actually think the sheriff's right. Why don't you pull off those blinders he has you wearing?"

"Forgive me, Alex, but you're the one who walked into that meeting with blinders on."

She refused to be dissuaded. "I've been tagged for quarantine like a sick dog."

Tucker's face gathered intensity. "You're not sick, damn it, and that's not the issue here."

"What is, then?" Alex asked.

"Fear."

"Fear?" Even as she said it, Alex knew that she was afraid. She hadn't stopped shaking since the news of Ken's death. Her mind backtracked to the morning of the murder. She'd bolted from the patrol car Tucker was driving as they rolled out of the parking lot to the murder scene. And she still hadn't been able to visit the place where Ken had been slain. "Are you labeling me a coward?"

"A scared deputy is a coward, and a coward is no good to anyone. But fear is a normal reaction to this sort of trauma. It doesn't label you a coward. Hell, fear isn't bad. It makes you careful because it makes you think."

"I have to go back out." Deep down, Alex wasn't at all sure she could pull it off. But she had to try for Ken's sake. "Ken deserves better than what he's getting."

"Alex, let go. Nothing will bring Ken back. Let the experts handle the investigation. They'll turn up something," Tuck insisted.

"I can't let go. We're missing something, Tuck. I feel it."

"Ken was human. And you've got to accept that. Alex, he didn't suffer, not nearly as much as you are."

She wanted to scream. Instead, she made a face. "I'm suffering more than Ken? We're talking about his flesh and blood here."

"Has it occurred to you that for all your suspicions, you're ignoring the obvious?"

Her mind sprinted around, but for the moment, the connection Tuck was making eluded her. "The obvious?"

"The killer pulled off the perfect crime and, here's the rub—he did it by accident. Ken wasn't a hit. His was a random murder. But a murder nonetheless. I think it was an unplanned encounter."

Alex knew no one could touch Tucker when it came to analyzing a crime scene, but she wasn't sure Ken's death was a random murder. "Maybe you're right," she said with quiet but desperate firmness. She could at least consider Tucker's theory. An even more terrifying realization washed over her. With a sense of conviction she said, "In that case, the killer may be the only one who can exonerate Ken."

"That road is on a safe track off of U.S. 89. It could have been anyone traveling on it. And bingo, we have our motive. A fugitive on the run."

"A fugitive on the run?"

Tuck nodded. "Maybe."

A big maybe, Alex thought. Still, that would validate her theory that Ken had pulled off the highway because he'd spotted something unusual. "Isn't it a little more complicated?" she asked. "What happened to the perfect crime?"

"Thirty years on the force has taught me one thing. There are no simple answers. You never learn as much as you want to. Even Ken couldn't have told you all the answers. If he could have, there probably wouldn't have been a murder. Accept it, Alex. You'll feel better."

"I'm fine," she lied. Alex was anything but fine. Eventually, she would have to deal more fully with the pain and hurt of Ken's death. But not now. "Will you give me a chance, Tuck?" she asked. "I'm not sick. I'm ready to come back to work, on active duty. It's the only way I can test my courage. Please. If it doesn't work, then put me on a desk."

Tucker pointed his finger at her. "Okay, but I want your word—no interference in this investigation. Report for duty tomorrow morning."

Tuck's capitulation came too easily and for a moment, the suddenness of it caught Alex off guard. Was she being paranoid? How else could she rationalize this unfounded suspicion she felt toward her old friend? "Thanks," she said, knowing she could make up her mind later about whether or not to participate in the investigation against Tuck's wishes.

"Oh! I forgot. This is for you," Tucker said, reaching into his pocket. He handed her a piece of sketch paper.

She unfolded the sheet. In spite of herself, she chuckled. The drawing was of Sheriff Wainwright. He was praying-

mantis thin, with a bulging forehead and beady eyes. And
it was just like the old Tuck she knew and loved. Parody was
his speciality.

"Thanks," she said. "I think I'll keep it."

"Hey, you," Tucker called out as she walked away.

"Yeah?"

"Sometimes you have to bend so you don't break."

GAGE PUSHED THE KEY into the lock of his room at the
Rancho Grande Hotel and stepped inside. *Damn,* he
thought, as he closed the door behind him and locked it. He
sank onto the sofa and leaned back, frowning, searching for
answers. But there were more questions than answers. This
job was getting to him. This case was getting to him. It was
forcing him to confront old ghosts. His ghosts.

The image of Alex's serene face formed in his mind. He
should have talked to her after the meeting. But at a time
like that, how could he have told her that he was beginning
to suspect her partner of gross negligence? That would have
shattered her. Why did he feel so protective of her? There
was a certain irony in it. First, because he was here, in part
to investigate her. Not that he really believed she had anything to do with Forney's death, no more than Sheriff
Wainwright really believed it. And second, because he
wasn't much of a protector. He'd failed in that duty to his
wife. Alex's denial was obvious. Death wasn't an easy thing
for anyone to accept. Murder, worse. Maybe it wasn't just
denial that allowed Alex to be so strong now. She really believed in Forney with esteem and soul-deep admiration.
Gage respected that kind of strength, which came from be-
lieving in somebody.

Before putting his briefcase aside, he opened it and removed the pathology report. Wearily, Gage stretched out on
the couch and massaged his temples. Why couldn't there

have been a better reason for all this? Things were stacking up against the dead officer. For Alex's sake, Gage hoped he could turn up some other conclusion besides the dismal one that emerged each time he read the reports.

Gage could still see Alex clearly in his mind, her violet eyes, dark and troubled. He had a gut feeling about her. She seemed genuine. So far, all her answers had been spontaneous, and they matched what he already knew. He returned to the dreary coroner's report. He wasn't grabbing something. And it had to do with the position of the body as it was found in the patrol car. Had the force of the gunshot laid the deputy down on the car seat?

He kept trying to figure out how one of the most massive criminal investigations in the state of Arizona could have so few clues. The unlikeliness of a chance meeting on a deserted road between Forney and his shooter nagged Gage constantly. It made him think that the deputy had been drawn to the desolate area by something he'd seen. That theory didn't get Ken off the hook, but it narrowed things down. Still, why hadn't he called for backup? That judgment error had been his only crime, but it had cost him his life. Again, Gage considered the possibility that Forney had been corrupt and on the take. That might help explain the connection between the forty-five-minute radio silence and Forney's murder.

Gage replaced the preliminary pathology report and pulled out the deputy's personnel file. It was so clean, it squeaked. Gage read unenthusiastically for a while, then slapped the folder shut and tapped it against the palm of his hand. The file could have belonged to Snow White. There were no fast tracks to a solution, but he felt certain the deputy hadn't been involved in anything. So forget the organized crime theory, Gage thought. Forney's record painted a picture of an ideal man who was churchgoing, community involved, and who had a commitment to his job more genuine than Gage had at first realized. No. Ken Forney must have spotted something that night.

Like it or not, Gage might be forced to wind up this investigation on the basis of what he thought, without facts. That his reports sometimes necessarily included conjecture, was something that didn't sit well with him. He prided himself on handling each case the same way and in the most ethical fashion he knew. Gage subscribed to the idea that the truth reserved a place in his report, and nothing more. But so far, he'd found no truths, no facts. None at all.

ALEX EMERGED FROM HER Bronco and lifted her sunglasses. As difficult as it was, she knew she had to take a look at the murder scene. And, after that, she would visit the morgue. The bright sun gave the desolate area a bleached out appearance. She'd driven the hairpin road up Yarnell Hill to gain an aerial view.

She was wrenched by conflicting emotions—she felt grief from her loss, resentment because an Internal Affairs investigator had been sent by the sheriff to implicate her partner in his own undoing, guilt because she hadn't been with Ken, and protectiveness, too. She refused to sit by and see Ken's integrity buried with him. Tucker might not want her on the case, but what Tucker didn't know wouldn't hurt him.

"They haven't even scratched the surface yet," she mumbled to herself, frustrated with the lack of clues and dissatisfied with the investigative follow-up. The silent litany that had been playing over and over in the deepest recesses of her mind started again: *Find the shooter.* Up to now, Ken had been the focal point of the investigation. If he continued to be, the shooter would never be found.

The way Alex saw it, there was no common ground to be shared between her and the Internal Affairs investigator. And if Gage Morgan thought she was going to make his dirty work any easier, he was wrong. Dead wrong. He didn't have to defend her during the meeting with Tuck and Wainwright. Why had he? He was the natural enemy, so why wasn't he acting like it? And why did he have to be so handsome? He wasn't the kind of man that women would put off. Before this grizzly investigation was over with, she'd have to deal with Gage Morgan. Not because he was handsome, but because she intended to clear Ken's name.

Wickenburg lay in the distance, nestled in foothills that protruded from the desert floor below Alex. The northernmost part of Maricopa County was the perfect setting for the perfect crime. But there was no point in going over the possible scenarios of the brutal murder again. Real, tangible evidence was all that mattered.

From the top of Yarnell Hill, Alex studied the desert floor and thought about what had happened there. Ken wouldn't have surrendered his gun to an unarmed perp. And the gun was missing. Where was it? Had it been discarded in the desert? Was it out there right now? Alex made a mental note. When she returned to town, she would buy a metal detector and begin to search.

What had drawn Ken out here? she wondered. Something didn't ring true. Why would he have taken the Inspiration Mine turnoff? The gold mine had been abandoned as a commercial operation years before. The snaking, macadamized road that led to it amounted to little more than a cow trail. The road skirted a mountain of rock and eventually disappeared into the foothills. The occasional car that drove over it left behind displaced rocks and little else. Never any discernible tire tracks. The marks near the crime scenes were almost unrecognizable, as if they'd been erased by rain. But not a drop of precipitation had fallen since the slaying. Perhaps the shooter had swept the tracks, or perhaps the desert wind had covered them. In either case, tire tracks weren't going to be of any help to her. Besides, other vague traces of tracks crossed the desert now, and they belonged to law-enforcement officers' vehicles. Alex's head felt squeezed, and it hurt.

Five minutes later, she was edging warily down the side of the Yarnell Hill for a closer look. She gazed at the ribboned off spectacle of the murder scene. Where the hell was Digger while all this was happening? It had never occurred to her that he might have killed Ken, but he could have seen something. When he wasn't at Inspiration Mine, the old desert rat was prowling the sand dunes, scavenging food and anything else he could get his hands on. Oh, he was harmless enough, but her partner had often threatened to take the old miner in for poaching. Finding him had been the problem. It still was.

Right now, she was grasping for straws, and it was far too hot for standing around on this mountain. There was no shelter from the beating sun here. Alex stepped back off a rock ledge and onto a crude trail. She moved upward again, each fluid stride taking her toward the top of Yarnell Hill and her Bronco.

Out of the corner of her eye, Alex saw a moving shadow. She quickly whirled around. Not a stray soul in sight. A little shiver ran down her spine. In confusion, she listened for another movement. The Bronco was still about ten yards away. She suddenly realized she was doing something very foolhardy and dangerous. But then, what else was new? Alex had always possessed an intense interest in anything new and foreign to her experience.

It was just nerves, she thought. She still couldn't shake the vaguely anxious feelings she'd been having ever since Ken's murder. Today, she'd had the oddest feeling that she was being followed. It was crazy. It made no sense. She was supposed to be okay now. Back on track.

A bullet cut through the silence around her. It cracked into a saguaro cactus a few inches from where she stood. She dropped to the ground, crawling between prickly pears and dear horn cactus, a sob breaking from her throat. A second shot whizzed past her head. It twanged off a rock and ricocheted into the dirt. She froze for a moment like a cornered rabbit. Forcing down her panic, she moved into a crouch and drew her weapon. She was damned if she was going to just hang around and wait for a fatal bullet to hit her.

"Alex?" Skip Tucker, the lieutenant's eighteen-year-old son, called to her from a grove of saguaros near the road. The tall figure headed toward her. Dressed for the weather, he wore a T-shirt and shorts. Though still young, Skip was a big man like his dad. He was six-foot-four or five and broad across. A full head of curly red hair framed his freckled face.

Alex felt a flash of relief. Trembling, she holstered her gun. Utterly relieved to see Skip, she continued moving up the hill toward him. His enormous hands dangled at his sides. The index finger was conspicuously missing from his right hand due to a shooting accident.

Alex's shock yielded quickly to fury. She looked at Skip and shook her head in disgust. "You nearly blew my head off," she growled through clenched teeth. "What's going on around here?" It was hot and she could feel the perspiration running down her back. She reached the top of the hill and confronted Skip.

"I—I'm sorry, Alex," Skip said, predictably paling. "We thought we saw a mountain lion and stopped to squeeze off a shot."

"We?" Her mind beginning to clear, Alex shuddered.

"Hey, Alex," another deep masculine voice called out. "You okay?"

Her eyes shot open wide with surprise. "Marvin! Who's running the garage? Is there a mechanic on duty?" If cleanliness was next to godliness, this greasy mechanic was not destined for heaven. Marvin's thick lips were moist, and his eyes held a wild glint.

"I jumped ship," he answered. One corner of his mouth pulled into a slight smile. "Don't worry, I checked in with the lieutenant before I took off."

"Did the parts come in for the roadrunner?" Alex asked, referring to the department's off-road vehicle.

"I drove down to Phoenix and picked them up. The lieutenant has the Blazer back at the substation," Marvin answered.

"None too soon," Alex said.

"The deputies have been making a road map out there," Marvin said, looking down at the desert floor where the barely discernible tire tracks snaked in all directions. "Want to hear the payoff? Wes snared an illegal-alien guide and, believe it or not, the wily coyote was clean. Anything new in the investigation?"

Practice had taught Alex discretion, and she chose to ignore his question. Three law-enforcement agencies shared the substation building. Everybody knew Marvin because he'd been around for a while as a police informant. He'd opened his garage hoping to get the vehicles from all three agencies in Wickenburg. He'd done well for himself.

"We'll have to finish this conversation later," she said, dismissing any more talk of the alien guide. "But, speaking of the law, you know you're supposed to be a quarter mile off the road before you can discharge a gun."

"I guess instinct took over..." Skip said.

"You still haven't told me what you're doing up here," Alex said.

"We're on our way to scout our deer area," Skip answered.

"When the season's almost two months off?" Alex asked.

"We put in for the early bow hunt."

"Bow and arrow?"

"Uh-huh."

"Be careful with your firearms," Alex cautioned.

"You sound like Dad," Skip said in a grudging voice.

"Does Tuck know what you're doing?" Alex asked.

Skip swallowed hard, trying to manage a feeble answer. "Uh . . . well . . . no." He hesitated, measuring her for a moment.

"And you probably programmed all the computers at school to account for your absence," she said. "Right, computer whiz kid?"

"You're not going to tell Dad about this, are you?" Skip asked, regarding her quizzically.

"No, I'm not, but no more target shooting." Her voice rang with command. "And no more cutting school."

Skip stared bleakly at her. "Okay," he said finally, giving in. He gave Alex a rueful look. "But I'm not too happy about it."

"I'm not too happy about almost being killed."

Skip's sober expression was almost pained. "Sorry," he mumbled. "I was talking about cutting school."

"You haven't told us what you're doing here," Marvin said suddenly.

Alex sighed. "Just sorting things out . . . and I've got to go. I want your promise you'll be careful. I'll be watching you," Alex said with a quiet emphasis.

Skip cocked his head. His gaze was hard, hostile, his whole manner changed. "I can't believe you're actually keeping tabs on me," he said incredulously. "I'm eighteen years old. I can take care of myself."

Alex glanced at him and scowled teasingly. "Good, but I'll still be watching every step you take. But just in case you step out of line, so don't get paranoid."

"Gee whiz," Skip said. "We gotta get going."

Alex simply nodded. She watched the two walk away, their feet breaking brush as they went. In spite of the intense heat, she shivered.

After a moment, she walked the short distance to her Bronco, unlocked the door, and slid into the driver's seat. The murder scene had distracted her and she had been completely unprepared for the wild imbroglio with Lieutenant Tucker's son. Skip was a good kid, with all the usual energy of an eighteen-year-old. Still, she had an uneasy feeling about his appearance at this site, and about the close call.

Shrugging her unease off as melodrama, Alex sped along, her eyes frequently shifting to her rearview mirror. The narrow road hurtled toward the desert basin below. She proceeded to accelerate through a series of hair-raising turns. After reaching the bottom of the mountain, the rollercoaster ride finally settled down to a calmer cruise.

Alexis Sinclair made a sudden decision, which wasn't unusual. All of her best decisions were made quickly. Going it alone would be too dangerous, but she could work out the logistics later. If Digger wouldn't come to her, she would go to him. Unless he was sharing a rock with a rattlesnake, Digger would be at Inspiration Mine.

Chapter Three

The morgue was small and private, with just one entrance. Catching her breath, Alex opened the door and went in to the foyer. She saw Gage immediately. A moment of startled silence passed between them. She looked around and saw that no one else seemed to be here with him. He was alone. Tentatively, she moved toward him. She had his full attention. His eyes meshed with hers across the sterile space. Their dark gray depths seemed filled with questioning, wanting and loneliness. A gentle smile creased his face.

"What are you doing here?" she asked him, even though she knew she should have expected his presence. *No interference in this investigation.* Tucker's words were stinging in her mind.

"I was going to ask you the same question," Gage countered.

Alex hesitated, then decided to just play this one out. Simple question. Simple answer. Alex perked up. Suddenly she was a cop again. "Sorting out facts," she answered casually.

"Starting with the pathology report?"

"Yes . . ." She hesitated. "That's right. I wanted to see if Skinner could add anything new."

"Funny, I had the same thing in mind," Gage said. He studied her for a moment. "I need a favor, Alex . . . Is it all right to call you Alex?"

"Alex is fine," she answered, refusing to be distracted by his good looks and expressive eyes. "What sort of favor?"

His lighthearted manner disappeared. "You knew Ken Forney better than anyone besides his wife. I need to know what was going on with him right up until the moment he died. Can you help me?"

Was this man crazy? "But the sheriff doesn't want me on the case."

"You don't have to be afraid of me," Gage said, trying to put her at ease.

"Afraid? Hardly. But I know the cardinal rule for a good cop—know your enemy."

"What makes you so sure we're enemies?"

"You work for Internal Affairs. That puts us on a collision course."

"The obstacles could be avoided," he said. "Look, I'm convinced that there's more to this than either Tucker or Wainwright suggest. We both represent the law, so how about it? Will you grant me the favor? I could use you in my corner."

"I appreciate what you did back there with the sheriff, but—"

"I know what you're going through," Gage said, interrupting.

"Then you'll understand that I want to be alone."

"My investigation involves a murder. I'm going to be around for a while."

Alex wondered if he was baiting her. He was obviously a bold man, a clever man, a man of extraordinary force. But he was also from Internal Affairs, and she had to figure that he would come up with a real surprise. She knew she shouldn't trust him.

"Think of me as the enemy if you have to, if it makes you handle your own grief better. But I think you could use a friend right now, and as I said, I could use you in my corner." He studied her thoughtfully.

His straightforwardness was disarming. Alex scolded herself. Maybe she *could* trust him, after all. If for no other reason, she should cooperate with Gage Morgan to get to the bottom of Ken's murder.

"You're right," she said, relenting. A look of sadness stole across her face.

"You miss him a lot, don't you?" Gage asked.

"He was a good friend and a good deputy." Alex pulled in a deep breath and looked Gage directly in the eye.

He stared at her for a moment, then looked down at the white knuckles of her clenched fist. "You're trembling."

"It's the uncertainty, the not knowing what went wrong that's driving me crazy." Alex felt her lungs constricting. What if she wasn't able to overcome her fear of active duty again? Common sense told her not to address this subject with total frankness with an Internal Affairs official, but she couldn't stop herself. "And . . . I'm having a little trouble getting my confidence back."

"There's help, you know."

"If you mean the department psychologist, forget it. I don't need therapy."

"You'd feel better if you talked," Gage persisted.

She crossed her arms over her chest defensively. "When I know what I want to say, I will. Right now, I can work this through on my own." She tried to tell herself that Gage Morgan wanted to help her. He wasn't like the sheriff. But she couldn't stop the instinctive recoiling to protect herself.

"Can you?" he said, refusing to drop the subject.

"I appreciate your concern, but it's the investigation that needs help, not me. Shall we get started?"

"Then you'll help me?" he asked.

"My partner always said that we have all the laws we need to put the criminals away, but that too few bureaucrats are willing to put their necks on the line to enforce them." Alex's wide mouth was firmly set. "So how can I help you, Lieutenant?"

"All right, we've got theories, but theories amount to no more than speculation. First, we have to examine the facts. Given the nature of this investigation, there's a likelihood that I'll wander into jurisdictional gray areas regarding departmental rules and regulations. But sometimes you have to put your neck on the line." Gage swallowed hard. "Are you up to helping me?"

Alex thought for a moment, then crossed the foyer and buzzed for someone to unlock the inner door. "I want answers, too."

SKINNER'S FACE EXPRESSED a great deal of confidence. Rumor had it he liked his work. That made him good. Still, Alex had always considered him a butcher because of the rumors she had heard. Now, she thought that the short, squat man seemed too eager. Even though his work was necessary, Alex felt somewhat repulsed.

Skinner crooked his finger and by tacit consent, Alex and Gage followed him down an antiseptic corridor of the morgue. Alex willed a strange calm over her senses when they entered a familiar glass-enclosed room. She had been here once before. The same old steel desk still rested in one corner. For the first time since Ken's death, she felt a furious anger rising in her, a cold hatred for her partner's murderer. Death had a certain smell, and it hung heavy in the room. Her throat seemed to close up. A raw and primitive grief overwhelmed her. Tears threatened to fall down her cheeks.

"You all right?" Gage was speaking to her.

The soft sound of his voice released her. She felt able to move and speak again. She crossed her arms tightly in front of herself before looking into Gage's face. It was a strong face. From it, Alex could tell that he had a capacity for great compassion. "Yes," she said, giving him a reassuring nod. Releasing her arms, she rubbed her damp eyes, then clamped her hands together. They felt damp, too. She shivered from the chill in the room.

"You cold?" he asked. Gage swung his arm around her and laid his jacket across her shoulders. Her mind told her to resist, but her body refused. Both Gage's concern and the warmth of his jacket felt good. She'd known there was something special about Gage from the beginning.

"I still can't believe it. I can't accept the fact that he's dead. And, I've got to know why before I can put it behind me." More desperately than ever, Alex wanted to put all the pieces together.

"That's why we're here," Gage said. "To find out why."

Alex turned her head toward Gage. A troubled expression drew his lean, rugged features downward.

"Why?" Skinner echoed. "A .38 slug was crowding his brains." Skinner's voice held a rasp of excitement. "Specifically in the left parietal bone of the victim's cranium. Powder burns indicated the bullet was fired from extremely close range. But the body was clean otherwise. No contusions, no lacerations. Obviously, no struggle."

A soft gasp escaped Alex. Skinner's enthusiastic manner irked her. But she was resentful of the entire situation. She could almost hear the shot ringing out as the medical examiner spoke. The roaring in her head started again.

"You don't have to be here," Gage reassured her.

"I know," she said. "But I'm a cop, too. I'm supposed to take this."

"Okay, I understand," he told her. His attention focused on Skinner. "Did you find any trace of drugs, alcohol or disease in his body?" Gage asked.

That's a ridiculous question, Alex thought. It irritated her, but she realized that it was a standard question.

"Zilch," Skinner answered. "I've got the pathology report right here." He reached into a pile of folders on top of the desk. "Photographs of the body are included, no extra charge," he said dryly.

Alex drew a ragged breath. So Ken Forney had been preserved for posterity.

"But the only thing you'll see in the pictures," the medical examiner continued, "is mottling skin with the purplish striations of lividity caused by the way blood reacts to gravity when the heart no longer pumps. By my estimate, the victim died at approximately one-thirty that morning."

Alex cringed, even though Skinner was offering no new information. "Then," she began with caution, "Ken made his last radio transmission forty-five minutes before he was shot dead? You're absolutely sure about that?"

"Uh-huh."

Forty-five minutes. That nagged Alex. It all nagged her. *Help me, Ken. What is it we're missing?* Maybe he'd been filling out his report. But that wasn't possible. His notepad was clean.

"Anything else?" Gage pressed.

Listening to Skinner talk was a little like taking a crash course in forensic science. Skinner continued talking, explaining the terms of his trade as he went. "The modus operandi, m.o., or the manner in which the perpetrator carried out his crime, was by contact wound. Or almost. Stippling—by which I mean powder and debris from the gun barrel—was present around the entry area."

Alex listened attentively while Gage hurled a barrage of questions at the medical examiner. Skinner took it all in stride. Nothing daunted him. Death least of all.

He continued. "Along with powder and debris, we found pooled blood. Victims who have been shot will lose blood in a high-velocity manner. A coroner expects to find pooled blood if the victim has been dead for any length of time."

Alex stood woodenly, stark white but dry eyed, and listened. Skinner's horror-inspiring words just kept flowing.

"Give me a real nugget," Gage said. "Some good hard, physical evidence."

"You'll be lucky to get circumstantial evidence. So far, no one looks like a good suspect. No hard, fast evidence leapt out of this one."

"I need something that a jury can see or hear or touch or smell, something tangible. I need something so incontrovertible that its very existence links the killer with the victim at the moment of the crime."

"I've got one battered bullet and no gun to match it." Skinner paused, replacing the folder on the sterile looking desk.

"Not enough," Gage said.

"But sufficient to put a chink in Forney's armor," Skinner added.

The thought froze in Alex's brain, momentarily halting her thinking process. With almost certainty, ballistics could determine that a bullet had been fired from one and only one weapon. Alex had aced her exam at the academy. Every gun except a shotgun had rifling machined into the barrel to make the bullet's path truer. The rifling could identify the gun. Had Ken been shot with his own gun? Why would he have surrendered his weapon? Alex chided herself for assuming it was the murder weapon.

"Even if a bullet was not fired from a particular gun but was merely worked through the magazine, there would be distinctive tool marks left on the slug's casing," Skinner said. "The firing pin in a gun leaves marks by the gun's extractor and ejector. And I can tell you from the lands or high points that mark the bullet, that it passed through the barrel of a Smith & Wesson. This make has five lands and grooves and right-hand twists."

"How can you be sure Ken was shot inside the patrol car?" Alex asked.

Skinner began reviewing the report of what had been found when the patrol car had been processed. "When a gun is fired," he began, "some of the smokeless powder fails to ignite and is blown out the end of the barrel. We found gunpowder particles on the driver's door panel and the driver's seat. The remainder of the car was clean. Had the victim been shot outside his patrol car, the interior of the car would have been free of powder."

"Are you suggesting Ken knew the perp?" Alex asked.

"Could be he knew the creep," Skinner said, and shrugged. He paused, considering his next chore. "It's standard procedure in an autopsy to ascertain the height of the shooter, his position and the position of the victim."

Hearing the gruesome details of Ken's last seconds of life was horrible to Alex. For Skinner, the opportunity to demonstrate his expertise just seemed to make him happy.

"Barrel debris will travel two, maybe three feet. Ken Forney had heavy stippling around his wound." Skinner looked at Alex, then continued. "The sodium rhodizonate test turns purple in the presence of lead. Results from that test indicated the shot had been a near-contact wound. The path of the bullet indicated the angle of the gun."

"And?" Gage probed.

"And it followed a straight trail."

"Meaning?" Alex asked, curious herself.

"Meaning the shooter was either a midget, or he was so tall, he had to kneel down next to the car door in order to shoot. But that position would have made him vulnerable, which is an unlikely situation for a perp. So, I figure he knew Ken."

"And Ken confronted him," Alex said, feeling relieved. "Something he wouldn't have done had he been sleeping."

"From the back spatter that hit the driver's door, I think it's clear that Ken was sitting upright in the seat when he was shot."

"An unlikely position for someone asleep," Alex said.

"I think somebody was clever," Gage said. "Given what you've said, my theory is that Ken was caught off guard, a victim of the element of surprise. And that was his one big flaw."

"Things are not always as they seem," Alex said.

"What do you mean?" Gage asked.

"Theories have to be proven. You're wasting time dwelling on Ken's weaknesses."

"That's my job," Gage asserted.

"The focus should be on the killer," she insisted.

"Ken's actions are the only clues we have to lead us to the killer," Gage said. "It just doesn't wash that he surrendered his weapon. I'm a cop, too, and a cop never gives up his gun if he wants to keep drawing breath."

The dead seriousness in Gage's voice startled Alex at first, but she had to admit that his logic was faultless. "Ken was no coward," Alex said. "Anything we might suppose about my partner and what he did that night is still just unproven conjecture." Alex didn't want to revive her antagonistic relationship with Gage. Not over what was speculation at this point. After all, they'd called a truce of sorts.

Gage greeted her reaction with calm acceptance. "Then his mistake was in not shooting his assailant," he suggested.

"Skinner," Alex quizzed, "did you test Ken's hands for trace metals that might have been left had he fired a gun?"

"Inconclusive results," Skinner replied. "His hands were swabbed with a five-percent solution of nitric acid. It's a routine test. But smoking a cigarette, or using toilet tissue could leave similar residue."

"Ken didn't smoke," Alex mumbled, her face as devoid of expression as a papier-mâché mask.

"Was the body bound in any fashion?" Gage probed.

"No," Skinner said flatly. "Forney appeared to be a willing target. The minimal evidence keeps bringing me back to the same conclusion."

"And what's that?" Alex asked with no lack of sarcasm. Skinner's so-called conclusions hadn't gotten them anywhere.

"Either he knew the assailant or he was caught off guard."

Gage was slow to answer. He shook his head. "I doubt the suspect list includes friends and relatives."

"Correct me if I'm wrong," Alex said, "but the missing link here is the motive."

"Robbery, revenge, a crime against the establishment— none of these motives apply," Gage insisted. "What's the scoop, Skinner. You holding back anything?"

"You won't like this," he said, giving Gage his full attention, "but I don't think the perp intended to cool him. I'm not positive the intruder came prepared, but we won't know what gun wasted Ken Forney until after ballistics."

"And for ballistics, you need a gun," Alex pointed out. The thought barely penetrated her mind before another followed. An even more terrifying realization washed over her. Both Skinner and Gage were right. Ken must have known his assailant.

"On the phone you said you had something for me," Gage said with a vague hint of disapproval. Apparently, he, too, was put off by Skinner's eagerness.

The medical examiner groaned and began leafing through papers. Abruptly, he pulled out a sheet. Spreading his mouth wide, he grinned triumphantly and stabbed his finger to the paper.

"AB negative," he touted. "Ken Forney had AB negative blood."

"I'm missing something here," Gage said.

Alex wasn't impressed, either. "Ken's identification bracelet told you his blood type," she said. Disconcerted, she crossed her arms and pointedly looked away.

A shadow of annoyance crossed Skinner's thick face. "The forensic chemist found traces of blood on the outside of the patrol car..." His voice held a note of impatience.

"That's not unusual when a .38 slug 'crowds' a man's brains," Gage said.

"Moving his body could have left blood behind," Alex mumbled.

"No," Skinner said. "This was cast-off blood."

"From the back spatter?" Gage asked.

"No," he said in a low, matter-of-fact voice. "You know, from a dripping sleeve."

Alex cringed.

"Animal blood," Skinner said, enunciating each word.

"Animal blood?" Alex echoed. She hesitated, blinking with bafflement. Apprehension coursed through her as her mind jumped on.

"I can't believe this. What are we dealing with here? A satanic cult?" Gage asked.

"I don't think so," Skinner said. "They usually make their presence known by some sort of symbolic gesture. Like cutting out a heart. You know, gory stuff like that. The forensic people made their findings based on the breakdown of the molecular construction in the blood sample. The size of the red cells and the visual difference in the eosinophils substantiates the distinction between animal blood and human blood."

"In layman's terms . . . ?" Alex asked.

"It's not Ken Forney's blood," Skinner said. "Not what was on the outside of the car, anyway. It's not human blood. In all likelihood, it belongs to a four-legged animal, possibly a coyote."

"It's worse than a clue," Gage said. "It's one of those horrible stray details an investigator has to cope with. What we need is real evidence. Like I said, we need fingerprints or a match from ballistics. We need the shooter's gun."

"I need some fresh air," Alex said. Suddenly, she desperately needed to retreat from the region of the dead.

"I'll see you to your car," Gage offered.

He was slow to comprehend and it irritated her. *He* was part of what she wanted to get away from.

"No, thanks. I can let myself out."

Outside, she sucked up fresh air, but it didn't help. The morgue visit had failed to satisfy her. At first, the significance of the animal blood had eluded her. It abruptly struck her then, as she gained her first clear view of the situation, that even though poaching didn't always involve animals, it often did. She played catch-up in a hurry. A trucker may have been spotted making a drop for an airlift in the desert.

"You all right?" Gage asked, emerging from the building and startling her.

She nodded yes. But she wasn't. She couldn't think of a single part of her life that was all right at the moment. But no matter how grim the subject, plotting the investigation made her feel that she was back among the living. Ken's murder had been a grizzly experience, but it was one with which she had to deal.

"I think we should account for the truckers in the region that night," she said, hoping that would turn up a motive.

"Always thinking ahead," he replied, giving her an intent look. "Okay. You take the Interstate Commerce Department and I'll take adjudicated poaching cases."

Alex was surprised that Gage would help her, that he'd let her participate in the investigation against Tucker's wishes. Excited, she continued, "Our next move should be to—"

"Our *next* move?" he cut in.

Without warning, he clutched her hand with both of his. His mere touch sent a warming shiver through her. Then his hands relaxed, resting lightly on hers. She felt the power coiled within him colliding with her own.

"Your safety tops the list." His gentle eyes looked hard, piercing. "At this point, there's nothing but animal blood to point to organized crime, but we haven't eliminated it. You could be in danger. I can't leave you hanging on that kind of hook."

"I can take care of myself," Alex said. "I'm a cop, too, remember?"

"So was Forney." Gage spoke grimly, all levity gone from his rugged features.

She sighed. This Internal Affairs investigator was a really good-looking man, and he appeared concerned about her welfare. He seemed human, and that contradicted everything she'd conjured up in her mind about both him and Internal Affairs. Revising her opinion of Gage Morgan was becoming a familiar scenario. But she could be reasonable.

She had assumed he was here to implicate Ken in his own undoing. Maybe she'd been wrong.

"All right," she said. "You've made your point."

"You're probably safe enough," Gage assured her. "But it wouldn't hurt for someone to keep an eye on you."

"A bloodhound! Just what I need."

"How about an Internal Affairs investigator?"

Gage released her hand, leaving Alex conscious of where his warm flesh had touched hers. "It makes sense, and it doesn't seem like I have much of a choice."

"I'm glad we've found something to agree on," Gage said, his unspeaking eyes prolonging the moment.

"I am, too, though it doesn't exactly get me off the hook, does it?" With or without Gage, she knew she would be in danger.

ALEX DIDN'T GO HOME. It was too late to call the Interstate Commerce Department, so she ran an errand. In town, the local hardware store informed her it would take as long as six weeks for a metal detector to arrive. Great, she thought, but she ordered it anyway. After that, impulse took over and she drove to a lookout point on the Hassayampa River. The sight had always served as an inspiration to her. And this visit, her spirits were out of tempo.

She sat on a huge boulder and tried to conjure up some serenity. She closed her eyes and tried to force her emotions into order, but a tumble of confused thoughts and feelings assailed her. She couldn't think of a single reason for Ken to be on that deserted road in such a remote part of the desert unless he'd seen something. She fought to control the frustration rising within her.

She'd learned from Ken not to jump to conclusions when investigating a case and to examine all the angles before tackling the job of putting the facts together. He'd taught her professionalism. He, like this lookout point, had been an inspiration to her. She didn't want to act like a small-town cop with hurt feelings. On the other hand, she didn't care what the evidence said, she would search until she found the truth.

She wasn't betting the farm on a lone gunman. But Alex was the kind of cop who took a theory as far as it would go. Three types of suspects could have qualified: a felon, an indigent, and a local. Possible scenarios detailed themselves in her imagination, and elimination came swiftly.

Ken would have made the felon. But conspicuously missing tracks and the fact that there was no sign of a campsite all but eliminated the probability of such an encounter.

An indigent? Alex would have dismissed this possibility but for her partner's missing weapon.

And, except for poaching, a local appeared to lack any motive at all at a crime scene that was so clean, it squeaked. She thought about that. Gage and Skinner seemed to think that Ken knew his killer. Whatever the case, it was increasingly clear that an intimacy existed between Ken's slayer and the desert. And the desert was the kind of place where airstrips seemed to be born out of sand.

She flicked her thumb back and forth across her lower lip. Mob influence in Wickenburg? Had Gage been serious? They had hardly gone looking for gangsters under every rock. The Mafia? In Wickenburg? Wickenburg was an oasis on the edge of a desert. It was inhabited mostly by people on Social Security who were afraid to go out after dark. Sun City separated Phoenix from the resort town and competed with Wickenburg for the tourist trade. No, she thought. The little Western town was hardly a war zone for druggies and gangs.

Deciding to concentrate on something else for a change, Alex stared down at the Hassayampa. A golden-hued palomino broke through the water in a smooth, low and seemingly effortless run. Its head was carried proudly on a finely arched neck, and its feet were lifted high and placed firmly and precisely. The horse, its eyes glinting, reared and pawed the air with its hooves. Sweat glistened on the muscles moving in the horse's powerful flanks as it charged out of sight.

For the moment, Alex put her thoughts of Ken aside and allowed the events of the day to play through her mind like a favorite song. She could still see Gage's dark eyes turned toward her with kindness in them. What was it about him that she couldn't shake from her thoughts? Her eyelids closed and she pictured him in her mind. Who was he? What was he really like? Inside. Was he married? A wife? The last thought jarred her. Even though he was from Internal Affairs, Alex wished she could have met him under different circumstances, without this black cloud of death hanging over them. He hadn't even asked for her address. But then, he was a cop. He didn't have to.

The striations of sunset in the desert sky faded from peach and yellow to deep black over the mountains. Exhaustion crept into her body like an unwelcome guest. It was time to go, and she would, she thought, in a minute. Alex remembered asking Ken once if there was a reason for everything bad that happened. His answer could be summed up as human error. "There are no free rides," he had told her. "Screw up and you take the consequences. But maybe you learn something...."

"Damn you, Ken," she whispered.

Chapter Four

Gage drove directly to the substation from the coroner's office. He didn't consider the animal blood a lead, but he didn't exempt it, either. Right now, it was all they had to go on. He intended to squeeze every possible ounce of evidence out of it that he could.

He slid out of the county car and climbed the steps to the substation's rear entrance with purpose. It required effort to heave the steel door open and step inside. The substation possessed an eerie calm, and the cold gleam of fluorescent light radiating from a dingy cciling added to the sterile atmosphere. Empty halls and the absence of clanging phones struck an odd harmony.

Gage strode into a room that was broken up by two booths. Each booth housed a computer terminal. Computers were not his field, but he'd learned enough to use them efficiently. He sat down and hit the appropriate keys. *Okay,* he thought. *This shouldn't be too difficult.* Computers were supposed to organize data. It was taking forever to pull out the information. He'd asked for a listing of all reports filed within the past ten years.

He waited. And he pondered the situation. He should just write his report and get it over with. He had nothing to prove here. Maybe the sheriff was right. Maybe it was a

ringer. Maybe the only blame lay with Forney. That's really
what he was doing here, wasn't it? Trying to protect the deceased. No. That was only part of it. Now there was Alexis
Sinclair. He was trying to protect her. *You're trying to prove
something,* whispered a small voice inside him.

A beep sounded from the terminal, grabbing his attention. His gaze slid toward the screen. At the beginning of
each line, a letter distinguished between a felony with an *F*,
and a misdemeanor with an *M*. The next letter determined
the offense, poaching with a *P*, loitering with an *L*, and so
on. Then the case number appeared, a dash, and the year.
Okay. Easy enough. He began scrolling down, line after
line.

An hour later, he was still there, his eyes plastered to the
screen. He pulled up four possibly significant cases. The
most recent one was a year old. He shut down the terminal
and headed for the basement to pull the actual reports.
Anything over a year old was purged from the files and
stored downstairs. Three of the cases jumped out at him.
Not so of the fourth. It simply wasn't there. He checked for
transposition. He checked in case it had been misfiled under another year. Nothing. The file was missing. He checked
the sign-out sheet to see if someone had it. No.

He slammed the file drawer shut and headed upstairs with
the other files. What difference did it make about the fourth
file. In the end, would it really matter? In the end, the result would be the same. A deputy sheriff would still stand
accused of dereliction of duty and he would still be dead.

PROOF. THE MISSING LINK in establishing a motive. Alex
was now fixated on the contents of Ken's last radio report.
She knew that the tape of his last transmission had been re-
viewed and studied. Still, it was possible a minute detail had
been missed, some sort of audio malfunction, for instance.

It was possible that something had gotten lost in the translation from dispatch to tape—something only she could distinguish. Her fingers traced the shape of the minirecorder on the night table. If she could listen to the tape, the missing clue might surface—and with it, the proof.

Alex rubbed gently at the base of her neck. What was it with Gage Morgan? Did he believe in Ken's innocence? She couldn't just sit around waiting to find out in his report. The time for waiting had long passed. Alex had to do something. She couldn't put off the task any longer. Gage was probably staying at the Rancho Grande. It was the hotel nearest the substation. She started to dial the number for the hotel, but hung up before she finished. Then she dialed again. This time, she asked for Gage's room, and listened as the operator rang his extension.

"Hello." The sound of Gage's voice momentarily lightened the gloom.

"Gage, it's Alex."

"Anything wrong?"

"No." *No*. She repeated the word to herself, testing it, trying to reassure herself. "Are you alone?" She chided herself for her own diversionary tactics. Why didn't she get to the point?

"There's no one here, if that's what you mean," he said.

"I thought your family might join you for the weekends."

"I don't have a family," he responded matter-of-factly.

"I'm sorry, I had no right to pry."

"What's on your mind?"

"The tape of Ken's last radio transmission, is it part of the file?"

"I just got it out."

Alex beamed in satisfaction. He was thinking the same thing she was. It was in his voice. Somewhere in her subconscious, she experienced a sense of calm for the first time since her partner's murder. She really wasn't alone in this thing.

"I want to hear it," she blurted out. Her voice held strong and her words tumbled out, bumping into each other. "I might pick out something you've missed." The overwhelming need to hear the tape resurfaced. She felt it was the same kind of compulsion that had sent her to the crime scene earlier.

"That's a moot subject," Gage responded.

"But Ken was my partner. If I could hear the tape, study it—"

"The answer is no," Gage said firmly.

"So you're one of those men who draws the line?"

"I guess you could say that. I just have to keep moving it." Silence followed. "I happen to believe that the last few moments of a man's life are private business. The tape would make great news. The media would try Forney in the papers and on television. Exploit him. Pin the blame on him. I won't have it."

"I agree with what you say," Alex said. "I'm trying to protect Ken, too. It's all the more reason to share the tape."

"The answer is still no," he said. Silence again. "Alex?"

"All right," came her reply. "I'll bow to your decision."

"I appreciate that," he told her.

"But I don't have to agree with it." With that, Alex hung up the phone and was alone once again with her frustration.

IF THERE WAS ONE THING Gage Morgan hated, it was waiting. *She's not going to call back,* he thought. And they needed to talk. He'd been too short with her about the tape. He'd listened to it repeatedly, trying to uncover some new shred of evidence. And he always returned to the same conclusion. Ken's only crime had been breaching radio contact when he failed to call for backup.

The next morning, before seven, Gage called Alex, but only got her answering machine. Not too happy to hear a recorded voice, he reluctantly left a message for her to call him. He finished dressing and gulped his last bit of coffee before heading downtown to the substation. Alex had to be somewhere.

Gage saw her the moment he entered the building. Tucker was giving her a thumbs-up sign, signaling his approval. Surely she wasn't going out on active duty, Gage thought. Not when she'd already expressed a confidence problem. Not when her face was a portrait of denial. Even as he asked himself if she was returning to duty, he knew the answer. He looked at her for a moment, measuring the suppressed terror in her eyes. As frightened as she was, she was still lovely to look at. Why couldn't she be someone else? Someone who wasn't involved in this investigation. From the moment he'd laid eyes on her, he'd known he was playing with fire. And now, at the sight of her again, his amazement deepened.

Alex was teetering on the edge. Gage recognized the signs. That was part of his job as an Internal Affairs investigator. But she was not a loser. She just needed a little time to cope with the fact that her partner was dead.

"Gage," Lieutenant Tucker said. "I didn't expect to see you here today."

Without meaning to ignore him, Gage continued staring at Alex.

"There's another consideration in this investigation that we haven't discussed," Tucker was saying.

Gage raised his hand to silence the lieutenant without taking his eyes off Alex. "Excuse me, Tucker. I was just—" He turned back to face the lieutenant, frown lines ridging his face. "Is Deputy Sinclair on the duty roster to-day?"

"She wasn't scheduled, but she's ready."

Gage's expression seemed to alert Tucker to the fact that there was a problem. "Are you aware of her condition?" Gage asked.

"I know she's been under some stress since Forney's murder," Tucker said, showing no signs of concern. "But she's assured me that she's okay. Why? Is something wrong?"

"Yeah," Gage said, wondering why Tucker would suddenly defy the sheriff's suggestion that Alex be put on a desk job. Tucker had the final say, of course. It was his substation. Still, Alex clearly wasn't ready. Before Tucker inquired further, Gage left the lieutenant and wove through a few idle deputies toward Alex.

"Lieutenant Morgan," she said.

"Could you use some company?" Gage asked. Alex's first instinct was to smile, and Gage tried to relax his authoritative expression. "Will you stop with the lieutenant," he said. "Please, call me Gage." He set his clipboard down on a desk and rubbed his forehead. "You okay?"

"Fine," she said, nodding. "I'm fine."

"You're not going out today?" he asked suddenly, complete surprise still on his face.

Alex snapped her mouth shut, obviously stunned by his abruptness.

"Well . . . yes," she answered. "I'm ready now."

"Like hell, you are," he said with a critical tone in his voice. Gage reached out and caught her hand in his. "You don't have any business in a patrol car when you're trembling like this," he growled. "A deputy sheriff with complete confidence doesn't shake like a rain-soaked dog."

Alex jerked her hand away. He had touched a nerve.

"Stop it," she replied in a low voice taut with anger. "Just stop it."

The back door slammed shut. Gage turned. A tall, blond man dressed in a deputy's uniform and cowboy boots entered the substation.

The man stopped dead in his tracks and stared wide-eyed at Gage. Then the deputy offered Gage a distracted nod and turned his attention to Alex. "You're a hard lady to pin down," he said. "I've been calling your apartment for two days. All I get is your answering machine."

His greeting contained a strong suggestion of reproach. Gage heard Alex swear under her breath just before she acknowledged the lanky deputy sheriff. "Hello, Wes," she said.

"You going to introduce me to your friend?" Wes asked.

"Lieutenant Morgan, meet Deputy Sheriff Wes Davenport," Alex managed to say.

"Good to meet you," Gage said, proffering his hand.

"The lieutenant is a crack investigator from Internal Affairs," Alex explained.

"Investigator?"

"Yes," Gage said, and paused.

There was a protective air about Wes as his gaze settled on Alex. But as far as Gage could tell, she took no comfort in Wes's presence. His condescending attitude would have irritated anyone.

"Then lucky for us he was available," Wes said, turning to look at Gage. "You do much investigative work like this?"

"It's my specialty, but it's not often that I get a case as interesting as this."

Alex seemed almost oblivious to Wes, and Gage himself could barely catch a word the deputy said. Was he really feeling jealousy? Was it really Wes's attentive glances at Alex that were blocking everything else out?

Eyes narrowed, Gage concentrated on sizing up Wes Davenport. The deputy stood about two or three inches taller than Gage's six feet two inches. His blue eyes were framed by tiny squint lines. Gage supposed lots of women would find Wes Davenport attractive in a basic, earthy sort of way. He found himself hoping Alex wasn't one of them.

"This investigation has been the lousiest piece of police work I've ever seen." Wes stared contemptuously at Gage. "It's damn well not the way I do things. But in my book, if a man can't take care of himself, he shouldn't be wearing a badge."

"Ken did everything in his power to—" Alex began.

"He still got killed," Wes reminded her, cutting in.

Without warning, she bolted toward the rear door, but stopped short of it, retreating into the radio room. Gage followed after her, leaving Wes behind.

Alex stood at a window, hunched and defeated. She stared at a patrol car that had just been dispatched to duty.

She clearly didn't want pity. He knew this. He'd been there. Making mental notes about her behavior, he continued to watch Alex. She hugged herself in a comforting manner. She was trembling noticeably. A look of pure misery settled over her delicate features. It appeared to require sheer physical strength for her to straighten her sagging shoulders and drooping head. Gage moved into the room and toward her.

"You're at the bottom right now," he said softly. "The only place left is up. Look, I know it sounds simple." At the sound of his voice, Alex lifted her head and listened. Gage didn't hear Tucker walk up behind him, and the lieutenant's voice startled him.

"I think you're out of line here, Lieutenant Morgan," Tucker said, tossing the words out like stones. "This business doesn't concern you."

"That's where you're wrong," Gage fired back. "It's my business when a deputy sheriff creates a dangerous situation for herself and others by placing herself in a vulnerable position."

"Alex is a conscientious deputy—"

"Then how could she consider going out today?" Gage asked. He was hardly impressed with Tucker's vote of confidence.

"Stop it! Both of you," Alex demanded. "I'll do my job, Lieutenant Morgan, and you do yours." The color drained from Alex's cheeks.

"I happen to be doing my job," he said. After all, instincts were a natural part of his work as an Internal Affairs investigator. And if a deputy sheriff showed signs of instability, it was his job to know it and report it. It wasn't just the pull of whatever magic force was in her eyes that led him on. It was duty.

"You have no authority here," Alex said in clipped tones. She looked to Tucker, whose pock-marked face was turning red. "Tell him, Tucker," she demanded.

"She's not ready for active duty," Gage said, his voice uncompromising, yet oddly gentle. "What you're suggesting is irresponsible. And it's dangerous."

"Wait a minute—" Tucker said.

"You don't know what I'm ready for," Alex said. "And you have no right to come in here and make judgments."

"Just yesterday, you told me you had a 'confidence problem.' And that's an exact quote," Gage said without relenting. "What changed overnight?"

"You betrayed me!"

"This isn't about loyalty, Alex," Gage said, looking at Tucker. "I strongly recommend you put her on a desk job until she proves to one of us that her confidence is back." Gage's eyes caught and held Alex's.

"I'm sorry, Alex," Tucker said.

Alex continued to stare at Gage. "How many lives will you ruin before you're through?"

"I'll keep you on the payroll in spite of that remark," Tucker mumbled.

Before Alex could find her voice, Tucker had vanished into his office. She'd been left alone with Gage. Wes walked by the glass-enclosed radio room and stuck his head through the doorway. Gage watched him give Alex a commiserative look.

"You okay, Alex?" Gage asked, trying his best to ignore Wes.

"Everyone within earshot of a police radio just got a blow-by-blow account of a deputy sheriff grounded by an Internal Affairs investigator," she said. The last place she should have come was the radio room, but there was nothing she could do about it now.

Alex's face flushed with humiliation and anger, for him or herself, Gage wasn't sure.

"One of these days," Wes said, "they're going to listen to me and replace that transmission tower on top of Yarnell Hill. That signal sounds like it bounces off the moon after it gets here." Wes moved away from the radio room's door. "I didn't hear a thing," he told Alex without taking his eyes off Gage. "I'm just across the hall if you need me."

Gage stiffened at the challenge in Wes's eyes, but met the accusing gaze without flinching.

Alex sent Wes a careless wave, dismissing him. "I'm sure you've got work to do," she said with easy defiance. She might be under pressure, but she still intended to resist Wes with every means in her power.

Wes uttered a muffled word, then turned and left.

Rage fueled Alex's body now, and her cheeks blazed as she turned her attention back to Gage. "Damn you!" she whispered. "I trusted you, and you were baiting me. I should have known you'd use what I told you against me."

"Alex—"

She rushed past Gage before he could finish. Without one word, she pushed open the steel door and stomped out without excuses, without goodbyes, without questions.

Chapter Five

Alex felt embarrassed and angry—angry at herself and at everybody who had the slightest connection with her humiliation. Internal Affairs. The words rocked in her ears. Whatever it was Gage Morgan was here to do, it would be without her help! Contempt slowly replaced Alex's rageful mood as she drove home.

The apartments where Alex lived were two-storied boxes that had been built for economy. The units hulked around a cul-de-sac and faced the Hassayampa River. In the dark, they were colorless, and in the daylight, they were all the same dull brown. Fortunately, the apartments' interiors were cheerier than their exteriors. Usually, anyway. Alex thought of all the housecleaning she needed to do. It would be all right now, Alex thought. In just one short minute, she would be inside the safety of her home. And she would be mercifully alone, she told herself as she unlocked the door.

A locked door meant Jill hadn't returned. Her roommate and close friend was a flight attendant who was gone most of the time. Right now, Alex didn't want to face her. She was determined to straighten out the mess in her life without anyone's interference. Inside, she took time to study the disastrous mess she'd made of the living room. Gone was the once-cozy atmosphere the apartment possessed. The closeness and clutter everywhere appalled her. She knew she should clean, if only out of consideration for her roommate. After wrestling with herself and determining that she couldn't summon the strength to tackle the mess, she sank onto the couch. It was a pattern she'd followed since Ken's death.

When the door opened suddenly, Alex snapped her head around to see who it was. "Jill! You're supposed to be in Denver."

"And you're supposed to be on duty," Jill said. "Oh, no. Alex...."

"I tried." Alex felt a scream of frustration rise at the back of her throat.

"What happened?" Jill asked. She fixed her gaze on her close friend.

"Nothing. Absolutely nothing. I've been grounded!"

"Grounded? By who?"

"Gage Morgan. The investigator from Internal Affairs. He said I was shaking like a rain-soaked dog. Well, he didn't actually ground me, Tuck did. At Gage's request."

"Oh, Alex." Jill's gaze embraced Alex with pity. Jill went to the couch, put down her suitcase and gave her longtime friend a hug. "You'll be all right. It's normal to be upset at a time like this."

"I don't need a mother hen to give me a lecture."

"Not a lecture, a pep talk."

"Whatever. It doesn't change the situation."

Jill tried to find some semblance of a smile with which to reassure her roommate. "Internal Affairs is here to investigate Ken, not you," Jill said. She paused to study Alex. "You're a survivor—so survive!"

With leaden arms, Alex raised her hands. She wiped her eyes, but it was impossible for her to forge a smile. "You're right and I know it. Don't worry about me, Jill. Really, I just need some time, and I'll be fine."

"Chris invited me to his condo in Mexico," Jill said. "I traded with a new attendant for time off for the trip. Think you could do without yours truly for a week?"

Alex hugged Jill. "Oh, Jill! How long have you waited for this invitation?" Chris Parks was a pilot for the same airline Jill worked for, and from the moment they'd met, Jill's attraction to him had intensified. "I'm happy for you, and of course, I don't mind being alone."

"I've got two hours to grab a shower and a fresh suitcase. I'm meeting Chris at the airport," Jill said. "We're hopping the one-thirty flight to Mexico City." She hesitated, measuring Alex for a moment. "But I could take a rain check."

"Absolutely not! I'm just going to take it easy for a couple of days."

Jill sucked in a deep breath and held it for a moment while she studied her friend. "Okay, but I'm leaving a number," she said. She fumbled in her purse. "Here it is. If you need me, use it." Jill started reluctantly for the bedroom, her suitcase in her hand. "I'll be back next Sunday," she said, stopping suddenly to turn and face Alex. "Are you sure—"

"Not another word! Now scoot," Alex said, feigning confidence.

"Okay," Jill said, raising her left hand. "I'll quit."

Alex remained on the couch and drew an afghan around her. She envied her roommate's opportunity to leave town. When would she get over this feeling of needing to find a secret hiding place away from all mankind?

Outside, it started to rain. August was crowding into September, but the monsoon persisted. Gusts of warm wind pressed against the windows. Alex didn't move. Since Ken's death, she'd spent more time in her apartment than she had the entire time she'd lived there. Spacious as it was, it began to close in on her. The feeling unsettled her. With the remote, she flipped on the local news.

Terry Pyburn, a Phoenix news anchor, was reporting on the freeway-expansion project. Alex's mind wandered back to the night almost two weeks ago when she had sat in the same room, listening to the same reporter, while Jill played nursemaid to her case of the flu. Alex had driven to the station and reported for duty that night, but had returned home after Ken assured her it was a slow night. He'd said he didn't want to take the flu home to his family. Alex had been lying on this very couch, warm and cozy, when she'd heard the report of a downed officer. Deputy Ken Forney, badge 913, had sustained a fatal bullet wound to the head.

Alex could still feel the panic that had gripped her then. She'd leapt from the couch and driven to the station, intent on proving the announcement erroneous. Not her partner. Not her friend. Not dead.

As soon as the door had shut behind her, as soon as she had seen the faces, she knew. Later, she found out that Ken's death wasn't the worst part. The speculation about the circumstances surrounding the murder had been even harder to take.

It had been more than Alex could stand when the press started to imply that Ken had been negligent in his duty. She still thought that there had to be another explanation. Common sense reminded Alex that her partner wasn't the sort to go looking for trouble. Ken must have seen something. He must have tried to call for backup. He would have attempted to resist his assailant. Ken wouldn't have surrendered his gun. It was out of character.

The television reporter jolted her back to the present. Alex stared into the calm face of Terry Pyburn. Then, she realized it was the mention of Ken's name that had drawn her out of her reverie and back to the broadcast. She pulled her head off the couch and listened. Ken's picture appeared in a small window on the screen.

"The investigation into the murder of Sheriff's Deputy Ken Forney still suggests the possibility the assailant surprised the deputy. An Internal Affairs investigator has been assigned.

"Lieutenant Gage Morgan is known across the state of Arizona for his investigative work. His preliminary report points toward the possibility that Deputy Forney compromised his duty. A twenty-year veteran..."

Alex stood and stomped over to the television. Anger replaced her despair. She slammed her clenched fist down on top of it, trying to swallow the emotion in her throat. "Damn it! It wasn't his fault!" The sting of hot, long-overdue tears were blinding her eyes and choking her throat. Suddenly, the torrent burst from Alex's eyes and rolled down her cheeks.

"Alex? What is it?" Jill asked. She came from the bedroom, showered and packed. Not knowing what else to do, she wrapped her arms around Alex. An eternity seemed to pass between them. Alex wept against Jill, then finally drew back, her sobbing gasps still racking her shoulders. She swallowed the despair in her throat and spoke in a low, tormented voice. "I should have been there," she said, defeated. Her misery was like a steel weight.

"Alex, we've been over this," Jill said, trying to comfort her. "If you'd been there, you might be dead, too. Ken was a good deputy. Something went wrong. No one could have prevented it. Your being there wouldn't have changed things. You've got to accept that." Jill took Alex by the shoulders and shook her gently. "Alex, do you hear me?"

An inner torment began to gnaw at Alex. She stood motionless in the middle of the room, and shook her head.

"No . . . I should have been there," she persisted. "Then all this wouldn't be happening." No matter how many times she was told differently, she'd never be convinced.

"Alex, you're suffering from a severe case of vulnerability."

She could only stare at Jill.

"And you're wearing it like a shroud."

"Maybe you're right," Alex said.

Once today had been enough. She wasn't up to another disturbing discussion. Although she had resented Gage's words at the substation, at least he had viewed her as a professional. Was that what kept drawing her to him?

"And what exactly are you doing about it? You don't see it, do you? Get a plan, girl. Fight back. Play into the IA investigator's hands if you have to."

It took a few moments for the full impact of Jill's words to sink in. "You're right, Jill." Alex was amazed at how calm she sounded now. A smile broke out on her otherwise sad face. "Damn it, you're right." Her voice had assumed a tone of triumph. Then her expression changed, as if she had begun to puzzle something out. *Assemble the facts first.* Ken's words echoed in her mind.

"You know, I've been thinking about this, too," Jill said. "What if there were two of them?"

"Two assassins?" Alex asked incredulously. "What . . . ?" No. Ken's murder was beginning to look like the product of organized crime. For what, she wasn't sure yet, but if poaching was at the root of it, the sheriff's electoral opponent was the expert in that area. Okay, she thought, she was just as anxious as Gage to get to the bottom of this case. "Gage isn't going to deny Ken a proper investigation," Alex finally said.

"And proper investigations take time," Jill chimed in.

Alex nodded in agreement. "Before this is over, hundreds of calls will be made, scores of meetings scheduled and all the appropriate police parlance will have knocked down all possible scenarios." Acting out her anger with this Internal Affairs investigator was childish. And Alex knew that now. A compromise was needed. It may as well be on her terms. Alex sprang up and made a grab for the phone. She had two calls to make.

"Good going," Jill said. "Still the same old Alex."

No, Alex thought sadly as a mental image of Ken momentarily blurred her vision, *not the same. Never the same again.*

IT WAS HIS LAST CASE, and it was turning into the lousiest piece of police work Gage had ever seen. As soon as he completed this investigation, he was hanging up his law-enforcement career. He shoved the remainder of a jelly donut into his mouth. After a feeble attempt at wiping the powdered sugar from his lips, he swallowed. Why couldn't he swallow his skepticism?

He had remained at the substation after Alex had left in defeat. Busting her from patrol duty had given him no pleasure. All afternoon, he'd pored over the reports hoping to find something he'd missed earlier. Nothing. He was dragging his feet on this investigation. He knew it and the sheriff knew it. So why didn't he just wrap it up? Everything pointed to dereliction of duty. And the identity of the killer had been buried with the deputy.

Gage shrugged. An archaeologist seeking to reconstruct the ancient past would have an easier time of it, he thought. Over and over, he had tried to reconstruct the crime scene. His investigative work had closed out false assumptions. He was very circumspect about his investigative work. Gage had dealt with enough cases over the years to know that crime scenes were often deceptive. He had tracked all kinds of criminals, too. Some were street people. Some moved in influential, wealthy circles and were polished and sophisticated. He'd been around long enough to know that things were not always as they seemed.

Gage knew from Skinner's post-mortem examination of Forney that the deputy had been shot only once. The wound had been fatal. After the shot, Forney wouldn't have lived long enough to react in anything more than a reflexive, involuntary manner. He might have had time to fling his arms out instinctively, or maybe even hit the door handle. But that was all. Still, Gage couldn't rid himself of the feeling that the crime scene had been a little too neat. That no clues had been left was suspicious in itself. Who was he kidding? The conclusion was the same no matter how the facts stacked up. Ken had seen something that night. And Gage was on the side that said he was killed because of what he had observed.

Why had Ken breached department policy? Why hadn't he used his radio? The dead man might as well have been on Mars during that silent forty-five minutes between his final radio transmission and his murder. Since the meeting with Skinner, Gage no longer believed that the deputy had pulled onto that lonely road to snooze. Still, it was going to be difficult to dig out a legitimate reason why Ken had failed to follow procedure.

For a minute, Gage wondered if Forney's radio had been working properly. But then he found a report of a standard check made of the equipment after the car had been returned to the substation.

Another possibility hit Gage for the first time. Could someone else have been in the car with Forney that night? A legitimate rider? Why hadn't the lab people dusted the inside of the patrol car for prints. That, too, was standard procedure. Mortimer Greer's laboratory, which had handled the case, had almost two decades on the other labs in the county. Mort wouldn't have missed something that important.

Gage had a theory. He believed the perpetrator always left something of himself at the scene of his crime and always carried something of the scene away with him. Forensic science was the backbone of a solid homicide case, and Gage hoped Morty could still come up with something concrete. He fished inside his briefcase for his phone book. He opened it to the *M*s and began scanning the page. His index finger tapped in the numbers on the phone. He leaned back in his chair, wondering if this would turn into a wild-goose chase.

"Hello," came the voice on the other end.

"Mort? This is Gage Morgan."

"What can I do for you, Gage?"

"I'm working on the Forney homicide case in Wickenburg. I've been looking for interior fingerprints from the patrol car. They're missing."

"Not missing," Mort said. "Nonexistent."

Gage nodded even though Mort couldn't see him. "Why?" he asked.

"The substation commander, a Lieutenant Tucker, excused us from the scene. Ran us off, actually. Said he was ready to move the car and if he needed the inside dusted, he'd get back to us."

It puzzled Gage that a thirty-year veteran like Lieutenant Tucker had made such a hasty assumption.

"I need a favor," Gage said. "A big one."

"Gage, you're not asking me to—"

"Mort, this one's important," Gage answered.

"They're *all* important," Mort said.

"I need some tangible evidence. I want this case to be crystal clear when I'm done."

"You don't know what you're asking me. The inside of that patrol car has been handled more times than the *Mayflower Madam*."

"Is that a yes?" Gage persisted.

"I'll call you," Mort said. "Don't call me. You got that?"

"Yeah, I got it," Gage assured him. "And thanks, Mort."

There was a click, and then the dial tone buzzed in Gage's ear. Gage sometimes wondered how he had ended up a cop. He had never thought of being one. A construction worker maybe, like his dad. He had been building things since he was old enough to pick up a hammer. Architects like Frank Lloyd Wright were his heroes, not cops. He had looked to law enforcement as an interim career at best.

He leaned forward, resting his arms on his desk. When the telephone rang, Gage thought his head would split right down the middle. The sharp, intrusive peal startled him. The phone rang again before his arm flew toward it. He pressed the receiver to his ear.

"Hello."

"Gage?"

The sound of Alex's voice surged into his ear, surprising him. Alex was the last person he'd expected to hear from.

"We need to talk," she said lightly, as though nothing had happened earlier.

"Frankly, I figured you'd still be upset with me," he said.

"For doing what you thought was right? Besides, I'm not the issue here."

"I'm glad you feel this way. There's no point in dragging this thing out," he said.

"So how about it?" she asked. "Lunch tomorrow?"

"Name the place."

"There's a small restaurant at the airport called The Hangar. I'll meet you there at noon tomorrow."

"We're on," he said.

A click and she was gone. Such undaunted optimism, Gage thought. He hadn't figured on it. He wished a little of her lighthearted attitude would rub off on him.

FEELING DISAPPOINTED and filled with trepidation, Alex entered the airport restaurant. Because the cool inside was like a benediction, Alex was glad she'd selected The Hangar over The Dude Ranch. She suspected Gage would prefer the indoors to the outdoor, pool-side tables at The Dude Ranch. Outside, the heat was setting records. Temperatures hovered in the high nineties, and the only reprieve was at night, between suns. The pale blue cotton dress she'd worn today turned out to be the best choice. It was airy and cool.

The restaurant wasn't paradise. The air smelled of coffee and grease, and the windows were smudged and dirty. But this was Wickenburg, and The Hangar's windows offered a view of the take-off and landing strips. What else could one ask for? she wondered. And The Hangar was always busy. Today was no exception. The air buzzed with lively conversation. Alex mentally crossed her fingers, hoping her other guest wouldn't be late. She was running out of options.

Alex saw him almost immediately. His sharp brown eyes and curly black hair made him handsome looking. But romantic? No. Detached? Yes. He was striding toward her. His imposing size intimidated some, but his laid-back style allowed him to move in and out of most situations without force. Howard LaRue was the type who had no reservations about letting people know when he regarded them as fools. He was running for Maricopa County Sheriff, and that made him Sheriff Wainwright's opponent. "What brings us together today?'' he asked in a no-nonsense tone. His straightforward manner allowed little room for idle chatter.

"Just a friendly lunch," she answered. Alex smiled, but refused to surrender the truth just yet. Secretly, she hoped Gage would appear soon. She dreaded sitting through this thing alone.

"You wouldn't flatter an old, worn out deputy sheriff, would you?" Howard asked.

"I wouldn't think of it."

"Sit down and join me, then," Howard said.

He took Alex by the arm and led her to a rear booth with a vase of artificial flowers in the center of its table. He signaled for the waitress. Alex ordered orange juice and a grilled cheese sandwich. Her blood-sugar level was erratic from her nerves. Howard LaRue had a fruit plate and asked for a refill of decaffeinated coffee.

"You've had a bad few days of it," he said, offering his condolences. "You okay?"

"Wounded, but not down," she replied warily. If they were going to discuss the murder, it was going to be hard to remain upbeat.

"You never were the weak-hearted type." A grin curved his lips. "How's the investigation coming?" he asked.

Alex looked startled, as though he had just read her mind.

"I read the paper, you know," he continued, swallowing a mouthful of coffee.

"A lot of gaps need filling," she said.

"What's the margin of error on this thing?"

"Ideals and principles are not the foremost concern here."

"Ideals and principles got trashed eight years ago," Howard said, "when Sheriff Wainwright took office. But then, you know that, don't you, Alex?"

She deflected the question with ease. "Has it been that long?"

"Let's not allow this to become tedious," he said, his tone serious. "When we talked last night, I got the impression that Gage Morgan was running a one-man investigation. What do you need from me?"

"There is something," she said.

"I'm waiting," Howard pressed. He lifted an indolent shoulder and rested his elbow on the table.

"We've got a lead," she said.

"What kind of lead?"

"Animal blood."

"*What?*"

"I checked out a hunch about truckers."

"And?"

"Zilch. We're still in the dark."

His thick fingers came together, and he touched the tip of his chin.

"Why tell me?" he asked.

"Because you're the environmentalist. And I guess I have problems with someone who thinks he's got all the answers." Her mouth grew dry. She glanced around the restaurant. Gage should have arrived by now.

"Lieutenant Morgan is not so bad, you know," Howard said.

Alex looked surprised. "You know him?"

"Not personally, but I've heard of him and his work."

She tried not to let that bit of information affect her. "It bothers me that Gage Morgan has so much power over Ken's life."

"Come on, Alex. Facts can stand alone without any help."

"Ken was your friend, too." Alex paused. "His reputation is riding on the outcome of his investigation. Can you help?"

"I'm flattered, truly flattered, but, no." Howard expelled an exasperated sigh. "Alex, you're sticking your neck out. Let the detectives handle this. An independent investigation could bring a world of trouble down on you and me. Anyway—" Howard didn't finish. He turned his gaze up to Gage, who was standing at their booth now.

"Gage! Hi," Alex said.

A pale yellow shirt emphasized Gage's deep tan. The short sleeves revealed sinewy arms, and Alex couldn't help but stare at them as he slid in next to her. Why did he have to look so handsome? And why did she pick a time like this to admire him?

Alex turned to her other companion. "I want you to meet Howard LaRue," she said. "He's running for—"

"Sheriff," Gage said, interrupting her.

He then shot Alex a withering glance. For a minute, she wanted to die. A knot of apprehension formed in the pit of her stomach. She watched Gage calculating. An especially narrow look emerged from his piercing, gray eyes. "I don't remember you mentioning anyone else," he said in clipped tones. Gage offered a reluctant hand to Howard, who rose and extended his own.

"Nice to meet you," the former deputy sheriff said with a tight, uneasy smile. "Alex and I were just having a heart to heart." Howard seated himself again.

"We," Alex began, "Lieutenant Morgan and myself, think Ken's murder could have resulted from his intrusion on some illegal activity."

Howard drew in a breath and held it. He didn't move. "*Illegal activity?* That's an intriguing idea," he said, and shrugged. "But it all depends on what you mean."

"The animal blood is substantial proof that something illicit was going on in the desert that night," Alex said.

Howard's expression said he knew there was more to it than that, but because of Gage's presence, he merely nodded. Gage refrained from saying anything. His stiff-necked attitude was making Alex uneasy.

"I don't know what to say," Howard began. "If you want to hear me say I think it's possible, I suppose I do."

"I'm not talking about a solitary poacher trying to put meat on the table," she said. "We could be talking about organized crime with a crew of—"

"Smugglers?" Howard asked.

"It's a consideration," she said, "until it's eliminated."

"Personally, I think you're wasting your time," Howard said.

Was she? "I don't think so," Alex responded dryly.

"Okay," Howard said. He set his coffee cup down. "Sounds like you've already made up your mind."

Even without the sheriff's title, Howard possessed power. It put Alex on edge. "If professionals are involved," she went on, "chances are their operation, whatever it might be, is still thriving right under our noses. We could have a dangerous situation here."

"I'm sure that won't stop you," Howard said.

Alex clicked her tongue.

"Where are you going with this?"

"I was hoping you could give the investigation new direction," Alex said. She glanced toward Gage for support, but he said nothing.

Howard turned his attention back to his food. He nibbled at a slice of apple he'd selected from the fruit strips on his platter. As he munched on two more crackers and a plump strawberry, he lounged back into an easy posture against the back of the booth. He seemed to realize how much Alex wanted his help, and he looked like he was about to offer her something good. "A year ago a file turned up missing," he finally said. "It was a case we couldn't account for. My case. The sheriff put surveillance on me. You know, like I was under suspicion. He assigned me to another substation in Cave Creek. That was too damn much to ask of anybody. I said no. The sheriff knew I would. He fired me."

"What kind of case?" Gage asked. Finally, LaRue had caught his attention.

"Small-time collar from the East Coast by the name of Frank Damato. Big-time smuggling offense."

Gage thought of the fourth case he'd pulled up on the computer. The file was still missing, and that nagged him. The criminals in the other three cases had alibis at the time of Ken's murder. "Smuggling what?"

"Birds. Talking parrots, including Brazilian macaws and cockatoos. Even Mexican Amazons. For as little as fifty dollars, they could fly the birds across the border, bypassing quarantine, and sell them for as much as a thousand dollars to breeders and private individuals."

"Who was the aircraft registered to?" Alex asked.

"It was rented."

"And the file?" Gage pressed.

"Nobody seemed to know what happened to it. I got suspicious when we discovered it was erased from the computer, too."

Gage tried to slow the words that rolled up his throat and forced their way out. "Are you suggesting the sheriff had a part—"

Howard held up the palm of his hand and looked to the ceiling as if that hadn't been his intention at all. "I don't think, under the circumstances, that I can make such an accusation," he said, effectively dodging the question. "The only thing I can tell you is that I don't understand what happened in the first place."

"How did you happen to find out that the records were erased?" Gage asked.

"The file never made it to the county attorney's office. No complaint was filed. In the meantime, the defendant vanished after the judge released him on his own recognizance."

"Sounds like your problem is with the judge," Gage suggested.

"I asked the Board of Supervisors to form a task force to investigate alleged corruption in the sheriff's administration," Howard said. "They voted not to. I wasn't buying it. The sheriff's soft stance on poaching was no secret, and Damato had been linked to organized crime. He didn't travel two thousand miles just to chicken-scratch Arizona and get a tan. There's a lucrative market in the East for nearly everything that's illegal to shoot or trap here."

Alex watched as Gage diverted his gaze downward. It was hard not to reject such an idea as absurd. But Howard appeared so confident, so sure.

"Look, Howard," Gage finally said, "with all due respect, we're weeks into a murder investigation, and all I'm hearing about is how to put a noose around the sheriff's neck. The suspect list doesn't include him, if that's what you're suggesting."

"That's exactly what I'm suggesting." Howard pressed his lips together for an instant. "And now, I've got to go." He scooped up the check and stood. "One thing," he said. "Has anybody questioned Digger?"

Gage hesitated, and Alex wondered whether he would say what he was thinking. There was something about Howard that prompted Gage to temper his honesty. He wouldn't want to admit to any further failure in the investigation, would he?

"I don't know what significance to attach to this man, Digger," Gage began. "This is the first time I've heard of him."

"Alex knows all about him," Howard assured him. "He's the desert watchdog." He extended his hand to Gage. "See you at the polls."

Howard disappeared, and Alex looked back at Gage. Accusation was rampant in his sterling eyes. *How could you?* they asked. She went limp against the booth.

"Okay, Sinclair, talk your way out of this one."

"I can't explain—" she began.

"You tricked me," he said in a calculated tone. "And, I'm leaving." He stood.

Her voice became a whisper. "Where are you going?" She pulled herself up to follow him.

"Consorting with the sheriff's opponent is hardly appropriate conduct for either one of us. There are those who regard Howard LaRue as a crazy environmentalist, one capable of anything that would swing this election campaign in his favor."

"Howard gave us a piece of valuable information."

"He's a civilian. And if he's got valid information to contribute, he's under suspicion!" Gage paused long enough to slap at his breast pocket, then continued. "I was under the impression that we had a few leads to check out ourselves."

"I called every trucking agency in the area. Then I called every rental agency that handles tandem trucks. I ran down every I.C.C. violation issued on that night. And I came up empty. It's ten days until the primary and this crime stands between the sheriff and the finish line. It's high profile. It's hot. The papers love it."

"Howard loves it," Gage retorted, "because the sheriff is forced to solve it or surrender to allegations of incompetence from his adversary."

"Look, Howard is a friend."

"Howard's a deputy sheriff gone sour! His pride has been wounded because the sheriff fired him. That could make him dangerous to this investigation. How can you expect me to take clues passed on from an embittered ex-deputy seriously?"

"If the sheriff's clean, he'll probably thank us for this."

"You're wasting your time, Alex. I don't have time for your games."

"Games?" she snarled. "My partner's reputation is on the line, and I'll do anything to save it."

"Dirty tricks won't work."

"I'm not above anything that'll clear Ken's name."

Gage stopped short of the door. When he turned to face her, he gripped her shoulders. Alex could feel his strength penetrating her body. So why was she going weak in the knees?

"Can't you understand that the truth is all I want?" he asked. "The truth. That's all." He released her in defeat.

"I wanted to tell you about this meeting."

"When were you going to?" he snapped in a sarcastic voice.

"If I had told you, would you have consented? I don't think so. Not voluntarily."

"I thought you were different," he said. "But you're just like everybody else in this town."

She was a professional and his remark hurt. "Nothing in law enforcement is ever cut and dried. I saw no impropriety in meeting with Howard LaRue. I didn't know if you would or not. I couldn't take that chance."

"All you had to do was ask."

Alex stared at Gage. It was hard to be defiant when she knew he was right.

"I'll give anyone an audience who can help me get to the bottom of Ken's murder," he continued. "It's my job. I don't work from a preferred list."

"Okay, I'm asking. Help me find Digger," she said. "Go to Inspiration Mine with me."

"What?"

"You just said you'd give anyone an audience who could help."

"Just who the hell is Digger?"

"Digger is a possible witness. If we can locate him, he could provide a fast track to the truth. And I don't see that we have any other choice. The police lab has failed to turn up any concrete evidence."

"I'm not so sure about that. Mort tells me that your Lieutenant Tucker dismissed his crew from the crime scene before they could dust for prints on the inside of Ken's car."

"Now wait a minute," Alex snapped. She couldn't believe that Gage was implicating Tuck. It was as though Tuck was guilty of a crime and she was his character witness. "If Tuck did that, he had his reasons. He's a top-notch investigator himself."

"What happened to Howard's vital clues?" Gage cut in. "Why look for Digger when you have those?"

She looked pleadingly at Gage. "I'm not discounting his information. If there's anything to this poaching angle, the collar he mentioned could definitely play a part in it. But we don't have time to sort through every arrest file looking for that case. Time is running out. You said so yourself."

"Is there anything else you're holding back from me?"

"I know this is out of the blue, but Digger could have seen something. We can't overlook that."

"No?" he said. "Everyone else has. You mind explaining?"

"Digger slithers around the desert like a rattlesnake. He lives in an old abandoned mine in the Bradshaw Mountains, northeast of town. Inspiration Mine."

Gage's eyes glistened once again, but his face seemed to lose all color.

"You're impossible."

He took Alex by the hand and pulled her outside with him. She kept revising her opinion of him. She didn't want to, but she couldn't help it. She liked him. And, completely against her wishes, she was attracted to him. Right now, she was far too aware of his masculine scent.

"First, you accuse me of not feeling for your partner and his family. Then, you refuse to cooperate with me. You set me up at a meeting with the sheriff's political opponent. Howard LaRue's looking for all the help he can get to grind his ax because the sheriff fired him a year ago. How do we know he didn't destroy the Damato file himself? And now you're asking me to travel to who knows where to find some man named Digger." He choked on the last words. "I'm an investigator, not Sherlock Holmes! I'm wrapping up this investigation. It's something I should have done a week ago."

"Give me more time," she said. "Please."

Alex had a plan, even if it was more like a last resort. All she had to do was find the old desert rat. Then what? Even if she found him, a rattlesnake might prove more responsive. In all likelihood, finding Digger would gain her nothing. She wasn't a magician who was going to pull a rabbit out of a hat. On the other hand, she had to try. She looked at Gage.

He studied her before he spoke. "I have a theory," he began. "I don't believe in a ringer, and this case is too cut and dried."

"Is that a yes?"

"I'll give you forty-eight hours—"

Well, that was something. Especially since Gage had been instrumental in having her grounded. She pressed him for more anyway, "I'd be lucky to pick up Digger's trail in that length of time." She sighed. "Ken spent twenty years serving the Sheriff's Department. How can you haggle over a few days?"

"Save the guilt trip."

"You know as well as I do that forty-eight hours is too soon to conclude your investigation. It might even be called negligent."

"Ten days, then. That's all, and I'm filing my report. By then, I'll have more lab results."

"Do you have hiking boots?" she asked.

"Hiking boots?"

"Come on. We're going shopping."

Chapter Six

Events had suddenly accelerated for Alex. She had agreed to pick up Gage at first light the next morning. He'd agreed to accompany her to Inspiration Mine. Somewhere deep in her heart, she felt a new and sinking fear. Ten days might not be enough time. She let out a sigh of pent-up frustration. Right now, she couldn't think. She didn't want to. But in ten days, she would be forced to accept the inevitable.

She drove to Marvin's garage, her head throbbing with hammer force. After pulling into an empty stall, she turned off the engine and climbed out of the Bronco. The garage was typical, with the usual amount of grease, dirt and noise. Marvin squirmed out from underneath the car he was working on and got to his feet.

"Hope this isn't an emergency," he said, rubbing his neck. His tone was as impassive as his expression.

"Sorry about the short notice. Could you check out the Bronco?" she asked hopefully.

"Something wrong with it?"

"No, and I want to make sure nothing goes wrong with it," she answered. "You know how engines play out in this hot weather. I need this favor, Marvin."

He glanced up at her. "Favor?" he said with a chuckle. "You need a miracle. You taking a trip?"

Alex deliberately cleared her throat. "Well—uh—you could call it that."

"Where are you going?" he asked rather insistently, staring at her without reservation now.

"A safari," she said quickly, struggling for an explanation.

His brown eyes narrowed. "Police business?"

Alex paled at the close reference. She reminded herself that Marvin had no way of knowing. He had simply taken an educated guess. "Marvin," Alex drawled, "you ask too many questions."

"Ah! Cloak-and-dagger games?" he said. He stepped forward with such deliberateness that she was forced to give ground. "How long will you be gone?"

"Oh, a few days," she said lightly.

"Isn't this a little sudden, even for you?" he asked, pressing for information.

She'd been chewing on her lip and suddenly bit down too hard. She resented his aggressive attitude and didn't care for the line of questioning, either.

Marvin looked down at her for a moment without saying a word. "You gonna tell me or not?" he asked flatly.

"I'm going to Inspiration Mine," she finally said, capitulating.

"You're not going alone, are you? There's a killer on the loose. You could—"

"Don't worry, Marvin. Just service the Bronco."

"Who's going with you?"

"You're in the wrong business," she said. "Did you know that?"

"You've done all you can to keep me in the dark," he said. "Whoever is going—"

"Who said anyone was going with me?"

"Come on, Alex. You wouldn't take off on a desert trip without someone. Who is it?"

"Marvin, will you stop with the questions," she said firmly. His tenacity was beginning to irritate her.

"I know!" he finally said. "It's that Internal Affairs guy. What's his name?"

"Gage Morgan. Lieutenant Morgan."

"You trust him?"

"I don't know," Alex said, exasperated. "But he is the one with the final say about Ken."

"As long as you trust the guy, I will, too. But I'm not sure it's a good idea to go on a trip with him."

Alex felt uncomfortable. The fact was that Marvin had spoken the truth. This whole thing could blow up in her face.

"You know you're probably wasting your time," Marvin continued. "Digger isn't likely to be there."

"Maybe not, but it's worth a try. I'll take the gamble."

"The sheriff must be getting you nervous. I don't imagine he believed for one minute that Ken was doing his job that night."

"He views Ken's murder as just one more stumbling block to the polls," Alex said. She began chewing unconsciously on her lip again.

"Don't worry about Ken," Marvin said. "He was too rigid to bend. He was honest. He'll come out on top."

And if he didn't, she wondered. Alex froze at that thought. Well, she had no intention of sitting around waiting for that to happen. Marvin was speaking again. Alex had been concentrating so hard on Ken that she hadn't realized it.

"Answers always have a way of surfacing," Marvin said now. "Take it from me, his name isn't ruined yet, not by any stretch of the imagination."

"That's easy for you to say."

A flash of hurt briefly crossed Marvin's features. Feeling guilty Alex closed her eyes for a moment and struggled for words. "I had no right to say that, Marvin. It was insensitive of me. Ken thought a great deal of you."

"Aw, forget it. I know what you mean," Marvin said, assuring Alex that it was all right. He assumed an authoritative position under the hood of the Bronco.

The desperation of her situation had made her reactionary, Alex thought. She had to find out what had gone wrong for Ken, but even that didn't justify hurting other people along the way.

"I guess I could work you in," Marvin admitted, straightening up after he finished his inspection.

"Thanks. That's one I owe you."

"No sense you killing time around here," he told her. "Why don't I drive you home and drop the Bronco off when I'm finished."

"Great."

Marvin walked over to his jalopy. "Hop in," he said.

They rode to her apartment mostly in silence, exchanging only occasional niceties. When they pulled into the parking lot, Marvin slowed to a halt. Alex flung open the car door and stepped lightly out onto the sidewalk. "Thanks for the ride and the favor, Marvin."

"I'll call you when I'm finished," he said.

"I'll be here."

Alex strode toward her apartment door. Her mind whirled in circles, making it hard to think straight. She forced herself to collect her thoughts. Setting her priorities was important. There wasn't much time.

Inside, she walked straight to the closet and pulled down a small duffel bag. She wasn't sure how long they would be gone, but she decided to pack lightly. She threw in enough underwear for a week, a change of jeans and a windbreaker. The weather was still very hot, but the desert always cooled at night.

When she finally dragged the duffel bag to the front door, she wondered if she'd overpacked. Well, if she had, it was better than underpacking, she decided. She went over to the sofa and flopped down onto it. She looked down at her hands, which were curled in her lap, then reached for an apple from the fruit bowl on the end table. She bit into it, her expression pensive. Ten days now. Ten days until the primary, and Gage was filing his report then. For better or worse, the stage was set. Her world had narrowed down to salvaging her dead partner's reputation. Nothing else mattered for ten days.

A PEAL OF THE DOORBELL woke Alex. She nearly jumped off the couch. Marvin? He said he would call first. Well, Marvin was a little strange. At any rate, he definitely had an overactive imagination, Alex thought. She pushed herself up and walked to the door. The lens of the door viewer distorted Marvin's features, but it was him nonetheless. Why hadn't he called, she wondered as she pulled the door open.

"Marvin! You said you would call first," she said with deliberate sternness.

"Did I?" he asked, curling his big hands around her throat.

Fear shot through Alex like a bolt of lightning. She waited for his thick fingers to tighten. Instinctively, she opened her mouth to scream, but nothing came. Above the roar in her head, she heard him speaking.

"Hey," Marvin said. "Don't you know better than to throw the door open without asking who it is?"

He abruptly began to massage the back of her neck. Alex went as limp as a rag doll when she finally realized Marvin wasn't going to hurt her. What on earth was wrong with her?

"I knew it was you," she said. "I looked through the viewer."

"You're as white as a ghost. What's wrong?" he asked, his concern genuine.

"I'm sorry, Marvin," she said in a painful voice. "I'm on edge these days."

"This little trip might be just what the doc ordered," he said reasonably.

"Did you service the Bronco?"

"Top-notch job," he assured her. "I don't want you getting stuck in that sand sea."

She frowned anxiously as he walked past her and headed toward the kitchen. "What are you doing?" she demanded. "Let's get going. I'll take you back to the garage."

"What does a guy have to do to get a drink around here?" he called over his shoulder.

"Just hurry up before I decide to charge you," she said. Marvin was only getting a drink of water. Why in the world was she so paranoid? Alex pressed her eyes closed in self-disgust. It also bothered her that Marvin had been able to goad her into saying so much. She straightened and slung her pocketbook over one shoulder. That uneasy feeling was back....

GAGE HAD AGREED TO THIS. And he had agreed to buy this tan safari shirt. It was thick, hot and ridiculous. He had a feeling he looked like a circus ringmaster. Alex was dressed in a pair of skin-tight jeans, a plaid blouse and boots. Her hair had been slicked back into a ponytail that made her look like a teenybopper. Still, nothing concealed the fact that she was every inch a woman.

In the future, Gage thought, he would have to be more careful about what he agreed to. The trip had sounded like an intriguing idea. But it wasn't even fully daylight when Alex picked him up, and he wasn't a morning person. What's more, he didn't even know the route they'd taken. Okay, maybe there was something to this Digger character. But why had the information come from the sheriff's opponent? Was this Howard LaRue's method of putting the investigation in a tailspin?

Gage couldn't shake his vaguely anxious feelings. So far, he had spent the trip looking over his shoulder. He had the oddest feeling that they were being followed. But the roads were virtually empty. It made no sense.

The dirt trail Alex turned onto looked like a web spun by a spider, he thought. It twisted so erratically that he was sure it couldn't exist on any map, but he wasn't about to ask Alex. He had his pride. It was hot, and he began to worry about the possibility of their vehicle breaking down.

"How dependable is this automobile?" he asked, checking the panel for the temperature gauge.

"Don't worry," she answered. "I had it serviced last night. Everything is tip-top." After pausing a moment, she continued. "You're not the outdoor type, are you?"

"What's that supposed to mean?"

"It means you're going to have to wash off that after-shave the first chance you get. And don't waste any water."

"What?"

"Every bee, mosquito and insect within miles will be drawn to us by the smell," she said.

"You're the first woman to complain about my after-shave," he informed her. But from the beginning, he thought, nothing had been ordinary about Alexis Sinclair.

"I'm not objecting to your after-shave. As a matter of fact, it smells nice, but the mosquitos will eat us alive."

"I'll take your word for it," he said. What choice did he have? She was the desert rat. And probably a damn good one.

Alex slowed the Bronco and stopped on a rise. "If the weather holds, we'll reach the Inspiration by tomorrow evening," she said.

"Weather? What's that got to do with it?" Gage asked.

"Rain's in the forecast," she replied.

"Sunshine is pouring down on us like melted butter."

"It's raining up north," she persisted. "The runoff could swell the washes and dry riverbeds down here. Flash floods would make the going tricky."

"So we avoid the washes," Gage said. "With water running down them, it shouldn't be too difficult figuring out where they are."

"It's not difficult now. Their banks are marked by stands of palo verde and ironwood trees. It's crossing them I'm concerned about."

"You have a way of inspiring confidence. But you're the expert."

Alex glanced at Gage out of the corner of her eye. From between the seats, she pulled out a road map. Unfolded, it was big, and Gage had to help her hold the map while she studied it. Her index finger tapped a spot at the top.

"Here's where we are," she said. Her finger traced a line up the page. "We cross the county line here and then bear northeast until we reach the Bradshaw Mountains. Inspiration Mine is encircled by high peaks, but none that are impassable." Her finger rubbed back and forth on a red line she'd drawn on the map. "Except for this stretch of road, it's easy going. We climb four thousand feet by the time we reach this pass."

"No wonder no one has gone after Digger," Gage said. He pointed to another mark indicated on the map. "The Inspiration?"

Alex nodded yes.

"I wish I knew more about where we're going," he muttered.

"The cavalry would have sent a scout ahead," she informed him, sitting in a relaxed position behind the steering wheel.

"Now that's an intriguing idea. Look, if this Digger is so important, why hasn't anyone else thought of him?"

"Maybe someone has," Alex suggested, gazing toward the protruding hills.

"You're really worried about this old piker."

"He's slick as a rattlesnake. But they can shed their skins and start over. Digger isn't getting any younger." Alex suddenly had a grim thought. "What if he witnessed something terrible? What if—he's dead, too?"

"An elusive desert rat doesn't sound that easy to catch up with." Gage wondered again, what were they doing going after Digger? He *was* going to be very hard to find.

"Maybe," she said, then folded the map and replaced it between the seats. "Ready?"

Ready? It was a little late to turn back, even though the logical part of Gage's brain flashed out warnings. The mountains stretched endlessly around them. In the distance, intervals of lightning speared the bluish peaks. Gage nodded and Alex began the treacherous ascent up the winding ridge route.

"It might have been a good idea to have filed a flight plan," Gage said.

"I told you before, the fewer people who know about this, the better. Have a little faith." Alex sighed and shook her head.

"I'm not anticipating trouble, but I like to plan for the possibility."

"Look, I couldn't reach Tucker, but I left a message on his answering machine." She wondered now if Tuck had gotten the message. He didn't always check his machine. "Besides, I was born and raised on this desert," Alex said. "That ought to stand for something."

Gage had an idea that Alex was a good deputy sheriff under usual circumstances. But now, she was also very much a woman who wanted desperately to prove something.

The path narrowed and so did Gage's confidence. What would happen if they met another car? The faintly marked road was barely wide enough for the Bronco.

The washboard road made the ride uncomfortable as the Bronco whipped over the narrow passage. A low rumble of thunder shook the earth. An ear-splitting sound much louder than thunder penetrated the air. The mountainside began spitting gravel. A stone pelted the Bronco, shattering the windshield.

"What in—" Gage began, but before he could finish, another curtain of rocks fell on them.

"Rock slide!" Alex called out.

"Rock slide? Nobody said anything about rock slides— I get claustrophobic!"

"Claustrophobic? You'll be lucky if you're not dead when this is over."

He could barely see the shrinking road in front of them. Red dust belched into the air. Rocks flew down and hit the ground.

The crashing, roaring noise from the rock slide exploded in their ears. Dislodged rocks plunged all around them, stirring up the earth again. Dust and dirt lifted off the ground like a thick fog, shrouding the Bronco. Gage cast a hasty glance around the headrest, through the rear of the auto. There was blockage behind them, and he didn't know what lay ahead.

"I can't see," Alex said in a controlled voice.

From the edge of the dirt road to the valley below, the drop was almost straight down. Gage shuddered. "Speed up and try to outrun the slide. If one of those—" Gage sucked in his breath as a giant boulder, half the size of the Bronco, bounced in front of them and over the side of the mountain. "Hang on to the wheel!" he shouted.

The Bronco lurched to one side. It balanced for an instant on two wheels as it clipped the edge of the road. For a heart-stopping instant, the vehicle seemed suspended above the sheer drop.

"I'm trying," Alex said, attempting to outdrive the slide. "I've never seen anything like it before." Gravel and dust spurted out from under the spinning tires. Alex was trying her best to outrun the crashing rocks.

"And you probably won't again," Gage said as they finally cleared the deadly landslide.

"What's that supposed to mean?" Alex stopped the car.

"I heard an explosion first. It must have started the rock slide."

"You think someone deliberately caused it?"

"Maybe."

"That's crazy," she said. "That's murder."

Gage nodded and climbed out of the Bronco. He scanned the ground above him. There was no hint of movement there. No sign of human presence at all. A swirl of wind blew dust into his face. He was definitely the biggest fool that ever lived. Never in the world should he have agreed to this trip.

He trudged along the ledge that Alex had insisted was a road. The ledge hung precariously over a deep gorge that was sprinkled with saguaro cacti. He was still berating himself for agreeing to this trip when he spied a metal object in the road. Before he stooped to examine it, he realized it was a crowbar.

Nothing unusual about finding the tool, he thought. But closer examination revealed a smattering of blood on it, fresh blood. Something was wrong. He stopped dead still and stared back the way they had come. Nothing. Anyone could have dropped it, leaving it behind, he thought. But he knew that wasn't true. A crowbar dropped conveniently one step ahead of a rock slide? It was too much of a coincidence. Gage felt a weight in the pit of his stomach. He picked up the tool, deciding to take it with him. You never knew what might turn out to be evidence.

He hadn't seen a hint of life, but that hadn't convinced him the rock slide had happened naturally. He felt certain he had heard an explosion. Scanning the slope again, he tried to push the unwelcome thought from his mind. Unconsciously, he slapped his breast pocket for cigarettes. They weren't there. *Damn habit,* he thought. He moved ahead looking for footprints, tire prints or a sign of human foul play. Little remained to be seen. There was no way of determining how many people had passed on the road.

"What do we do now?" Alex asked, thinking aloud.

"Get in the Bronco and wait for me," Gage told her.

"Wait? Where are you going?"

"Up that slope," he said, gesturing toward the steep incline.

"I'm coming with you," she said. "I'm not afraid." *Maybe you should be.* He made a clicking sound with his tongue and trudged back to the Bronco. He reached inside for his revolver. After a moment, he strode back and began working his way cautiously upslope. Alex was close behind. Storm clouds obscured the sun now, lending a shadowed murkiness to the daylight. Gage forced his body to move slowly. His mind raced ahead of him as he searched for prints. A terrible heaviness remained in his chest, and his head told him to get off this mountain before another rock slide buried him . . . and Alex. He glanced over his shoulder. She was still following. Good, he thought.

When they had scrambled halfway up the slippery, steep slope, he stood perfectly still, revolver drawn, and scanned the mountain. Nothing moved except the wind. Gage wiped his hand across his stinging eyes.

"Do you see anything?" Alex called out.

"No," he answered. "Let's turn back."

"To Wickenburg?" she asked.

"We should have never left there," he grumbled. He turned and looked downward.

He made no further headway in his attempt to climb down the mountainside. His next step never connected. He didn't know how it had happened, but he was sailing down the hill on his backside. Rocks, cacti, tree stumps and a huge anthill were in his path. When he finally plowed to a halt, he simply sat holding his head between his hands. He pressed his palms against his temples as if to prevent an explosion, but it was really the pain in his thumb that was giving him trouble.

"Gage," Alex called. "Gage." She made her way slowly toward him, taking great care not to lose her own footing. "Are you all right?"

"Hell, no, I'm not all right!" he snarled. In all likelihood, he realized, he really was all right. He seemed to be in one piece. "That was one nasty ride." He rubbed his hand across his cheek. Grit and gravel were embedded in his hands. He got gingerly to his feet, staggered, then lurched toward Alex for support. His legs felt rubbery beneath him.

"This is turning out to be a great trip," he said sarcastically. He already felt ten years older than he had that morning. And the incident only served to confirm what he had always suspected—the outdoors belonged to the animals and Davy Crockett.

"Are you hurt?" Alex pressed.

"You any good at digging out splinters? I shaved one off that mesquite stump halfway down the hill," he said, giving her a thumbs-up sign with the wounded digit.

"Oh," she said. She couldn't help but smile.

"You think this is funny?" he asked. "I got blood poisoning once from a splinter."

"No, it's not funny. You know," she said absently, as though her mind were tracking something, "I checked all the citations filed in the Wickenburg Justice Court for August 12 and 13, and no truckers were cited during that period on U.S. Highway 89."

"I know you didn't turn up anything. So what are you getting at?"

"Mesquite farmers," she said.

"If they were using that spot for drops from an airlift, they would have left behind shavings of bark and sawdust maybe," Gage said. He grinned wryly. "The kind of shavings that are now embedded in my body?" He winced against the annoying pain.

"But what if the exchange took place deeper in the desert? Maybe Ken followed the truck off the main road and—"

"You're talking major bust. Not your everyday routine arrest. For Forney to do it alone would have hardly been a courageous act. Unless he was closer to the shooter than we realize, I can't believe he would have allowed himself into such a dangerous arena without backup."

"You're right. And he acted by design, not impulse. He always did. I keep going back to the lone gunman who might have sneaked up on him. I've tumbled that possibility around inside my head over and over. I still have questions and they keep getting harder." Changing the subject abruptly, she said, "How's your thumb?"

"This," he said, pointing it in her face, "could turn into something serious."

Alex was hard-pressed to temper her humor. "Let me see it," she said. Her light tone broke up the seriousness of the situation. "Maybe I can pull that mesquite splinter out."

"Careful! I'm bleed—ouch!"

"Sorry," she muttered, licking her dry lips. "You moved and I broke it off."

"Great," he grumbled. "Where did you get your nurse's training?"

"I'm sorry. I was only trying to help."

"Never mind the help," he said, caring more for his thumb at the moment than for Alex's feelings.

Alex shook her head in disgust, the wind catching a strand of her hair and whipping it across her face. He watched her absently brush it back, tucking it behind her ear. He couldn't help but admire her spirit. Suddenly, he wished that their relationship could continue beyond these few days.

"Come on, let's get out of here," he said. The splinter wasn't the only thing that bothered him. The knowledge that there could be someone else out there—someone who was waiting for them to become careless, waiting for them to fall asleep—waiting to murder them—struck a chill through Gage. Maybe they were getting too close to something. Perhaps the rock slide was a warning. He couldn't get rid of the notion that someone was monitoring his and Alex's every move. And if someone was there, he or she wouldn't give up easily. Whoever it was was clearly brazen enough to attempt murder in broad daylight. There was no telling what would happen if the criminal became desperate enough. Maybe they should go back home. But how? The road back was now blocked.

Chapter Seven

Wes Davenport burst into Tucker's office without knocking. "Do you know where Alex is?" he asked. He stood with his long legs spread apart and shifted his weight from foot to foot. "Well? Do you?"

Tuck realized that it would require more than stern looks and a fearless demeanor to control Wes. And yes. He *would* control Wes. At whatever the cost.

"No. And I don't see how Alex's whereabouts are any concern of yours, either," Tucker answered. He didn't bother to look at Wes. He continued to paw through a stack of mail on his desk, then stopped abruptly and reached for paper and pencil and began to draw. The pencil almost gouged the paper as he pushed it along.

"Alex and Gage Morgan set out for Inspiration Mine earlier this morning," Wes continued. He stopped shifting from foot to foot and stood at rigid attention in front of Tucker.

"What?"

"Alex has some fool idea that Digger might know something about Ken's murder," Wes said. "She's hell bent on finding out if he does."

"That old miser?" Tucker responded.

"Even if he did see something, no one's going to know about it. He would never allow anyone to find him," Wes said.

"How the hell did you find this out?"

"Marvin told me this morning."

"As if I don't have enough problems," Tucker said with a snort. "She doesn't have any business out there with that city slicker. He's partially responsible for her being grounded, so it seems strange that the two of them would go out there together."

"Well, if you don't trust the guy—"

"I trust the guy," Tucker interrupted, "but he's got no business being on that desert with Alex. It makes me nervous. I know *she* can take care of herself. Him? I don't know." Tucker turned his attention back to his drawing.

"I'm not sure it was a good idea for her to go off with him," Wes said.

"An overactive imagination can be a curse," Tucker cautioned. "Besides, we don't know who went off with whom."

Wes walked tentatively to the partially open door of the office and shut it. Abruptly, he turned to face Tucker.

"I'm going after her," Wes blurted out. He lifted his Stetson. Sandy-colored curls strayed down onto his forehead, giving him a boyish appearance. The rest of his hair lay matted by his temples. Wes rubbed his sweating forehead with his arm.

Tucker didn't stop pushing his pencil, nor did he look up. His thick lips were drawn into a taut white line.

"They've put some distance between us by now," Wes continued. He began to pace in front of Tucker's desk. "So the sooner I get started, the better." Tucker's seeming indifference irritated him. The lieutenant was the most disciplined human being Wes knew, while Wes himself had to struggle to remain composed.

"No way," Tucker said abruptly. "You can't go after her like a bloodhound. She's a deputy sheriff and she can take care of herself."

The scant seconds of silence that followed were interrupted when Tucker pressed too hard and broke the pencil lead. Even then, he didn't glance toward the spot where Wes was standing.

Wes considered cursing out loud, then rejected the notion. "Why don't you do something?" he demanded. "There's still a killer on the loose."

"Even if I wanted to," Tucker replied, "we don't have the time or the manpower to go sneaking around after them."

"Okay," Wes said. "You've given your opinion. Now what?"

"Don't get cocky," Tucker cautioned. "Your shift ended three hours ago. Go home. Get some rest."

"Great! Just great. They're going to single-handedly crack the case. And I'm suppose to go home and get some rest," Wes grumbled. He replaced his Stetson. "I'm leaving," he said with a decisive tone.

"Go home, Wes!" Tucker ordered.

"Later, Lieutenant." Wes hurried outside and slipped into his truck with an increased sense of urgency.

"HOW DID I LET YOU TALK me into coming out here?" Gage asked.

Alex ignored him and gunned the engine, burying the Bronco deeper into the sand of the wash known as Date Creek.

"Careful," Gage said. "The engine is already overheating. I thought you told me you had this serviced before we left."

"I did." Alex frowned and stared bleakly into the horizon, endeavoring to control her jumping nerves. Storm clouds still shadowed the sky. She gripped the steering wheel with both hands, attempting to drive the Bronco across the dry riverbed again. A perfect campsite was on the other side. Below-average rainfall had allowed the sun to suck all the moisture out of the ground. Not even the four-wheel drive helped. She was burying the tires. She cursed under her breath, then a sigh escaped, as if from under the weight of her own powerlessness.

"Think you could bounce on the bumper?" she asked Gage. "I need the weight back there to free the wheels."

He looked at her as if to ask whether or not she was serious. His hand gripped the back of his neck and rubbed in order to ease the knots forming there. "Oh, no. You don't mean— You *are* serious!" he said incredulously.

"Leaving the Bronco in a wash wouldn't be the smartest thing to do," she said.

He looked at her, then the Bronco and finally relented. "All right, all right," he said, splaying his hands to the breeze. "I'll do it, but this is it. I've had enough problems for one day."

When Alex revved the engine, the bouncing Bronco sent Gage flying. Only one prickly pear graced the bank of the wash. He landed on it. Another pressing problem caught Alex's attention. The Bronco was not only stuck, but now steam was coming from under the hood. The radiator? It would have to wait until she saw to Gage. Alex wondered how one hunk of man could be so uncoordinated. She turned off the ignition and marched over to help him.

"I'm beginning to think you're jinxed," he said, struggling to get up.

"Here," she said. "Let me give you a hand."

"No, thanks, I can do it myself," he answered, getting to his feet. "You're trouble, you know that?"

"Will you stop being foolish and let me help you?" Alex's voice was filled with frustration.

"I'm not bleeding, and if I'm not bleeding," Gage said turning away, "I'll be okay."

"Let me have a look," she insisted. She circled around to his backside. Gingerly, she pulled his waistband out for a peek. He'd done even more damage than he had to his thumb earlier.

"Ouch!" he snarled. "What are you trying to do to me?" He inhaled sharply as her fingers slipped an inch or so down his Levi's. "You could hurt me doing that."

Alex explored where the tender flesh was punctured by cacti. "Get out of those jeans." It was an order. "I'll get the first-aid kit and spread a blanket," she said.

"What about the Bronco?"

"From the looks of things, it's not going anywhere. It'll stay put for the night. At first light, we'll dig it out. We'll make camp on the high side of the wash. We can set the cots up on that flat boulder at the mouth of the cavern," she said, gesturing toward a hollow opening.

"A cave?" he echoed. "Don't things live in caves?"

"The worst that could come out of there would be a mountain lion."

"A hungry mountain lion," he said, correcting her.

Alex simply looked at him and slowly shook her head, chiding him.

"If you're the camp foreman," he asked sardonically, "when do we eat supper?"

"As soon as we get the splinters out of you, so that you can gather enough wood to build a campfire," Alex said.

"Great," he said.

Alex walked over to the Bronco and retrieved a brown army blanket. She spread it beneath a palo verde tree on the high side of the wash. For a moment, she paused to glance across the valley. From here, civilization seemed faraway. And for all her fears, she hoped it was. Then her gaze fixed on the distant horizon. She cocked her head and strained to get a better look.

Gage crossed the wash and stood beside her. "Look at the dust devil," he said, pointing toward the distance.

"Oh! That's what it is." Alex drew a tremulous breath. "I thought someone might— I don't know what I thought."

"You okay?" he asked. He shifted from foot to foot. The cacti thorns stung against his skin.

She gave him a reassuring nod. Gage shrugged. The stillness suddenly unnerved her. No, Alex thought. She intended to keep her wits about her. She took a good look around. Sage and greasewood scents filled the air. The surroundings were peaceful, soothing, as only the Southwestern desert could be.

"Gage?"

"Yeah?"

"I've still got the oddest feeling we're being followed," she confessed. A chill settled at the base of her spine.

"It's not unusual for me to look over my shoulder in my line of work. I've been making you nervous. Look, maybe this trip wasn't a good idea," Gage grumbled, rubbing his backside.

"It was a very good idea," she insisted.

"A good idea? We could have been killed back there. And I've got a prickly pear cactus embedded in my—not to mention the fact that the Bronco is stuck and heating up!"

"Let me have a look at those cacti," Alex said.

"No way," Gage replied, gripping his jeans. "You've done quite enough for me, thank you."

She lightly touched his Levi's, putting pressure against his backside.

"Stop that!" he insisted. "Are you nuts?"

"I didn't know how else to get your attention." She grinned and pointed toward the army blanket. "Lie down on your stomach and I'll see what I can do."

"I'm full of red-hot splinters. And I don't lie on my stomach or loosen my belt buckle on command. Besides, anybody could happen along."

"Then you'd need your gun—not your pants." Alex felt hard-pressed to stifle her humor. "You're not really bashful, are you?" An unbidden chuckle erupted from her throat. Alex couldn't help it. A bashful man? It was refreshing, but it struck her as funny.

"Have you got a warped sense of hum—"

He inhaled sharply when she slipped her fingers below his waistband to assess the damage again. The tender flesh felt like a pin cushion.

"Ouch!"

"Hold still," she said. "You're making it worse by jumping around. All you have to do is let me get under the belt. It's hardly like I'm asking you to completely disrobe."

His pride had been seriously wounded by his predicament, that much she was sure of, but he was too distressed to offer any further objection. She followed him to the blanket, crossed her legs and sat down herself. She tried to ease the nagging ache in the small of her own spine. The ground was hard but, for comfort, far better than the bouncing Bronco.

"I'm waiting," she said, prompting him.

He didn't linger any longer. Nor did he apologize for the curses falling from his mouth. Gage jerked down the top of his pants with more swiftness than a gentleman would. He drew a harsh breath and stretched out belly first on the blanket. *Not bad for a city dude,* she thought after a sweeping glance that covered the length of his body. Lean, muscular legs seemed to stretch out forever. Alex tried to think of something to say that would rid him of his anxiety. It was no use. He had a behind full of cacti and she knew it had to hurt. Her own amusement over his predicament would improve the situation not one bit. She went to work extracting the unwelcome thorns.

"Oh," he said in a thin-lipped voice. Cold dignity created a stony mask of his face. "Careful," he said over his shoulder, "I think you're enjoying this."

"Be quiet!" Alex said suddenly, her voice snappy.

"What's wrong?" he demanded, craning his neck to see for himself.

"Nothing," she insisted. "Just hold still. Quit thrashing."

She rolled abruptly to the opposite side of the blanket. A snake glided effortlessly onto it and was getting nearer to Gage's feet. It slithered closer and closer.

Her sudden movement caught Gage by surprise. He lifted his head, eyes wide with fear.

"A snake!" he screeched, trying to get to his feet. His unbuckled pants made it impossible for him to run.

"Don't move," Alex said. To Gage's horror, she grabbed the creature and tossed it across the wash.

"I'll get my gun," Gage blurted out, jerking his pants up and bolting for the Bronco.

"No need to now," she assured him. She pranced like a cat after an adequate kill. "You tenderfeet need to learn the difference between a rattler and a king snake," she informed him. "The latter eats the former. And king snakes are harmless. So calm down. You're not hurt."

But she wasn't so sure that was true. Alex was familiar with the dull ache that cacti thorns could inflict. Gage had certainly endured his share of pain for one day. And they were barely halfway into the trip.

"I won't belabor the point," he said. His hands closed into tight fists as he fought for control.

"Better button up," she suggested.

Gage clicked his tongue. "I was just getting ready to," he said. "It seems to me that this whole thing was your idea."

Alex made a serious effort to hold back her laughter as she watched Gage buttoning his pants. "We've got just enough twilight left to set up camp," she said.

He groaned.

"Stand still and I'll have a look at your pants."

She pulled one more thorn from his Levi's before he strode toward the Bronco. There he withdrew his gun and tucked it under his waistband. He was trying not to alarm Alex, but he knew she read the concerned look on his face. After all, a man had been murdered on this desert.

Together, they unpacked their cots and bedrolls without episode. Alex didn't intend to embarrass Gage, but after he used an entire book of matches in his struggle to ignite the campfire wood, she knelt down and set fire to a handful of cow dung that she had gathered.

"I always thought people kidded about using cow chips to start a fire," Gage said.

"They work well in a pinch."

The fire Alex built was on a huge boulder at the mouth of the shallow cave. She cooked what Gage said was the best steak he'd ever eaten. After dinner, when the fire dwindled she rebuilt it. Gage sat on his cot in a relaxed position, watching the fire. Alex watched, too, as the small flames started to lick around the edges of the twigs. The blaze grew slowly at first and then crawled up and caught the bigger pieces of wood. As though hypnotized, she couldn't take her eyes from the leaping flames. She watched them grow taller and, as they did, she stared entranced into the orange-and-yellow center of the fire, feeling strangely purged.

Gage cocked his head questioningly and broke the silence. "Why hasn't anyone else bothered to look up Digger?" he asked.

"Digger is elusive," she answered. "An eccentric miser. A long shot. I suppose others have thought about him, but most realize it would be useless unless he wants to be found."

"What makes you think you can find him?"

"Just a hunch, but I don't see how we have a choice. Not when you consider the length of the suspect list."

A keening howl traveled across the desolate valley.

"What was that?" he asked.

"A wolf."

"We're going to sleep with wild animals on the loose?"

"It's not animals you have to worry about. It's man."

"Thank you, if that's supposed to make me feel better." He paused for a minute, studying the fire. "You mentioned once that Wes Davenport was an expert tracker."

"Besides Howard LaRue, he's the best," Alex told him.

"Wes is the deputy who came to your aid in the substation the other day?"

Alex nodded.

Gage continued to probe, looking for the answers he needed to fill in the blanks. "Do you care for him?"

She thought that an odd question. "I've known him since he moved to Wickenburg from Dallas," she said in a matter-of-fact tone. Gage was crowding her again, and Alex needed her space.

"Were you more than friends?" he persisted.

"Why do you ask?"

"He was overly protective of you."

"Once, about a hundred years ago," she said, "we dated."

"Were you close?" he asked unceremoniously.

"No." It was the truth. Now, anyway. "I don't see what difference that makes."

Alex sighed. Why was Gage always pushing at her emotional boundaries? Her rebuttal was stiffly indignant, as though his question had been intended to attack her virtue. Her private morality, she figured, was her own business. And what difference did it make? She knew Gage would draw his own conclusions. He reached out and stirred the fire.

"Your relationship with Wes doesn't matter as far as I'm concerned. But it would help me to better understand his motives." Gage recalled the jealousy he'd felt toward Wes in the radio room, but kept his face blank.

"It was over almost as soon as it started. Wes has a gigantic ego, but he doesn't nurture a grudge, if that's what you're thinking."

"Maybe not for you," Gage said.

"I don't understand?"

"If Davenport thinks he owns you, he could have followed us."

"Is that why you've been looking over your shoulder?" Alex felt Gage's anxiety. It was like being plugged into an electrical outlet.

"No. Just habit." He paused. "For a ten-year period, I found four poaching related cases. All felonies. I checked out three bookings. A fourth file was missing."

"The one Howard mentioned? The Damato file?"

"Maybe. The time frame was right."

"Is there a connection?"

"I don't know. But what I do know is that Davenport wasn't involved in any of the arrests."

"Neither was I," she said and lifted her eyebrows. "Does that implicate me, too, Sherlock?"

"If Davenport is the experienced guide you say he is, and if he knows this desert like the back of his hand, don't you think it odd that he's conspicuously missing from every major poaching arrest?"

"Maybe so, but it doesn't exactly put him on the top of the suspect list. There are a few good deputies on the force." A humorless smile quirked the corners of her mouth. "You're quick to pass judgment."

"I'm not in a position to judge," Gage said. His eyes hardened. "It's you who are passing judgment. And until you revise your opinion of me, you'll be digging yourself into a black hole."

"I'm simply trying to get through this the best way I know how."

"Why do you get defensive every time I start asking questions?"

"It's hard not to when you're constantly directing suspicion at my partner, my friends and probably even me."

"I'm just doing my job."

"Yes, I know." Alex also knew that he wasn't the sort of man to settle for half-truths.

"I have to ask these questions," he said. "Maybe it sounds like I'm taking a crack at everybody. But I'm not."

Okay. She could be reasonable. "You asked how well Wes knows the desert," she reminded him. "He knows it well, and I suppose you'd have to add Howard LaRue to that list, too. I went through those arrest records myself. Neither Wes nor Howard has been around when a major poaching offense has gone down." Alex knew that Gage was probing for answers he either had and wanted her to substantiate, or for answers he didn't have at all.

"Well, who knows," Gage said without conviction. "Maybe it doesn't mean anything at all."

"Are Internal Affairs investigators always so suspicious?"

Gage fixed his smoky gray-eyed gaze on her and leaned closer. "Just paranoid," he said. "Especially after rock slides."

"I've been a bit paranoid myself since Ken's murder. A couple of times I've thought someone might have been following me." Her voice drifted off while she studied the expanse of desert.

"I'm not so sure someone *isn't* shadowing us."

Alex jerked her head up to face Gage. He had startled her, but not so much that she couldn't feign control. Gage sounded sure that they had company. "Shall we turn in?" she asked, changing the subject. "We've got a big day ahead of us tomorrow."

"The way I feel tonight, you won't get an argument from me."

Maybe he wouldn't argue against getting a good night's sleep, but beneath his cool, controlled exterior, Alex sensed a man who was willing to risk danger.

Minutes later, they had spread out their bedrolls. Gage made a thorough inspection of the contents of his. It turned up no scorpions, lizards or snakes. He slid in and zipped up for the night. Alex snuggled in, too. Only three feet separated their cots. Alex found some comfort in the fact that they were both still dressed. "Are you sleeping with that gun?" Alex asked.

"I don't feel like I have a choice."

"You're going to end up shooting yourself in the foot," she cautioned. She lay her revolver down next to her cot.

Gage reached inside his sleeping bag and withdrew his weapon. He placed it on the flat rock beneath him, gave it a pat and then tucked his hand back inside his bedroll.

"Gage," she asked softly.

"What?"

"Why are you doing this?"

"Same reason you are," he answered. "I have to."

"It's not too late to turn back." That was bull and she knew it. It was too late the minute they pulled out of Wickenburg.

"I'm no quitter," he said.

Alex stared up at the stars and wondered if it would all come together in nine days. It would. It had to. She believed more from hope than certainty. But she had always prided herself on her own intuition. Nine more days, and she would know who had killed Ken.

IT WAS NEAR DARK. Wes hiked across the foothills on a well-defined track that dirt bikers used on the weekends. He could have driven his truck, but since the distance was greater by way of the road, he thought he'd save time this way. He didn't want to advertise his presence, either, so he had chosen to go by foot.

He had almost gotten to them once. He would just have to try harder tomorrow. His eyes strained through the deepening darkness. Only moonlight illuminated the trail, and that was no good. Guesswork wouldn't get him anywhere. He shifted the pack on his back and drew out his flashlight. It was no use. He might as well make camp and continue in the morning. He knew this desert like the back of his hand, and he knew that it was foolish to travel by the moon.

If only he could have gotten an earlier start, he thought. He felt certain they had made camp by this time. He set about bedding himself down for the night. Before dawn, he would be up and gone.

Chapter Eight

Gage didn't like creeping around this desert. He didn't like being here. He didn't *need* to be here. And he couldn't sleep. For over an hour, all he had done was toss and turn on his narrow cot. Tempting fate wasn't his favorite pastime. And unless a miracle occurred, the outcome of his investigation wouldn't be influenced by this trip.

"Gage?" Alex asked lightly.

"Yeah?"

"You awake?"

"Yes. You, too?" he asked.

"Uh-huh. I can't sleep."

"What'd you have in mind?" he asked.

He rolled over and propped himself up on his arm to look at her. The moonlight illuminated her face. In spite of himself, he had to admit that he enjoyed Alex's company. So what if someone was following them? Or worse, trying to kill them? Logic had vanished the moment he teamed up with Alexis Sinclair.

Two years ago, his life had fallen apart. Like an inept carpenter, he'd pieced it back together. Nothing had felt right since. The shape of his world became unrecognizable. Through Alex, though, he was being reminded that certain inbred tendencies he'd long since thought dead were alive and well. Alex aroused protective instincts in him that he hadn't felt in a long time. He hadn't felt them since he'd failed in his duty to his wife. But he didn't have anything to prove to Alex. And he wasn't here only to protect. A chill swept across Gage's neck at the thought. What if he failed her, too? Alexis Sinclair was rash. Determined. The way he saw it, she was on a collision course with disaster. And, she would probably need his protection. He remembered the bottle. "Brandy?" he asked, producing the liquor from beneath his bed roll like magic.

"What else do you have there?"

"Just brandy." Gage offered the bottle of dark red, cherry-flavored spirits to Alex. She gratefully accepted, pressed the bottle to her lips and tipped it. She returned it to Gage. He sipped the brandy, too, and savored the flavor as it slid warmly down his throat.

"I'm a third-generation desert rat," she told him.

She hadn't said as much, but Gage had assumed that her family had been near the desert for a long time.

"I'm curious," he said, changing the subject, "what drew you into law enforcement?"

"While I was in high school, I worked part-time for the Sheriff's Department, typing police reports. I got to know the deputies. Whenever I could, I rode with them." She paused. "It gets in your blood. And now, I've got five years on the force."

"I thought maybe you came from a long line of law enforcers."

"My dad died in Vietnam. I don't remember him. My mother raised me."

"Alone?" he asked.

"Lilly didn't have any family to help."

"Lilly?"

"My mother," Alex said. "She remarried and moved to Canada after I graduated from high school."

"How did you talk her into allowing you to live so dangerously?"

"I didn't. I had to sneak out to ride in patrol cars." She laughed lightly. It was pleasant talking to Gage about casual things. "The first time I was involved in a chase, Tuck tried to pull me out before the pursuit ended. I wouldn't budge. When he turned on the siren and we started to roll, I knew I was hooked."

"What do you do to relax?"

"I fly."

"You what?" Gage began to laugh, not a deep belly laugh, just an amused chuckle.

"What's so funny?" she asked.

"I'm sorry. It's hard to imagine you leaving your squad car for an airplane," he said. "The lady thinks aviation while she enforces the law."

"I suppose you could say it that way," she said, looking directly into his eyes. "A ride in the sky is the most peaceful thing I know."

"Alex," Gage began in a serious tone, "did you socialize with Forney?"

She snapped her head around to face Gage. "What?"

"I should have said Forney and his family. Can you elaborate on his personal life?"

"He was happily married for twenty years. Two years ago, he lost his daughter to leukemia. All Sandy has left is their son, Paul, and a stack of doctor bills."

"They were heavily in debt?"

"Their daughter was in and out of the hospital for a year before she died. The bills stacked up."

"When was the last time you saw Ken socially?"

"The night before his murder. Sandy had a birthday party for him, his thirty-ninth. She said they were going to ignore his fortieth. I guess she was right. I was already coming down with the flu, but I went anyway. Perhaps if I hadn't, I would have been well the next day and able to work."

"He made a night of it?" Gage asked.

"I don't know. The party was just getting underway when I left. I felt too ill to stay. I was there just long enough to drink a toast with them."

"Then he was a drinking man?"

"A birthday toast hardly means he was a drinking man."

Gage hadn't intended to vex Alex. And on the heels of her vexation came her defensive armor. But he had to ask these questions. A seventy-two-hour profile was standard procedure. It was part of the investigation. "But we can assume he drank the night before he was killed?" Gage persisted.

"You can assume anything you like."

"Alex, this is important. Is it possible Forney had a hangover the night he was murdered?"

"I told you I didn't stay. Besides, you know as well as I do that pathology checked for abnormal alcohol levels in his bloodstream."

"But wouldn't you know whether or not he would have continued to drink?"

"What are you getting at?" she snapped. "Ken wasn't a lush. What if he did take a drink? He was still able to put twenty-four hours between the party and his shift. It would have had no bearing on his performance that night. And Skinner said that there was nothing abnormal."

"Was there food at the party?" Gage pressed.

"Damn it! What difference would that make?"

"It would have a bearing on how he felt the next day." Gage had expected a defensive attitude. That was a normal reaction under the circumstances. But Alex had carried it to extremes. He couldn't help but wonder if she was trying to protect her partner from something. But what? "You know that the path people can slip up."

"Oh, I see," she snarled. "Now you've established he got drunk in spite of the fact that pathology turned up nothing."

"You know these questions are procedure—"

"Damn the procedure!" She stood up to face Gage. "Why don't you ask his wife?"

"I was hoping I wouldn't have to do that."

"Doesn't that fall within procedure?"

"I try to eliminate as many questions as possible before I'm forced to confront the family," Gage said. "I try to make it as easy as possible for them." He deliberately paused for a moment. "I seem to remember that really pursuing this investigation and finding Digger was your idea."

Alex blew out a heavy sigh. "I'm sorry," she reluctantly admitted, but there was no trace of apology in her voice.

"You've got to understand that the most important part of my investigation is finding out about Forney's physical and mental condition before his murder," Gage continued. "At the moment, all I know about the man is what happened after rigor mortis set in." He regretted the words the moment they were out. Alex squeezed her eyes shut in despair. He hadn't meant to be brutal, even if he had been unrelenting in his questioning. "I'm sorry."

"You don't have to apologize for the truth," she said. She sat down and stared at him from her cot. But this time, her eyes were open in a different way.

Gage wondered if she was allowing him partial entry into her deepest self. "It won't get any worse," he said, trying to reassure her. He'd completed the abrasive part of the profile. At least as far as she was concerned.

"Thanks for the wisdom, Lieutenant."

"It's one of the privileges of rank," he replied, holding her gaze. "Alex, please don't get upset over what I'm about to say. I want you to listen and think about it."

Her face grew serious and her eyes got even wider. Moonlight seemed to bounce off them, but she didn't say a word. In the warm night, they began analyzing what they'd learned about the case. And they did it well together. For her part, Alex had been careful about voicing all her opinions for fear of giving the case against Ken more validity, and perhaps even casting a negative verdict in stone.

"This is the hardest thing I've ever had to say, but we can't back off from any possibili.ies at this stage," Gage said. He unzipped his bedroll, swu ig his legs over the side of the cot and rested his palms on his knees for a minute. "It could be you didn't know Ken as well as you thought you did."

For the first time, Alex wondered if Gage was right. Ken had been a friend, a mentor, and her partner. But perhaps she had never really known him at all.

HOURS LATER, into the night, there came the dissonant noises of the desert. A coyote barked and a donkey brayed, but it was the sound of rushing water that aroused Alex from a doze. A breeze stirred the warm humid air. She smelled wet dirt.

She sat up groggily. Water slapped at her. She was soaking wet. Emerging from the cot, Alex looked furtively up and down the roaring wash. She reeled around at the sound of Gage's fierce call. He was up, taking a closer look at their current predicament. Raging water had begun to sweep over the flat rock they were camped on. It was as if the elements had waited slyly until night.

Lightning ripped down from the mountains. Thunder crashed with such a terrifying closeness that it sent a chill up

Alex's spine. All she could do was stand by her cot like a bedraggled little cat.

"Alex! Get back! We're being swept in."

Chunks of rocks dislodged from the cliffs above hurtled down around them.

"Run for it!" Gage ordered.

The Bronco had disappeared with a crashing, roaring noise. A waterfall had been created by the runoff from above, and, no sooner had Alex moved than the cots were swept downward by the water's rush. "Wait. In here," she shouted against the roar of the water. "Inside the cave."

"I'll be claustrophobic," Gage called back.

"You'll be dead. Come on." Alex had no intention of just standing there, waiting to be washed downstream.

Alex scrambled over the rock-strewn boulder and through the waterfall. Gage followed. They were both soaked. In another moment, they had made their way inside the shallow cave.

Alex's breath came in rapid gasps. Her chest burned and her eyes blurred from the water that dripped from her hair. "We'll be safe in here," she assured him.

"Are you all right?" Gage asked.

"I think so," she mumbled, staring out at the waterfall. Dazed but happy to be alive, she felt a flash of relief now. The cave would offer some shelter, at least.

"Glad you're all right," Gage said, "because I have something to say, and like it or not, you're going to listen."

"Indeed?"

He held up his hands to stop any further words. "From the moment we began this journey, you've treated me as if I were incapable of tying my shoelaces. You made camp and you cooked our meal, and I appreciate that. But being inexperienced on the trail, being a tenderfoot doesn't make me stupid.'' He sucked in a deep breath. ''We're going back, Alex.''

''I don't take orders,'' she said.

''You're going to take this one. We're turning back.''

A curious smile tugged at her lips. ''And if I won't? What will you do?''

''My, you *are* a feisty woman.''

''Look, the plain truth is that you're right about giving up our plans. Attempting to reach Inspiration Mine at this point would be impossible. It's too dangerous. But turning back is out of the question. That roaring wash out there may as well be the Missouri River.''

''Well, that's just great. Here we are in the middle of nowhere, with no food, no weapons and no radio.'' He snarled. ''Wait a minute.'' He slapped his rear pocket and pulled out the bottle of brandy. ''We've got something to drink.'' He displayed the bottle proudly.

''I wouldn't drink that if I were you,'' she advised him.

''And why not?''

''Alcohol will dehydrate you as fast as the afternoon sun.''

''All those old movies were frauds,'' he said, eyeing the bottle suspiciously.

She reached inside her shirt pocket and pulled out a book of matches. ''We've got matches,'' she said, waving them. Striking one, she assessed their new quarters. Amid the silty rocks were pieces of broken glass and bits of clothing. Here and there was an empty can.

''Do you see what I see?'' Gage asked, elated. There was a rat's nest.

''A tomb?''

''That rat's nest over there.'' Gage pointed toward a dome-shaped mound of twigs, cacti and bark.

"Oh, I hate rats," Alex confessed. Hating them was only half of it. They scared her to death.

"I didn't realize you were afraid of anything."

"I didn't say I was afraid—"

"Give me those matches," he said.

"You can't be serious." Was Gage really going to set fire to the nest?

"I'm soaking wet. We've lost the Bronco, our clothes, our food and our weapons. Do I look like I'm kidding?"

"If a rat is in there, it can only run out one way."

Gage pitched a burning match onto the nest. It went up in flames like a torched powder house. Every ounce of courage Alex had demonstrated earlier with the snake was absent when the pack rat scurried out to freedom. After emitting a scream that would have scared an alley cat, Alex lunged toward Gage.

"You're soaked to the bone," he said in a husky voice.

"I'm—I'm sorry," she mumbled, pushing away from his hard, rigid body. "I'm on edge. And I really hate rats."

"You're not only wet, you're muddy." He pulled her closer and brushed a strand of her hair away from her face.

His hand felt warm and loving, and she hoped he wouldn't take it away. That feeling confused her. But then, a lot of things confused her lately. Was she really falling for Gage Morgan? "What now?" she asked.

"We get clean and dry."

"I can't wait to hear how."

Gage chuckled as he looked down at Alex's solemn expression.

"You find this amusing?" Alex asked.

"I'm sorry," he said. "I was just thinking about you slinging that nasty reptile across the wash earlier." He paused for a moment. "Alex, this trip has been..." His voice dropped off.

In the dim light furnished by the small fire, she could see the tenderness in his eyes, but she refused to allow it to sidetrack her and she went on the attack. "Go ahead and say it," she said.

"Say what?" he asked.

"That this trip has been a dangerous folly."

"You've done all the chattering," he said. "Be quiet and come here." He pulled her shivering body even closer, into his arms, without giving her a chance to object. Her first instinct was to fight against the comfort he offered. But she both needed and wanted it. Just for the moment, she decided to give in and quit fighting.

"Why do you pretend to be so tough?" He spoke into her ear while his fingers threaded through her hair.

"I'm not pretending anything."

He felt so warm. And she was cold and nervous. He was brushing the hair away from her face in a soothing fashion, and for a moment, she was able to believe that everything would be all right. Her racing mind eventually slowed. Sanity returned and she pulled away from him. She hadn't planned a life of celibacy. It just seemed to always work out that way. And, perhaps, she thought, that was the best thing.

"Are you all right?" he asked, looking as though he might make another grab for her.

Alex made her voice sound even. "Yes, I'm fine," she said. "I appreciate your concern, but I don't need it." Even as she said it, she knew it wasn't true. Being close to Gage felt good, but it also frightened her a little.

"Here," he said, gesturing toward her with the bottle, "take a sip of brandy. Go ahead, one sip won't kill you."

She accepted the bottle and drank. But if Gage Morgan thought a bottle of brandy could get her back into his arms, he was mistaken. The warming effect soothed her frayed nerves almost immediately. She tipped the bottle again, more eagerly this time.

"Whoa there, better slow down," he warned. "Dehydration. Remember?" He tried to look serious.

"Right," she said. The truth of the matter was that Gage *did* scare her. She half considered throwing the bottle at him. But then, why waste good brandy? How was it possible for this man to arouse such a dizzying range of emotions in her? Had his eyes always been this vivid? Or was it just the firelight dancing in them? Alex trembled, but she was no longer cold. She gestured toward him with the brandy.

"Go ahead," he said, inhaling sharply. "You need it more than me."

She took another sip and handed the bottle back. She glared at him. "What's that supposed to mean?" she asked.

"Don't you know? I just want you to relax, to lighten up. You're cold." Gage paused. "And you're trembling."

"I don't trust you." *But don't take it personally,* she wanted to say. Every man in her life who'd meant something to her was dead. She didn't trust men. She wasn't sure she ever would.

"I know that," he said. "You demonstrate it every chance you get."

"And I don't want to hear this—"

"Alex, just listen to me for a minute."

"It's hard to take egocentric men seriously when they're always talking about themselves."

"What I'm trying to tell you isn't about me. It's about you."

"It will take more than a half-empty bottle of brandy for you to warm my bed," she informed him.

Gage reached out and pulled her to him in one sweeping motion. He sealed her mouth with his in a crushing kiss. She

PEEK-A-BOO!

Free Gifts For You!

*Look inside—Right Now!
We've got something
special just for you!*

GIFTS

*There's no cost—
and no obligation
to buy anything!*

We'd like to send you free gifts to
introduce you to the benefits of the
Harlequin Reader Service®: free
home delivery of brand-new
Harlequin Intrigue® novels months
before they're available in stores,
and at a savings from the cover
price!

Accepting our free gifts places you
under no obligation to buy
anything ever. You may cancel the
Reader Service at any time, even
just after receiving your free gifts,
simply by writing ''cancel'' on
your statement or returning a
shipment of books to us at our
cost. But if you choose not to
cancel, every other month we'll
send you four more Harlequin
Intrigue® novels, and bill you just
$2.47* apiece—and there's **no**
extra charge for shipping and
handling. There are **no** hidden
extras!

*Terms and prices subject to change without
notice. Sales tax applicable in N.Y. Offer limited
to one per household and not valid to current
Harlequin Intrigue® subscribers.

GALORE

Behind These Doors!

WE EVEN PAY THE POSTAGE!

It costs you nothing to send for your free gifts—we've paid the postage on the attached reply card. And we'll pay the postage on your free gift shipment. We charge nothing for delivery!

If offer card is missing write to: Harlequin Reader Service, 3010 Walden Ave., P.O. Box 1867, Buffalo, NY 14269-1867

BUSINESS REPLY MAIL
FIRST CLASS MAIL   PERMIT NO. 717   BUFFALO, NY

POSTAGE WILL BE PAID BY ADDRESSEE

HARLEQUIN READER SERVICE
3010 WALDEN AVE
PO BOX 1867
BUFFALO NY 14240-9952

NO POSTAGE
NECESSARY
IF MAILED
IN THE
UNITED STATES

tried to pull away, but it was no use. Then abruptly, he released her.

He was out of breath as he spoke, "If I ever 'warm your bed,' I'm sure you'll want to make love to me as much as I'll want to make love to you."

"Don't flatter yourself," she said. To her chagrin, her voice was cracking.

There was a kind gleam in his eyes when he spoke again. "You know what I think?" he asked.

"I don't care what you think."

"I think you don't trust yourself. Because if you did, you'd know I'm a friend—"

"You have all the answers," she said. "Except for the ones we really need."

"Okay," he said. "Let's get back to work. Right now, we'd better figure out what we're going to do."

"We can't do anything until daybreak," Alex said. Even thought it was she who pulled away from him, she felt put off by his businesslike tone.

"We'd better get some rest, then."

He eased down in front of the fire. Alex wasn't about to move away from the light. She hated rats. Feared them. She eased down next to him. Why was it **so** hard for her to admit to it when he was right?

"What would you say," Gage asked, looking over at her, "if I told you I've experienced your pain, that I've been there?"

"You?" A tentative stillness settled over Alex. Why did she keep reducing his interest in her to a merely professional level? It seemed so impossible to sort out her emotions right now. "When?" she asked.

"Almost two years ago."

The pain in Gage's eyes testified to it. He really had been there. "Did you lose a partner, too?"

"Sort of...."

"I don't understand," she said.

"I lost my wife."

Alex dropped her gaze. Compassion kept her from asking for any more details. "How long does it take? To get over it?"

"You don't. You just find a remote place in your heart and bury it. Time has a way of healing us. You'll wake up one morning and—"

"It won't hurt?"

"Not exactly. You'll feel numb, but you'll be able to go on."

She didn't respond. What could she say? Alex didn't believe she would ever be the same again. Fatigue crept over her body and she began to give in to it. Their situation didn't look good and now, she felt responsible. "We could use a lucky break right now," she said. At least, she thought, she was with Gage. And the extraordinary thing about Gage was his determination. She questioned her own decision about making this trip to Inspiration Mine. But in the light of disaster, this tenderfoot beside her had demonstrated enough strength for both of them.

"Everything will look brighter in the morning," Gage said. "Let's get some rest."

Alex was seriously beginning to wonder if tomorrow would look any brighter. Sleep eluded her. She lay there, watching the fire, thinking, wide awake. Maybe they should have turned back. But curiosity and determination drove her forward, as it did Gage. Alex resolutely denied any possibility of danger. But try as she might, she couldn't shake the vaguely anxious feeling that someone was out there. Someone dangerous.

Chapter Nine

Waking up came slowly for Alex. When she began to take account of her surroundings, she found herself facedown on a dirt floor in a hot, dark, foul-smelling place. She wished she could delay the coming dawn, wished this was another time and wished this was another place. Her mind kept recalling last night. She looked over to see if Gage was awake. He wasn't there. He was gone. Alex decided to get up and find him.

Before she had a chance to, he knelt beside her. "You awake?" he asked softly.

It was Gage's voice, but somehow different. She blinked her eyes sleepily and saw that his face was different, too. His expression was still and serious, almost somber. His dark eyes reflected urgency. He didn't give her a chance to answer. "Come on," he insisted. "The rain's stopped. We've got to go." His tense tone forbade any questions. He was already moving toward the mouth of the cave.

"What is it?" Alex asked as she struggled to get up.

"There's someone out there," he called back over his shoulder. He signaled Alex to stay behind him.

She stiffened. "It's probably help...." she began uncertainly. Fear, stark and vivid, glittered in her eyes. Perhaps the moment of truth had arrived. Perhaps Ken's killer lurked outside.

"It could be help," Gage said, "but I doubt it. Whoever he is camped across the wash is waiting to draw us out there."

"He? Are you sure it's a man?"

"I'm not sure of anything right now except that there's no phone to call the police."

"What are you saying?"

"I think we've got trouble out there," he said.

In the silence that followed, Alex contemplated what Gage had said. He was still peering outside. Alex was sure that all her worst suspicions were becoming reality. Gage swung back around to face her. His eyes were unrelenting, and Alex studied his tense expression. Then she walked to the opening to have a look. "I don't see anything," she said.

"His campfire burned out a while ago," Gage said.

"You called and left a message on Tucker's answering machine. It's feasible he mentioned our plans."

"That's possible, but it's also possible Tuck got worried and tracked us."

"I was just thinking the same thing."

"Wait a minute," Alex began. "Tucker is an old friend. There's no reason on earth he'd be out there, unless he meant to offer help."

Gage glanced at her. "Or unless he doesn't want us talking to Digger. There's only one other person who could know about us being here."

"Wait a minute. If you're talking about Howard LaRue, he has a campaign to run. I doubt he has time to traipse across a desert," Alex said. She was attempting to reassure herself as much as Gage.

"Whoever that is, they've had us staked out for hours. I've tried to minimize the facts, but they keep screaming back at me." Gage swallowed hard. "Alex, I think we're getting too close to something, and someone wants to eliminate us because of it. Yesterday was their first attempt. I think they're back."

"But why?" she asked.

"I'm not sure. There's something in this desert they don't want us to find."

Alex sensed a wariness in his tone. "It's got to be Digger," she said.

Gage stepped back from the opening, pulling her along with him.

"How long have you known someone was out there?" she asked.

"I was suspicious after you fell asleep last night," he said. "I walked outside to check the water. That's when I saw the light. He's stalking us. That raging wash would detour an army, but someone is determined to cross it. When they're able to, they'll make their move."

"A rock slide could turn this place into a tomb," she said.

Gage sucked in a sudden gush of air.

"Come on, don't go claustrophobic on me," Alex pleaded.

"We're getting out of here," he said. With a grim expression, he surveyed the dawn.

"Gage..." Alex began.

"What is it?" he asked.

"I just remembered something else. I told Marvin about the trip, too."

"Marvin?"

"A local mechanic. He repairs the county cars. I didn't intend to tell him, he just got it out of me somehow."

Gage drew another deep breath. He rubbed at the stubble on his face. "Then anyone could know we're out here right now."

"You're right," she admitted. She neglected to mention the sort of panic she felt. She wanted to try her best to remain calm.

"Let's get moving."

"Where to?" she asked, studying his face. Her insides clamped together. They'd had no breakfast and her stomach was gnawing hungrily on itself.

"This is your desert," he said. "I was hoping you could tell me."

Alex was taken aback by his remark. He wanted logic at a time like this? As quickly as he had assumed his take-charge attitude, he had backed off. He was leaving the decision-making up to her. Was he testing her? Or was she getting paranoid? He was gentle. He was strong. He was human. And right now, he was out of his element, she reminded herself. She was the desert rat.

"Come on," she said, taking Gage by the hand, "this is no time to dawdle. There could be a dangerous human being outside."

"Wait a minute," he said. "Let's clear up something. You are, without a doubt, the most dangerous human being I've ever met."

Alex refused to allow the remark to detour her from the issue. "I've got an idea," she said.

"Lady, it's your idea that got us here."

"The Martinez ranch is due south of here, on high ground. It's less than a day's hike by foot."

"Cat-and-mouse across a scorching desert? What kind of odds do you give us without water or weapons?" he asked.

He was forcing her to face facts that she would rather forget. "If we're careful and if we pace ourselves, we might make it."

"Might?"

"Look, I'm not good at guessing games," she confided.

"This trip is turning out to be more exciting than I'd expected."

"We've survived it all so far."

"We took a foolish chance coming." His voice was colder than an arctic wind.

"Haven't we been through this before?" she asked.

He glanced down at her, then glanced outside. "Let's get hiking," he said grimly.

Gone was the tender, sensitive Gage of last night. He was all business, cool and calculating. But right now, his terse manner gave her a much-needed sense of security. They moved swiftly and silently, Alex leading the way. Gage was right. There was no getting around it. They had made a bad choice when they'd decided to venture to Inspiration Mine. Now they had to accept the consequences.

The fact that their situation could have been worse didn't console her at all. Neither did it mitigate the truth. She was scared. She forced her defenses to descend around her like a protective glass dome. This was just one more hurdle, she told herself. And she would get over it. She would survive. She had to.

THIS FEAR WAS REAL. They had been without water for over eight hours. The early-morning sun had arisen higher in the sky, beating down on their hands. Even though the temperature was only in the high nineties by afternoon, a few scattered clouds added humidity. And the humidity created suffocating, heavy air. It felt more like a triple-digit day. Alex's head reeled from the heat. Sweat and jeans made an intolerable combination. The two chafed her thighs and waist.

Alex stopped to look up. A hawk cried. She felt apprehensive. Her defenses were down again and she was afraid.

Her mouth was as dry as the sandy desert. Her chafed lips cracked. She could taste the salty blood in her mouth.

Judging from the size of the mosquitoes swarming her and Gage, they were well fed. The company of insects didn't help make Alex feel any less miserable. One thing was certain. If anyone had managed to cross Date Creek and follow them, they would have known it by now. Until the flood waters subsided, air transportation was the only conceivable way to follow them. There was no place to sneak around on an open desert. Even so, Gage had been looking over his shoulder since they'd left the cave. His expression had been unreadable. To Alex, his stony silence was an admission of distress, fear and possibly regret. *Well,* she thought, *that wash they'd left behind will hold for at least a few hours.* Even then, it would be dangerous to cross.

They'd been hiking for two hours straight when Alex realized they would have to rest or she could never make it. Funny, she would have bet a month's pay that Gage would give in first. Under normal circumstances, when she'd had a decent night's rest, she would have had more stamina. She was hiking with a definite handicap today. Eight hours on the open desert was a very long time. "We'd better stop and rest," she said, feigning concern for him.

"I'm fine," he told her. "But you look miserable."

Certain things weren't worth fighting over. "I've got to stop, pull off my boot, and get my lucky penny out," she said. "It's killing the bottom of my foot."

"You pull off those boots and you won't get them back on those swollen feet," Gage warned.

He was right. She'd just have to endure it. Alex dragged to a complete stop under a sparse palo verde tree, where she could sit down. She dropped to the ground. Looking ahead, she could just make out the ridge of mountains that cradled the Martinez ranch. Sweat poured off her face, causing hair to cling to her cheeks. She pushed away the damp strands. Rapid water loss would dehydrate them in no time, she thought. They really had to slow down. She was too upset to take note of the gentleness in Gage's voice.

"This isn't your fault," he said, flopping down beside her. "No more than it's mine."

Right or wrong, Alex took little consolation in the admission.

"Here, suck on this," Gage said. He gestured toward her with something green and gooey in his hand. "Prickly pear, à la carte. It won't hurt you. Suck on the sap. It'll help keep you from dehydrating."

"I knew that," she said, and feeling too sick to argue the point, she took the cactus and put it to her mouth. "I hate prickly pear," she muttered. But it was cool and wet, and Gage just might have saved her life by offering it to her. She was supposed to be the desert rat, but he was obviously the survivor. She had to be honest with herself. Maybe she knew more about the desert, but he was the stronger one. She felt reassured by his strength.

She had been pretty hard on him during the trip. If he was giving the orders now, she had no choice but to take them. It was a strange reversal of roles. The desert had a way of distorting things, she thought.

Gage was speaking again. "Think of it as gourmet," he was saying in a deep exaggerated voice. His expression softened, and he stroked her face. "Hey," he said. "I'm sorry things worked out this way. Is there anywhere to rent camels around here?" He was hoping to draw a smile from her. "Come on, one little grin."

Something was tickling her. She started screaming. "There's a spider crawling under my blouse!" Screeching and jumping, she felt the horrible thing moving onto her shoulder. When it plunked down onto her breast, she ripped her blouse open and the poor creature fell to the earth. "A tarantula!" She tried to stomp on it. The hairy spider moved away with its usual lethargy. Alex quickly rebuttoned her blouse.

"They're harmless!" Gage said. "Let it be. It won't hurt you. Look. It's crawling off." Then he was beside her, pulling her to him.

"I don't care," she muttered. "I hate spiders."

"And rats," he reminded her.

"True," she said.

"It's all right, the spider's gone."

"You're going to think I'm afraid of everything," she said. "Are you sure it's gone?"

"It's gone. Here," he said, pointing to the palo verde tree, "sit back down."

Why was this happening to her? For the first time since she'd been grown, Alex thought she might cry. Tears teetered on the edge of her lower lid, but she blinked them back.

"What are you doing?" she demanded of Gage.

He was rubbing something on her arm and it felt like sandpaper.

"I'm rubbing dirt over your exposed skin. It keeps the mosquitoes and flies from biting." He inspected her arm, then dropped it, and picked up the other one. Then, gently, he applied the silty dirt to her face. When he was done, he threw his head back, and roared with laughter.

"It's not funny!" she moaned. A latent tear streaked a path down her dirty cheek.

"I'm sorry. It's just that you look funny!" He laughed again, this time a deep belly laugh, spontaneous and uncontrolled. It was catching. Alex broke loose, too. More tears rolled down her cheeks, making mud of the dirt on her face. Gage laughed even harder.

"You look like a little girl when you're dirty," he said, wiping his eyes.

"I haven't been this dirty since I *was* a little girl."

Alex looked at Gage, into his gentle eyes. For a moment, she wished he was someone else. Anyone who could make her forget instead of demanding that she remember. Anyone but an IA official. Anyone except an IA investigator implicating her partner in his own undoing.

When their laughter was spent, Gage took on a serious look, trying to keep any trace of humor from his expression or voice. He handed her another piece of prickly pear cactus. "Here," he said, gesturing toward her with the sticky, green goo. "Take this with you. When you begin to feel dehydrated, suck on it. We'd best get moving. We've bought some time, but just until that wash runs down."

She opened her mouth to object, then clamped it shut. She could definitely keep up with him any day of the week. And the sooner they reached the ranch, the sooner she could take a hot soak, sip lemonade and relax in the shade. So in a rapidly weakening state, she got up and plodded along beside Gage. This time, she walked under the shelter of his arm, acutely aware of their steaming clothes and their perspiration-dampened jean-clad bodies. To her relief, Gage had slowed his pace. Alex was still fighting exhaustion every step of the way.

Just when she thought things couldn't get any worse, they trudged down a rise. The silt valley below had turned to mud from last night's watershed. Her boots sank deeper with every step, squishing on their way down. Pulling them free became increasingly difficult.

She tried not to think about her thirst. Her throat felt as though it were swelling shut, and she found it difficult to swallow. The hands of her watch seemed to be standing still. They had barely moved since the last time she looked. It was still three o'clock, the hottest part of the day. *Get a hold on yourself,* she thought. *You can do this.*

In the past hour, she'd noticed that Gage was wearing down fast. Like hers, his steps were becoming increasingly heavy. She'd heard the fatigue in his deep, labored breathing. "We'd better rest again," she suggested, more for his benefit than her own.

"Can't. We've got to go while we can. I'm not spending another night on this desert up against the elements. No way."

Fear surged through her. She thought back to the wash and the stranger who was waiting to cross and come for them.

"I SEE IT!" ALEX SHOUTED. "I see the Martinez ranch."

Gage's breath was coming short. He scanned the ground around him. His eyes froze. Something big and black was running toward them. Wild dogs? It was a horrifying moment. He considered running. But where? He considered screaming, but he couldn't find his voice. The thundering in his chest was his heart. He thought that it would leap into his throat at any moment and strangle him. He had agreed to this trip. Voluntarily. Was he crazy?

"Do you see those—"

"Dogs," Alex finished calmly. "They belong to Hector Martinez."

"You know them?" he asked. He took a careful step backward. His fear made him feel as if a fist was being driven into the pit of his stomach.

"Don't move," she said cautiously.

He tried to reply but had trouble making his throat move in speech.

The afternoon sun was beating down on them even through the heavy cloud cover. Gage felt a shiver scurry upward from his lower back. The pure black dogs were gliding gracefully closer. Gage glanced surreptitiously at Alex.

"Just tell me one thing, do they bite?" Gage's normally husky voice had grown high and faint.

"If you don't stand still, you're going to find out."

In a twenty-four-hour period, had they survived a rock slide, a raging flood and a night stalker, only to die at the teeth of flesh-eating dogs? What the hell! Gage was going to climb a tree. He didn't mind dying a coward, but he did mind dying. Frantic, he looked about. Straight ahead stood an ironwood with a low, sloping branch.

"Gage!" Alex called out to him. "What are you doing?"

"Getting out of chewing distance!" Gage jumped onto the branch.

"Dobermans," he related in a stunned tone as he clawed his way up the splintery tree to a higher level.

"Coors and Flossy," Alex said.

"They're pet dogs?"

"I told you they belong to Hector."

"Call them off. Please," Gage said. He could barely make himself heard above the noise they were making. But all the noise wasn't coming from the dogs, he realized.

"This branch is breaking," Gage said in clipped tones.

"Grab ahold of the branch above you and hang on," Alex cautioned. "If you startle them, they're liable to chew your nose off."

"My nose?" A crackling sound pierced the air. "Oh, no. I'm slipping," Gage cried out.

"Can you get your legs around the branch?" Alex asked, feigning calm.

"I don't think so," he answered.

"Don't you ever work out?" she asked.

"You're comforting in a crisis," Gage said. He stared down into the two pairs of carnelian eyes. The Dobermans yelped and growled, lunged and showed their teeth. They were ferocious. After a struggle, Gage managed to clamp his legs around the higher branch. "I did it!" Gage called out.

"Good," Alex said. "Now try to swing yourself over the branch and hang on."

"Do you think you could go for help?" he asked desperately.

"You sound hysterical," she told him.

"Imagine that! I'm about to die and I lose control." He forced himself to take slow, deep breaths.

"Gage," Alex said in an exaggerated voice. "Concentrate. Make eye contact with the dogs and talk."

"Talk? I was thinking about praying." The whites of their eyes and the whites of their teeth were all Gage could see of the Dobermans now. The dogs came closer to him each time they jumped. They snarled, whined, and snapped their teeth. "Just call them off," he begged in a croaking voice.

"Talk to them," she ordered. "Don't you know anything about dogs?"

"I haven't spent much time around the big ones," he admitted with an edge to his voice. "But I understand they're connoisseurs of bones."

"Nice Coors, nice Flossy," she coaxed, extending her hand.

"Why are they acting like man-eating killers?"

"They respond to kindness. Try and say something nice to them."

"I'm trying, damn it!"

A big black raven swooped past, checking the situation over. Gage turned his face up to look. A spat of rain hit him. A cloudy sky had loomed in the distance all day. And the rain would come now, after they'd spent so many hours under the hot sun. Gage figured all the moisture had been dumped last night, but apparently not. The droplets grew larger and began falling faster. Within minutes, it was pouring down rain. The curtain of water doused the dogs' spirits and they tucked their tails and ran back toward the Martinez ranch.

"Okay, I think it's safe to climb down," Alex said. "Come on, you don't have to be afraid."

"I'm slipping—" Gage free fell past her to the ground and landed with a thud. The desert floor reached up and slapped the wind out of his lungs. For a moment, everything turned black. When he opened his eyes, Alex was holding his head in her lap and staring down at him.

"You okay?" she asked.

"I don't know," he answered. "The dogs—where are they? He remembered watching them vanish back toward the Martinez ranch. He stared out into the air for a moment before attempting to get up. As quickly as it began, the rain seemed to be clearing up.

"The dogs are gone," Alex said. "Calm down. Don't get up too quickly. Sit up and breathe through your mouth. You were pretty frightened."

"I always freeze up in a life-and-death situation. Especially when it's my life."

"Here, I'll give you a hand," she told him.

"I can do it myself," he said, and pulled himself up without the aid of her arm.

"You're welcome," she said with a sarcastic edge to her voice.

He tried to be gracious. "Thanks, but no thanks. Every time you try to help me, I end up almost getting killed."

Alex tossed her hair back over her shoulder and met his gaze directly. "Let me rephrase that," she said. "*We* almost end up getting killed."

"Do you think it's safe to go into the ranch?" he asked.

"We don't exactly have a choice."

"What do you make of those Dobermans? I mean I almost had the feeling that someone let them loose on us," Gage said.

Alex shuddered. She squeezed her eyes closed and tried to shut out the little voice echoing in her head. The voice said something was wrong.

"I don't know," she answered. "Hector usually keeps them inside, but he wouldn't have had any way of knowing that anyone was on the grounds."

"I'm getting paranoid," Gage admitted. "But we've been gone about thirty-six hours and have had too many close calls. It just seems like too much of a coincidence."

"We need to talk about that," she said. "But first, I need a hot bath and dry clothes. Let's go." Alex bit at her lower lip. "Everything will be all right once we reach the ranch house," she insisted.

She felt relieved as they neared the Spanish-style ranch, even though she didn't believe that everything was going to be all right, not really. Still, right now, the most appealing thing she could think of was a cool drink in the reassuring company of a nonthreatening friend.

Chapter Ten

The Martinez ranch was nothing short of a legendary place. Alex hadn't visited for sometime, but she took comfort in the fact that it had remained the same. It was a constant in an ever-changing world. She'd just finished the longest hike of her life. Hot, humid, buttery sunlight had melted around her, through her, and scorched the top of her head, not to mention the back of her neck and arms. The rain had felt good, but it had stopped just as quickly as it started. Rain or no rain, Alex was still so parched, she could barely swallow. Fear had speeded up the dehydration process.

"Who drives the pickup?" Gage asked as they made their way to the front doors.

Alex eyed the mud-covered truck. Not even the license plate was visible. "It belongs to Hector," she answered. There was no bell on the massive entrance way to the house. She knocked on the carved wooden doors, wondering how anyone could hear her feeble attempt at entry.

The door opened, swinging wide. A small, delicate man greeted them. The silk, lime-green shirt he wore did little to detract from his ruddy complexion. "Do come in," Hector Martinez said.

Alex made the introductions, and then Hector escorted them through the rock-walled Arizona room.

"What a surprise, Alex," said Hector.

"You're a welcome sight," she confessed. "But I apologize for the intrusion."

"We met up with a couple of ferocious dogs on the trail," Gage said. "Do they belong to you?"

"Ferocious?" Hector echoed.

"You'll excuse me if I sound hysterical," Gage said, with a tinge of sarcasm in his tone. Gage figured that he was entitled to a little sarcasm. Two man-eating dogs had attacked him.

"The Dobermans? They're pussycats," Hector insisted. "Come, we will sit in the courtyard. That flash rain just quit, and the sun's just about ready to set. You'll probably want a cool drink before getting out of your damp clothes." He led them outside.

The courtyard was spacious and shady. A small round fountain dominated the center. Water, a precious commodity in these parts, spewed freely from it. Hector poured drinks from a sweating pewter pitcher. He passed the filled cups to them.

"Take it easy," Hector cautioned, waving his hand lazily. "Sip it slowly, my friends."

Alex forced the pewter cup away from her mouth. It was pure torture not to take giant gulps. She looked down at her cup and shooed a fly from the rim. Another sip. She looked closely at the cup in her hand, noting its primitive beauty. Hector leaned forward with the pitcher and refilled the cup.

"I'm so pleased to see you, Alex," he began. "Since my dear wife's passing, it gets very lonely at times. Your room is always ready. But I am curious. What brings you here under such treacherous conditions?"

"We were looking for—"

"Alex—Deputy Sinclair," Gage broke in, "was kind enough to take me on a desert outing."

Alex looked at Gage over the rim of her cup, calling him a liar with her eyes. She wasn't sure what she saw in his electric, gray gaze. His eyes remained unreadable. She'd slipped up somehow, but in the next moment, she recovered admirably. "We were on the wrong side of the wash when the flash flood came up." It wasn't a total lie. Since crossing Date Creek had hardly been the wisest decision she'd ever made, it wasn't really a lie at all.

"I have a rather unusual hobby," Gage added. "I photograph reptiles. I'm afraid we strayed a bit too far."

"Do you prefer those auto-focus jobs?" Hector asked. "Personally, I like the old manual thirty-five millimeters better. Since you like reptiles, I must show you Rojo, my pet Gila monster." The rancher gestured toward a garden area. "Look closely. See him? Since he is primarily nocturnal, he sleeps during the day. He's just waking up now."

Alex looked down at the creature. It crawled slowly away from them. Its face was black. The small beadlike scales on its back were surrounded by broken blotches, bars and spots of black, yellow, orange and pink. She'd always thought that the distinguishing characteristic of the Gila monster was its blunt tail.

"But where is your camera equipment?" Hector probed. "Do you not wish to take a picture? There is still some light."

Alex followed Gage's lead. "Lost," she said. "When the flash flood swept away the Bronco, we lost everything. Our food, our clothes, our weap—" She drew in her breath and held it for a moment. That was a careless slip. She hoped Hector hadn't picked up on her mistake. She wasn't sure why it made any difference whether or not Hector knew the truth about their trip. Still, Gage seemed to think it mattered. And, against her common sense, Alex was beginning to trust him.

"A terrible storm," Hector said, picking up the thread where Alex had dropped it. "The road is washed out and the phone lines are down. If not for my generator, conditions at the ranch would be primitive, indeed."

A plump, smiling maid entered the courtyard from the Arizona room. Shifting her weight from foot to foot, she placed a hand on her ample hip and nodded her head. With a thick Spanish accent, she announced dinner.

"Pilar," Hector said, "our guests are exhausted. After hot baths, they might prefer meals in their rooms."

"*Sí, señor*," the maid replied.

"You read my mind, Hector," Alex said. What an un-dreamed-of pleasure! A hot bath and supper on a tray.

"But perhaps you would enjoy a drink first?" Hector suggested.

"Nothing for me," Alex said. "Thank you."

"Pilar, show Alex to her room."

However well-intentioned Hector was, Alex felt appre-hensive about leaving Gage. But his expression hadn't re-vealed the slightest hint of concern. His eyes were warm and reassuring, and for an instant, she felt a pleasant camara-derie with him. She made a willful decision to relax. At least for tonight.

"We'll talk later," Hector told her. "I'll send a bottle of your favorite wine to your room. Drink it and you will sleep soundly, little one."

"You're a dear, Hector," Alex said. She stood up to leave.

"*Pobrecita*," Pilar said. The portly maid took Alex by the arm and led her out. She wore her black hair in a tight bun on the exact top of her head. Except for her flashing brown eyes, the severity of her hairdo robbed the maid's face of any warm expression.

A strange tightness gripped Alex's chest as she followed the maid down a corridor. The flagstone floor was decorated with Indian scatter rugs. The stucco walls were dimly lit, but Alex was seeing with her mind's eye now. She could see the Dobermans. They were jumping and snapping. But that was over, she reminded herself.

She entered the room to which Pilar directed her. Then real fatigue set in. The sleeping quarters were furnished with a double bed that was covered with a heavy Indian blanket. The bed looked welcoming.

"You'll want to freshen up," Pilar said. "The bath is through that door. You will find towels and soap. Everything you need."

"Thank you, Pilar. You can go now."

The maid nodded acknowledgement and turned to leave. Alex could no longer ignore the growing stiffness in her muscles. She would draw a hot bath and have a long, slow soak. It worked every time. Alex looked into a wall mirror. Her reflection shocked her. She did look like hell. Gage had seen her looking like this? That she felt bad about. About what had happened last night, she did not. She'd found pleasure in his arms and she didn't feel guilty about it. But why had she pulled away from him? Today, right now, she felt as though she trusted him.

She walked into the bathroom. It looked like pure heaven. The sunken tile tub sparkled. She hadn't had a proper bath in two days. Everything else could wait. She was filling the tub with hot water when she heard Pilar reenter the bedroom. Alex wasn't offended, just startled. Pilar hadn't knocked.

"Where would you like this?" Pilar asked. She held up a tray with an open wine bottle and a glass.

"In here," Alex answered. "Next to the tub."

"*Sí.*"

"That will be all, Pilar," Alex said, dismissing her. "Thank you."

The maid waddled out. Relieved to be alone, Alex stripped off her dirty clothes and dropped them in a pile. She tested the bath water with her toe and then eased into the tub. Glorious. After a moment, she sat up and tipped the wine bottle. Luscious red liquid gurgled into a crystal glass. She put it to her lips and sipped. It slid down her throat smoothly. It was warm and sweet. She wanted to tilt the bottle again, but she refused to give in to temptation. She needed her wits about her right now. She leaned back in the tub and stretched out her long, slender legs. Alex closed her eyes for a few minutes.

Almost immediately, the wine had dulled her senses. It was tricky, trying to bathe yourself like this, she thought. Her motions were slow and exaggerated. The wine had had a real effect on her, she realized. She tried to sort out the events of the trip, but as her logic slipped away, it became a real effort. Eventually, she gave up. She simply wanted to sprawl in the tub and sleep.

Instead, she stepped out and dried off. Drowsiness crept over her body like a heavy weight. It required sheer effort to make it to the bed. Once there, she fell across it with the towel still wrapped around her. How could one glass of wine make her so tired? Perhaps it was just the exhaustion from the trip overtaking her. Eyes closed, Alex groaned and rolled over onto her back, the damp towel tangling around her body. The only thing she could comprehend at the moment was that her brain was not fully functioning. Eight more days, she thought. She only had eight more days. A light inside her went off and she began to drift away.

GAGE NEVER DREAMED he would regret this trail's end. They had traveled so far in such a short time. He had learned a great deal about himself. The outdoors was the last place he'd ever expected to find out anything, especially about Gage Morgan, but he'd discovered magic in the desert wilderness.

The rancher looked younger than Gage had figured he would, despite the gray in his thinning hair. Early fifties, Gage guessed, and ambitious. There was a bright glint of shrewd intelligence in Hector's eyes that Gage found disturbing.

"And you, Gage? What would you like to drink?" Hector asked.

"Coffee sounds good. Black." Then, as an afterthought, he added, "Please."

"Coffee it is."

When Gage was comfortably seated in an oversized leather recliner, sipping coffee, he casually asked Hector about the ranch. "Quite a spread you've got here. Modern ranchers need a chopper for quick access."

"Yes, if you fly, it's a good idea," Hector replied. His voice implied that he didn't fly. He continued, "This ranch is a family heirloom, you might say. My grandfather acquired Del Rio through a Spanish land grant. The American government honored the requisition. Federal land borders us on all sides. I lease that land, too, from the Bureau of Land Management. This, my friend, is a working ranch."

Odd, Gage thought. He hadn't seen a single head of livestock.

"I noticed the antenna," Gage probed. "I thought you might be a ham operator."

"You are very observant, *señor*. Weather is an important factor if you want to survive in this remote desert. The radio allows me immediate access to the outside world in hazardous conditions."

"I've experienced the hazards of this desert firsthand," Gage confirmed.

"You are fortunate, indeed, to have reached Del Rio. As for the radio—unfortunately, it's not reliable. It's been down since the storm. Now, tell me, what brings you to Wickenburg?" Hector asked.

"I'm investigating Ken Forney's murder." Gage chanced trying out the truth—or a portion of it. He might learn more from this rancher if he did so, and perhaps Martinez might blurt out some information that could be used.

"A very terrible thing," Hector said, shaking his head and rubbing his hands together with a soft squishing noise. His grim visage and clamped lips indicated he wouldn't spill any new information.

Gage hunched his shoulders in a shrug that said he was tired. "I hope we're not imposing. We're grateful for your hospitality. But you must excuse me, I'm very tired."

"Of course. I'll show you to your room. You will find it very comfortable. We are remote, but not primitive in our life-style."

Gage wasn't picky. Anything would do tonight. "You won't get a complaint from me," he said.

Hector led Gage down an oversized hallway. White plastered walls supported the ten-foot ceilings. Twelve-inch thick adobe bricks insulated the interior of the house against the raging heat outside. When at last Hector pointed him to his room, Gage was grateful to shut the door behind him.

The silence in the sprawling house seemed fitting. It was quiet as a tomb. Alex had explained that Hector was widowed and without an heir to the sprawling estate. Gage picked fresh clothes from the closet and carried them across the hallway to a bathroom. He closed the door and turned on the shower. He'd gone two days without benefit of a bath. So much for the outdoors. He welcomed the hot water, standing mesmerized under its flow. When steam started rolling through the room, he turned the water off and stepped out.

He yanked a fresh towel from a hook and pressed it to his face. Weakness crept into his body. The hot water had served to drain the blood from his head, leaving him drowsy. *Easy does it. You'll be all right,* he assured himself. He peered into the mirror, but it was fogged.

He slid the bathroom window open and gazed out through the evening dusk. The view wasn't great from here—just a string of foothills in the distance that seemed to rise up and meet the window. Although he couldn't see the airstrip, he knew a single-engine plane was taking off. A landing strip was nearby. His auditory sense followed the plane as it hurtled overhead, piercing the still air. Help? Not this quickly. Anyway, the plane was leaving, not arriving. It must have been here when they hiked in. Gage felt an inexplicable flutter of panic in his chest. Hector had said his radio was out. Gage realized that no one knew they were here. He wondered if they had been missed.

He shrugged into the clothes that had been provided for him. He was relieved they weren't as fancy as the silk shirt and dress pants Hector wore. On his way back to his quarters, Gage heard voices down the hall. He caught sight of Hector and another tall figure striding into one of the rooms. Wanting a better look at the stranger, Gage slipped down the corridor, edging his way up to but just short of the doorway.

"It's feeding time. Hurry up. You'll barely have time to finish before it gets any darker. I don't want the lights turned on tonight."

"I'm on my way."

No, Gage thought. *Not more dogs.* How many mouths were they feeding? Gage couldn't help but wonder what the mouths belonged to. He didn't recognize the second voice. But it clearly belonged to a much younger man. Hector was coming out. Gage realized it too late. Where could he hide?

"Gage?" Hector said. "I thought you'd be sleeping off the effects of the desert by now. Anything wrong?"

"Uh—no. I was looking for the kitchen. A glass of milk always helps me fall asleep."

"I'll send Pilar with one," the rancher said. Hector's chilling smile said he didn't believe for a moment that Gage had just happened into the hallway.

WES WENT STRAIGHT to the substation when he reached town. He swung his mud-caked truck into a parking spot and jumped out. Inside, he encountered the desk sergeant first. The stocky man had the appearance of a bulldog. "Bullneck, where's the lieutenant?"

The desk sergeant cocked his thumb toward Tucker's office. "Inside," he bellowed.

Wes stalked in. Tucker only looked on impatiently.

The lanky deputy began by firing questions. "Do you realize Alex is in trouble?"

"Trouble?" Tucker asked, nervously fingering the pencil on his desk. "Wes, you're beginning to get on my nerves."

Wes gritted his teeth. "Alex needs help, damn it. I think she's being held against her will, and if I get my hands on—"

"Did you see anyone holding a gun on her?" the lieutenant quizzed.

"Well, no," Wes admitted.

"Then explain to me why you think she's being held against her will."

"I tracked her and Gage Morgan as far as Date Creek. Water runoff came down from the north before I could cross. But they weren't anywhere near the mine road. I need the Blazer."

"Like hell you need the Blazer. Now listen to me, Wes Davenport!" Tucker stood up. "You're going to follow orders and that's all you're going to do. Alex can take care of herself. And if she can't, she's in good hands."

Wes frowned. He wasn't interested in what Tucker was saying.

"Are you listening to me?" Tucker asked.

Wes nodded silently.

"You're letting emotions screw up this investigation," Tuck said coldly. "Stay out of it or I'll relieve you of your duty. You understand?"

Wes stared at him with anguish in his eyes. He was only trying to help. What was with the lieutenant? "I don't understand your attitude," Wes said. "I'm only concerned for Alex."

"Get out of here. We've had this conversation before, and this is the last time we're going to have it. Go home and get some rest."

"Is that an order?"

"If that's what it takes."

Wes walked slowly to the door, wanting to appear calm. There was more than one way to skin a cat. He had no choice. It was nearly dark. He would have to hurry.

Chapter Eleven

Groggily, Alex heard the shuffle of feet and the click of the lock being disengaged. Suddenly Gage stood in the doorway, staring at her. She didn't know how long she'd been asleep, but she had neglected to dress. She lay sprawled across the bed naked except for the towel. The effect of the wine hadn't completely worn off and she fumbled with the sheet in an effort to cover herself.

He looked different. Something was wrong. Lately, his appearance seemed to shift constantly, hour by hour. The geography of his face grew tight with concern now. But his eyes remained the same, reflecting light like polished silver. They crinkled at the corners as his morose expression turned into a smile.

She tried to sit up as Gage approached the bed. Without words, he sat down and reached for her. He took an afghan from a nearby chair and folded it around her.

"Is something wrong?" she asked. The throbbing inside her head slid from one temple to the other.

"I'm sorry if I woke you," he said, pulling her to him.

"You don't have to apologize for anything," Alex said in a husky voice. She snuggled up against him. "I'm glad you came. I had this stupid notion…" Her voice trailed off, and she nuzzled her head on Gage's chest.

"Where are your clothes?" he asked, half amused.

"They seem to be missing," she answered, drawing the afghan more tightly around her.

She'd always been shy about her body, but right now, her throbbing head was all she could think about. That and her stomach which now felt queasy. Had Hector put something in her wine? But, no, she thought, that was a crazy idea. Gage gently disentangled himself and drew away. Her eyes followed him as he rose from the bed.

"You all right?"

He sounded as though he was speaking through a tunnel. His words bounced off the walls. The spinning room made her dizzy and punctuated the throbbing inside her head. She pressed her palms to her temples and attempted to steady herself. It didn't help.

"I—I think so."

"No wonder you're sick. You didn't eat your supper."

She ordered herself to think, but there was a storm brewing in her stomach. *Not here. Not in front of Gage. Please, don't let me throw up,* she thought.

Suddenly, Gage was clutching her. "Steady. You almost fell off the bed."

"The wine must have done it."

"What wine?"

"The bottle Hector sent." She shook her head to clear the fog, but it didn't help.

"How much did you drink? You look awful."

"Not that much. A glass, but it must have really hit me."

Gage strode over to the closet and pulled a man's robe out. He returned to Alex and draped it around her.

"Come on, we're going to sober you."

He lifted her from the bed and guided her toward the bathroom. Her legs felt rubbery, and regardless of what she wanted them to do, they were out of touch with her mind.

Gage sat her down on the side of the tub and turned on the water in the sink. Then he lifted her to the basin and told her to splash water on her face. "More," he said. "This isn't working." He eased her back down onto the side of the tub.

"What are you doing?" Alex asked.

"Come on, you're taking a cold shower," he informed her. He tugged at her robe. "I didn't get you across a desert to have you crack your head in a bathtub. You're not going to get bashful on me now, are you?"

"What?"

"A cold shower works every time."

He yanked back the shower door, turned on the shower, shucked his shirt and leaned in under the icy spray. The water was running and his arms were around her, pulling her into the frigid torrent. She ordered her body to stand up, but it still wasn't receiving messages. At the moment, she wasn't sure of anything except how strong Gage felt. Was she really naked in the shower with Gage's arms holding her up? Was this the same Alexis Sinclair who had trouble stripping in the gym class? She wished she were fully dressed.

"Oh!" she moaned from the shock of the water. "You're trying to kill me."

"I'm not, but I think it's being arranged."

She couldn't stand this. She felt awful. What had made her sick? "I've had enough of this." The spray of cold water had cleared the fog in her head. She felt shaky but rational, and she wanted out of the shower and into some clothes. "Please get out," she said. "I think I'm okay."

"All right," he said, exiting the shower, "if you're sure."

When she stepped out, her head still hurt, but she felt better. Gage had taken his shirt into the other room and was presumably dressing. She wrapped a large bath towel around her. *Just take it slow,* she told herself. Every step made her head throb and brought on a rolling queasiness. Not sure if she could make it past Gage without showing her embarrassment, she clutched the robe to herself and headed for the closet. A few careful steps put her in front of it and she peered inside, trying to figure out what would fit her. She extracted a gray sweatsuit. It would have to do. Clean and comfortable was all she was interested in right now. She slipped back into the bathroom to dress.

"How well do you know Hector?" Gage called out to her.

She knew from the hesitation in his voice something was wrong. And his question was loaded. Her answer was quick and assured.

"As well as anyone, I suppose," she said, walking back into the room. "What are you getting at?"

She set her mouth in a tight line. Gage had to be wrong in suspecting Hector. She had nothing more than instinct to go on, but she trusted it.

"Who else lives here with him?"

"Not anyone I know of. Why?"

"I overheard him talking to someone. A much younger man."

"What's so unusual about that?"

"I'm not sure. It seems odd he didn't introduce us when we arrived. Did you know he has a landing strip on the ranch?"

"This is a remote spot. There's nothing unusual about an airstrip."

"There is if a man doesn't fly."

She searched for a plausible explanation, but came up with nothing. A sharp uneasy silence ensued, which Gage finally broke.

"Hector lied to us when he said his shortwave set was out. I'm certain they were using it."

A moment or two passed.

"I don't know why he would lie," she said. A chilling recollection of the Dobermans hit her.

"I'm not sure, either." Gage walked over to the window and looked out. "How well do you know the ranch?" he asked, turning.

"I can give you the nickel-and-dime tour, if that's what you mean. But I'm not sure how we can get out without being noticed."

"Right there," Gage said, gesturing toward the window behind her.

Alex looked at it, catching a glimpse of the black night against the glass. "I don't know. How would we explain this if we were discovered?"

"It might not be us needing to explain," he said. "What about the dogs?"

"Hector usually keeps them inside at night," she said.

"Good." He paused to look at her. "I'm glad you found some comfortable clothes. You might be needing them." He smiled. "I think I liked you the other way better, though."

"Consider us even," she said, remembering his encounter with the prickly pear. Still, she felt embarrassed. Color flooded her face. The shyness was back, full force.

"Are you okay now?" he asked gently.

"I'm fine."

As much as she loved adventure, a part of her dreaded what they might find on this treasure hunt. The best thing to do would be for her to act as if this was no big deal. Treat it all lightly. After all, Hector was a trusted friend. She wondered again how such a small bit of wine could have made her so sick and glanced at the window. "What do you want to do now?" she asked.

"We passed a good-sized barn when we hiked in. Lots of fresh tire tracks were leading to it," Gage said. "And besides those two Dobermans, no signs of life were visible. Let's check it out. You first.''

He was already prying the window open. Sweat glistened on his head. He frowned. Carefully, Alex crawled onto the window sill and perched to jump. The ground dropped off below and she snapped her eyes shut for a moment. She couldn't believe she was doing this. But then, what was new? She was always up for adventure. She leapt. Her feet thudded on the ground. She felt the air slap out of her lungs on impact. She tottered and fell on her behind.

Gage landed right behind her. ''You okay?'' he asked.

''I think so.''

''Get up, then!'' he urged, lending her a hand. ''We can't hang around here. Those dogs could show up any second.''

Before them the desert stretched out forever. Like a cat in the dark, Alex crept along with the greatest of ease. They reached the barn. Alex tried the door while Gage peered around the side of the structure.

''Look what we have here,'' he mused.

Alex left the door to join him.

''Haven't you heard?'' she asked. ''Choppers have replaced horses.''

''For a man who doesn't fly, Hector's sure got a lot of airstrips and planes. It seems like too much of a coincidence.''

If it was, it was a big one, Alex thought. It was the small ones that she worried about, the ones she tended to ignore. ''Gage...that chopper has a radio—''

''I think I've underestimated you,'' he said, playing catch-up with her mental gymnastics. ''Okay. We've got an alternative, but it will have to wait. I think we should check out the barn first.''

''Good idea. We could just be taking disconnected facts and connecting them to support a preconceived judgment," she said. She still wanted to hold out for Hector's best intentions.

Alex and Gage stepped deeper into the barn. Total blackness wrapped itself around them. Alex's breath was coming short. She tried to adjust her eyes to the darkness. A swirl of wind blew the odor of wet straw into her face. As strong as the smell was, she couldn't determine where it came from.

It was the humming sound in the dark expanse that really diverted her attention. She imagined a blanket of insects covering the floor. The thought made her skin crawl. "What are you doing?" she asked Gage in a less-than-even voice.

"I'm putting a match to this lantern."

The buzz in the room continued. It sounded like bees around flowers. The lantern brightened eventually, illuminating the interior of the barn. Then her heart missed a beat. She was staring into the eyes of creatures whose heads looked like miniature dinosaurs with blinkless eyes.

"Snakes!" Gage said, his screech paralyzing Alex.

She stopped motionless, one foot frozen above the ground. Stepping back, she called in a deceptively calm voice, "Don't move. They all look poisonous."

"All? Not all of them?"

Stacked rows of cages lined either wall, each filled with various species of dangerous snakes. Inwardly, Alex was as near to being hysterical as she had ever been, but outwardly, she was calm.

Gage was at her side now, and he was trembling. "I hate snakes," he said. "Snakes are your department. I handle the rats. Remember?"

"Then wait outside for me."

"You want me to walk back to the door alone? Oh no, you don't. I'm not going anywhere."

"All right, then. Hold that light up and stay right behind me."

She put off moving again for a moment. She felt the snakes move all around her. A swarm of flies hit against her face, making her wince. Finally, she forced herself to move, but not until, with the aid of the lantern, she had scrutinized every inch of their surroundings.

The bundles of freshly shed snake skins smelled badly. But the smell bothered her less than the faint sound of voices. The voices drifted toward them from the rear of the barn. It was the only area they hadn't explored.

They inched their way to the other end of the expanse and found a door. Alex picked up a small twig with which to push it open. She wasn't about to touch anything with her hands. Even without looking at the slithering creatures in the wire cages, she could see their lidless eyes open and shut on either side of her. The door squeaked open, and for a second, she stood rigid, not moving a muscle. She imagined that rattlers were crawling all over the floor inside the next room, and she imagined herself going insane, bit by bit, as they got her.

Feeling queasy and weak-kneed, she listened to a new sound. Wings flapping? Birds! Relief flooded her. She was unwilling to admit it to Gage, but she wasn't sure she could have faced another room full of reptiles. They stepped inside to spy the collection of parrots under the lantern's dim light.

The sight of it all caught Alex off guard. She was slow to recover.

"I'm beginning to understand," Gage said. "Damato—was that the case Howard mentioned?"

"I can't believe Hector could be involved with a man like that. Hector could be a breeder, perhaps...."

"Alex. Open your eyes. This is a sophisticated operation."

"Not Hector! He wouldn't be a part of this. He's a well-known person in this town. Respected. Liked."

"He's a human. I know you don't think he would commit a crime—"

"I have complete and absolute confidence in his judgment and integrity—"

"Alex!" Gage said with a take-charge tone. He put the lantern down and gripped her shoulders, drawing her closer. "I'm sorry you had to find out like this."

Alex stiffened. She nearly screamed at him. She began reviewing what they'd seen, wondering if she'd seen right. Among those snakes were fish rock, twin spotted and ridge nose, all protected species. They could be sold to interested parties for a fortune. It looked like Hector Martinez *was* in the smuggling business. She would have turned on her heel and left, but she didn't want to pass the reptiles again. They had to clear out, but she wasn't sure how. There had to be another route. A terrible heaviness weighted on her chest. She wiped a hand across her face, swallowed and tried to clear her mind. Closer inspection revealed a door straight ahead. They weren't trapped, after all.

Before she was able to make her legs work, Hector's voice cut through the silence. "Can I be of assistance?" he asked.

Alex's heart thudded painfully in her throat, and for once in her life, she was rendered speechless. She wanted her feet to move, to run, but it was no use, her brain wasn't sending out messages. It had gone numb. In one move, Hector was next to her. He placed one hand on her shoulder while training his gun on Gage.

"This is awkward," Hector said. He released Alex's shoulder and held the gun with both hands. "I thought the wine I sent would put you out cold."

She flinched. Shock coiled inside her. Hector had drugged her wine. *Why?* she wanted to ask. But the words didn't come, wouldn't come, so she just stood there, looking at him.

"I'm sorry," Hector continued. "Things could have been so simple, indeed." He turned his attention to Gage. "I'm very good with this gun," he warned. "One move, Lieutenant, and you are history. Do we understand each other?"

Gage held up his hands with the palms turned outward and nodded compliance. "Sure," Gage said, trying desperately to buy time.

"Shall we take the young lady back to the house?" Hector said to Gage. "It will be easier for you there," he said to her.

"I don't expect anything of you, Hector," she replied, hating the sliding note of desperation in her voice.

"Just don't do anything foolish, my dear." He purred like a cat. "I don't want to hurt you."

Alex felt the nauseating sinking feeling of fear. It was easier not to believe that this was happening. Not her Hector Martinez. Not her old friend. She forced herself to hold her tongue. She had no intentions of acting foolish. In her peripheral vision, she noticed someone else approaching. How many others were involved?

"Hurry up, Skip!" Hector ordered.

Skip? Oh, no, Alex thought, half in anticipation, half in dread. Wave after wave of shock slapped her. Floundering, she fought against the nightmarish scene unfolding before her. What was Skip Tucker doing here?

"Skip; tie the lieutenant's hands before the cop in him does something stupid. I don't want to have to resort to drastic measures. You wouldn't want that to happen, would you, Lieutenant?" Hector didn't allow Gage a chance to answer. "Quickly, get them back to the house."

"I can handle them," Skip assured Hector. His boyish voice was too soft, like an undercooked egg.

"Overconfidence breeds complacency," Hector cautioned.

They stepped outside. The night was black. But not as black as Alex's world was right now. Her mind raced forward and all her thoughts were unbearable. Panic gripped her. Then despair.

"Almost done," Hector said. "Just one thing more."

BACK INSIDE THE RANCH house, in the Arizona room, Alex tried to relax. Hector's long, spidery fingers came together and caressed the end of his chin. What hurt her most was not really that Hector had committed these crimes. It was his betrayal. She had believed in him totally. Ken had, too. Ugly stuff, smuggling. Murder, worse. Compulsively, as her instincts for survival took over, she tried to calculate how this might end. Whatever friendship she and Hector Martinez had shared was clearly over. He had vengeance planned for anyone who interfered with his scheme.

Alex raked her brain for a way out. She tried desperately to sort her thoughts into a logical stack, but the stack kept collapsing. First one emotion, then another swept over her. She agonized over how she was going to outwit her old friend. And the sight of Skip holding a gun on them numbed her senses. She turned her attention to Gage, who sat opposite her on the couch. Hector's smile made Alex feel sick, made her feel dirty.

"Why, Hector?"

"Because I'm tired of running my legs off for the ranch I'll never have. Patented land means taxes. I was forced to over-graze, choking out the grass. Now the land is worthless, and I'll do anything to save it." He sounded impenetrably sad and pitiful. He continued: "My dear, without wanting to sound philosophical, allow me to assure you that not all human misbehavior is the result of character defects.''

''The trail of skeletons you're leaving behind is a high price.''

''I have known you throughout your life. You are very dear to my heart, but I am confined by powerful restraints. This is a nasty, but lucrative business.''

''I don't condone what you're doing, not for one moment, Hector. It's a disgrace.'' There was no misinterpreting her meaning.

''I didn't want to hurt you, Alex, but you got in the way. You shouldn't have nosed around. You don't know what it's like to lose your home, your land, a ranch you've built from scratch. And then to—to have the opportunity to save it. I had to do it. I was about to lose what I love most in the world.''

''You already did. When you shot Ken, you lost any remaining shred of humanity.''

''Me?'' Hector replied. He said something in Spanish that she couldn't understand. ''Give credit where credit is due.''

''I didn't expect a full confession.'' Her voice was unforgiving and cool. She bit at her lip and blinked back tears.

''I did not kill Ken Forney, if that is what you are thinking.''

His words hit Alex like rocks. They were absurd. A bad joke. Of course, he had killed Ken Forney. But there was no humor in Hector's face. Hector's voice became more animated as he spoke, and his forefinger pointed at her like a witching rod drawn to the ground. ''When I last saw Ken Forney, he was alive and well. He was driving around town, alone in his patrol car.''

Comprehension burned through her mind like a streak of lightning. "You were there—at the murder site—the night he was killed."

"I didn't say that."

"Yes, you did. Because that was the only time in more than three years Ken rode alone in that patrol car."

She looked toward Skip, who had remained quiet throughout the conversation. The silence became tight and uncomfortable. Skip's eyes darted from Alex to Hector to Gage, then back to her.

"You're fishing," Hector continued, "but I'll tell you this. We did see him pull off the main highway. He must have picked up a beam from our lights."

"How could you have known it was Ken Forney in that car?" Gage asked with no lack of skepticism.

"The moon lit up his car like a Christmas tree. Skip recognized the number on it. Nine-thirteen, if memory serves me right."

Alex trained her eyes on Gage. There. It was out. Proof that Ken had pulled off the road because he had seen something. But it was not enough. She wanted more. Hector had been there. And she would continue to pull the secrets of that night from him. He might provide her with a small, overlooked detail that would help identify the killer. The only thing she was interested in was Ken's slayer. "Who else was in the desert that night?"

"For the time being, I will have to leave that concern to you."

"But—"

"I told you," Hector said, clearly losing his temper. His color rose. "No one besides Skip and myself were in that desert when Ken Forney pulled off the road." As suddenly as he had lost control, he regained it. "You know me, Alex."

Until now, she'd thought she did.

"Nothing escapes my eye."

"Then there were two autos out there, yours and Ken's."

"Three, counting Skip's. In retrospect, if I could catapult myself backward in time, I would remain to see who killed him. I've wondered about it myself."

"What are we gonna do with them?" Skip asked nervously.

"From the moment they arrived, I have been wondering that very thing. And the sad solution is that we must eliminate them." Hector's voice was smooth and unruffled.

Alex looked to Gage in horror. His expression revealed no surprise. Alex wondered which was worse, the grief constricting her heart or the possibility of death.

"You can't kill everyone," Gage said.

"As you no doubt perceive, I am most uncomfortable with this situation." Hector looked to Alex. "I know you would rather die than corrupt your position as a deputy."

Her head jerked up.

"Forgive me," he continued, "but I make this decision from the heart."

"You intend to kill us in cold blood?" Alex demanded.

The remark drew no shame from him. "No, not in cold blood, in self-defense."

A sharp, uneasy silence ensued. Alex examined his response in her mind's eye. It disgusted her. Had she really hoped for remorse?

"You have my solemn promise that you will not suffer," the rancher said. "It does not take long to snuff out a life. A few seconds, and it will be mercifully over."

Skip hunched his shoulders. He seemed to think that Hector was talking nonsense. Hector reached out to touch Alex's cheek.

"Don't put your hands on me," she declared recklessly. She couldn't keep the revulsion from her voice.

He stroked her chin with the back of his hand.

"You must be brave," he assured her.

Her reaction was quick. Alex spat in his face. Hector's palm connected with her mouth, splitting the skin like a grape. Although his hands were tied, Gage headed for Hector as quick as a flash. Caught off guard, Hector toppled over, kicking and squirming. Then Hector slammed his revolver against Gage's head. Gage slumped.

"Gage!" Alex screamed. Her shock yielded to fury as she ran to him. "You've killed him, damn you!" By the time she got to Gage, he lay in a motionless heap at Hector's feet. Alex crouched beside him.

"Get back or I'll finish him right there!" Hector ordered. He reached down to help Alex up. She suddenly came to life, snarling and hitting him. Hector grabbed one of her flying hands and pulled Alex to her feet. He flung her back onto the sofa. Alex got up. Drops of blood trickled off her chin.

Gage was coming to, but he remained groggy. "Touch her again," Gage said, "and if it's the last thing I do, I swear I'll kill you!"

"For a man about to die, you are very boastful." Hector's laugh was dry and cynical.

"There're people who know where we are," Alex said. "By now, they are probably looking for us."

"An unfortunate rock slide has delayed their efforts," Hector said.

Alex looked at him, trying to mask her horror. She had forgotten about the rock slide.

"Skip is careless and compulsive as only the young can be, but he did well with the explosives."

"You started that slide?" she asked, looking to Skip. She tried to swallow, but her mouth went dry.

"No one was supposed to get hurt," Skip snapped glaring at Hector.

"We could not allow the two of you to stumble innocently onto our operations."

"Smuggling and murder operations," Gage added. "Right, Hector?"

"Murder requires not only skill," Hector boasted, "but creativity. One must understand his victim. It's that way when any predator stalks and devours its prey."

"Why, Skip?" Alex pressed, stunned and sickened.

"Money is a tremendous motivator," Hector said. "And the boy got greedy, didn't you, son?"

"Don't call me son!" Skip retorted with cold sarcasm. His lips drew into a thin white line. "Alex..." His voice faded, losing its steely edge. "I didn't have anything to do with Ken's death."

"Quiet." Hector ordered. He paused a moment and then resumed his calm demeanor. "Human cargo doesn't fit into our line of work. Ken Forney's untimely murder was a nasty threat to my operation."

"What about Tucker, Skip?" Alex asked.

"You mean more to him than I do," the boy snapped. "You and that job. I got sick of waiting for him to come home. Mother died waiting. He killed her."

"That's not true, Skip," Alex said.

"Dad should have been there for her."

"Skip, don't go through with this...." Alex pleaded with a gentleness in her voice.

"I'll do whatever I want." Skip replied. His voice broke and he held his trembling lower lip in his teeth, determined not to let down his guard.

"I believe Skip is fed up with being told what to do," Hector said. "Now quiet! All of you." His arm shot out, striking the end table.

Alex's stomach made a slow revolution as another realization hit her. "Skip, you stole the Damato file and erased the case from the computer terminal." Her pulse started to climb. The inside of her mouth turned to cotton and her eyes burned.

"Skip's genius for computers advances the proficiency of our operation considerably," Hector said. "But a boy always finds it necessary to stand on a man's shoulders to keep from drowning."

In her peripheral vision, Alex saw Skip waver with his gun. If he was feeling remorse, he might be their way out of this. Her mind tried desperately to apply logic to this chaotic situation.

"Tell me, Hector," Gage said, "what do you have in mind for us?"

"Why not tell you, Lieutenant?" Hector's tongue slipped across his lower lip. He removed a handkerchief from his shirt pocket and blotted his neck and forehead. "What kind of monster would deny a dying man his last request. It is my sad chore to inform you that you are more dead than alive." He continued to hold the gun on them, prepared for any further imbroglio. "Skip! Are you listening?"

Skip's head bobbed up and down.

"This must look like an accident," Hector said.

"What kind of accident?" Skip probed.

"A natural one, of course. We shall fly our guests to the rocky cliffs over Date Creek and give them a closer look."

"But there's no place to set the chopper down," Skip replied.

"Exactly," Hector said. "When they're found, it will look like they were attempting to reach higher ground, away from the rain-swollen creek."

Alex's palms were clammy. She stared at Gage, searching his eyes for a clue. Someone had followed her and Gage at least as far as Date Creek. If it wasn't Skip, then who? She wondered if Gage had any new guesses.

"I don't like it," Skip protested.

"You don't have to," Hector snapped, his patience obviously spent with the boy. "Just do it." He paused to regain his composure.

The short-wave radio screamed out, shattering the tension. Hector looked startled, but kept his weapon trained on Alex.

"Answer the radio," he ordered Skip. "Everything is on schedule."

Skip nodded and left the room.

"Get up, Lieutenant," Hector ordered. "You're going to the attic where Alex is going to tie you up. Then she is going to her room. I hope you won't try anything foolish, my friends. No more shows of bravado, Lieutenant. That would only hasten your demise."

Alex racked her brain for an alternative to what Hector had proposed. There must be some way to escape.

"I'm an excellent shot at this distance. I won't hesitate to kill either of you," Hector said.

Gage hesitated and Alex knew exactly what he was thinking. He wasn't going to let another life be sacrificed. "I don't believe you," Gage challenged.

He was going to make a move, but Alex didn't know what he had in mind. He had called Hector's bluff. Now what?

"You are being most difficult, Lieutenant," Hector snarled. "But I do not intend to kill you just yet. Only after Alex has been permitted the comfort of death will you enjoy the same. I find this most distasteful, but a bit of blood on my hands will not make much difference to me. I'm already a criminal." He pulled the hammer back. "I'll count to three. One...two..."

"THEY WHAT?" Sheriff Wainwright asked, using that now-familiar argumentative tone with Tucker. "I warned Sinclair."

"I don't know who recruited who, but I think they both used bad judgment," Tuck said into the phone.

"You *think*. What the hell's going on there?" A brief, uncomfortable silence followed. The sheriff broke it, his voice cool and unforgiving. "You're going to have to do better than that, Lieutenant, if you want to stay in command."

The words burned into Tucker's ears like hot light. Every nasty word he wanted to say to the sheriff slid up his throat, waiting to be unleashed. Pain squeezed at his head, tension gnawed at his patience, but in the end, he didn't curse, he didn't speak, he didn't slam the phone down. He just stood in his office, emotion twisting his insides. Allowing the sheriff to set him straight about things made him feel tired. Very tired.

"THE VERDICT'S IN!" Gage said, leaping down into Alex's room from a crawl space in the attic. He moved with surprising swiftness. "Let's get cracking. We're getting out of here."

"Gage! How'd you free yourself?"

"Sorry I kept you waiting," he said. "But it took me a while to persuade Pilar to untie me. She's very fond of you."

He grabbed Alex's arms, untied Alex and pulled her up. She gave a shaky laugh and wondered how she could ever thank Hector's long-time servant.

"Houdini couldn't have done it any better," Gage said.

Suddenly, Alex wished she were somewhere else. She wished Hector were someone she didn't know or care about. It was impossible to swallow the lump in her throat.

"I feel so betrayed," she admitted.

Gage touched her shoulder and she flinched.

"I—I'm sorry," he stammered.

Alex's head jerked up. Tears—huge, blinding ones— bounced off her cheeks. She held her hand up, then bit her lower lip to steady it. "You don't have to apologize for anything. My misplaced trust is my problem...." Her voice trailed off.

"Hey," he said, pulling her chin up, forcing her to look at him. "We're in this thing together. And time is running out. We're getting out of here and that's our escape route." He gestured toward the window. "Let's get moving."

Their situation appeared desperate, he thought, but together, they might make it.

"Wait," she said. Pulling free, she raced across the room and grabbed her lucky penny from the bureau and dropped it in her shirt pocket.

"We've got to buy enough time to figure out how to get off Hector's property," he said. "Just one thing. Where the hell are those two Dobermans? I'll be damned if I'll be a meal for the likes of them." Suddenly he grinned. "Don't get me wrong, I ordinarily love animals."

"I heard them barking. I think Hector's turned them loose," she said.

"That's bad news. Really bad." Gage thought for a minute. "You wait here. I'll be right back."

"Where are you going?"

"On a mercy mission," he said. "Come here. Help me move this dresser. I'll need a hand getting back into the attic."

Together, they moved the chest of drawers under the attic's crawl space. Gage climbed on top of it and lifted himself into the attic.

"Be careful," Alex called after him.

Gage poked his head back through the opening. "What do you think those man-eating beasts enjoy devouring the most?"

"Red meat, I'd think," she said without hesitation.

"Why doesn't that surprise me?" he asked. Then he was gone.

Alex waited for what she felt was an eternity. *Don't let anything happen to him,* she thought. Her world was already crashing in around her. Ken was dead. Hector might be involved in his death. And how would she tell Tucker about Skip? Her imagination ran wild. In all the chaos, Gage was someone she could rely on. *Something must have gone wrong,* she thought. Just when she'd decided she couldn't wait a minute longer, Gage stuck his head through the crawl space's opening, flaunting two T-bone steaks.

"Well done, wouldn't you say?" he asked, waving them proudly.

"Well done, indeed," she answered.

Gage lowered himself to the dresser, and then to the floor.

"Come on, give me a hand," Alex said. She climbed through the window. "I've got an idea." She jumped clear of the house, landing on all fours.

Gage was right behind her. "Okay, let's hear it," he said.

"Follow me."

Gage hesitated, and Alex knew exactly what he was thinking. He didn't want a repeat performance of their run-in with Hector and Skip. "Come on," she coaxed, "will you have a little faith in me?"

"Where to?" he asked.

"The chopper pad!"

"The chopper?" he echoed. "That's the first place they'll look."

"I'm flying us out of here," she said.

"You fly choppers, too?"

Alex cocked her head and looked at Gage. "There's a little Houdini in all of us."

Gage didn't have to think about that. Alex Sinclair was full of surprises. "I could get used to you," he said.

His grin made her feel like she could take on the world. "First, we've got to disable their truck," Alex said. "I'll jerk the coil wire off the engine while you slip inside and cut the short-wave radio antenna."

"Good thinking," Gage said. Damn good. It was something a hot-shot detective should have thought of.

Keeping a close watch on the ranch house, Alex ran for the truck. Once under the hood, she yanked the coil wire free and then looked for Gage. After a moment, he appeared and signaled an all clear.

"Quick, let's make a run for the chopper," Alex said. She was out of breath, more from nerves than exhaustion.

"What about the other pickup truck?" Gage asked.

"Forget it. Without four-wheel drive, they won't get far in it."

"We've got company!" he said, gasping in horror as the Dobermans leapt toward them. "What are their names?" he asked in a husky voice.

"Coors and Flossy. Throw out one steak. They'll fight over it while we make a run for the chopper."

None too soon, he pitched out the meat. The dogs made a dive for it. "Quick," he prompted. "Let's get moving."

Gripping hands securely, Gage and Alex charged toward the fence that confined the chopper. Alex felt the muscles in her legs stretch as she ran to keep up with Gage. They scrambled for the gate, and Gage rolled it open just enough so that the two of them could slip through. Within seconds, they were inside, with the gate closed and locked behind them. Alex quickly scanned the expanse between the chopper and the barn.

"Let's get this bird in the air," Gage snapped, "before anyone hears the Dobermans."

"Right," Alex said. She covered the remaining distance and hopped inside.

Gage was close behind. Alex settled in and busied herself with the instrument panel. Gage kept watch on the house.

"All clear?" she asked.

Gage nodded. "But hurry. When Skip discovers we've cut the antenna, he'll alert Hector. They'll be coming any minute."

"We're in luck," she said. "The key is in the ignition."

"That's what I like about you," Gage told her. "I never know what to expect, but you always come through in a pinch. So what are you waiting for?" he asked.

"Would you just be quiet and listen for a minute? I've got something to tell you," Alex said.

"It can wait," Gage assured her. "First things first. Nothing can be more important than clearing out of here. Let's put some blue sky between us and this ranch."

Alex jerked her head around to face him. "Here, hold my lucky penny. You're going to need it." She pressed the coin into Gage's palm.

"When's the last time you crashed a chopper?" he asked. "On second thought—don't answer that."

Chapter Twelve

"Wickenburg Air Flight One is cleared for takeoff. Please extinguish all smoking materials and fasten seat belts," Gage said mockingly. He slapped his breast pocket for the cigarette package that wasn't there.

Alex tried to smile in response, but couldn't. The terror she felt wasn't for herself. Instead, she was concerned about the possibility of endangering Gage's life. She swallowed the knot in her throat, sucked in her breath and began mentally coaching herself on the preflight checklist. *I can do it.* She leaned back against the seat while her mind rallied. If she panicked now, they were certain to die.

Her breath came in short gasps as she checked the controls, instruments and fuel. "Okay," she murmured. Hands trembling, she tried the engine. It fired on the second attempt. There was no time to waste now. The rumbling engine was sure to draw attention. *I can do this,* she reassured herself a final time.

"Can you speed this thing up?" Gage asked. "We've got company."

A shot exploded into the chopper. The bullet was so close to their heads, they heard its passage. In the next split second, Alex thought she heard another shot. Then it registered: Hector was trying to kill them. She looked through the chopper's windshield. Hector was running toward them, firing blindly. One of the Dobermans leapt and connected in midair with a stray bullet. The animal fell back to earth like a limp rag.

Alex grabbed ahold of the control stick, pushed up on it and advanced the throttle. The bird lifted into the air toward safety.

For a moment, she and Gage shared a mutually locked silence, enjoying the steady hum from the engine. The water-soaked desert rushed by beneath them.

"We're airborne!" Gage said, his eyes gleaming recklessly. "I'm game for anything now." He tossed Alex a grin.

"What did you have in mind?" she asked in a lazy, sexy voice. "San Diego? Mexico? Hawaii?" If he knew of the crazy, romantic notions she'd been having about him, he would probably laugh. She knew he didn't owe her anything. Wrapping up his investigation was all that mattered to him. To Gage Morgan, she was Ken's partner, nothing more. And she would be better off keeping everything else from her mind. Still, his kiss was hard to forget.

"You just put this bird down at the Wickenburg airport and I'll take you an a world-class cruise." Gage paused. "I've got a confession. I never thought I would be so glad to see Wickenburg."

"I've got a confession, too."

"Nothing could upstage today's events. Shoot."

"We're not going to Wickenburg."

THE FIRST LIGHT of morning streaked across the sky. Alex caught a glimpse of a swaybacked old cabin below. A tipsy-looking barn was outlined against the yellowish dawn. Suddenly, the chopper hit an air pocket and dropped. Alex gripped the controls tighter until her knuckles were white.

"Son of a—"

"Just an air pocket," she reassured Gage. Then she said, "Are you a gambling man?" She could already feel his mood icing over.

He trained his gaze on Alex. "Your cloak-and-dagger methods are going to get us killed," he snapped.

That wasn't too far from the truth. She realized Hector and Skip could reach Inspiration Mine by auto in a few hours if they managed to repair the truck. And she knew she'd have to set the chopper down some distance from the mine and hike in. That meant that time would be lost. But it was the only way they stood a chance of nailing down Digger.

"Wickenburg tower. Come in Wickenburg tower." Alex spoke calmly into the mike. "Wickenburg tower this is Deputy Sinclair with the Maricopa County Sheriff's Department. I'm requesting a dispatch to the Wickenburg Sheriff's Department. Over."

"Alex! Are you all right?"

Alex glanced over at Gage. His surprised expression reflected her own.

"Ten-four. What's your twenty, Wes?" she asked. "You sound like you're next door."

"Where's next door?" Wes's voice came over the radio.

"We just lifted off from the Martinez ranch, bound for Inspiration Mine," Alex said.

"I tracked you to Date Creek. The runoff stopped me. I just crossed the creek and I'm traveling east on Inspiration Mine road—looking for you," Wes said. "You've had us worried, young lady."

Young lady? Never mind, she thought. In spite of Wes's chauvinism, she knew that he was trying to help. Alex glanced at Gage. His obvious relief reflected her own. That explained the intruder at the creek. And it was lucky for them that Wes was there now. The tower hadn't picked up their signal.

Wes continued. "A rock slide forced me to camp on the ridge the other night. At first light, I hiked down to the creek's edge and waited for the water to recede."

Alex looked to Gage. Something wasn't right about what Wes said. The ridge? If Wes hadn't camped across the creek, who had? "One thing more," she said. "Where's the lieutenant? Over."

"On the north rim of the Grand Canyon, trying to get some rest and relaxation."

"When's he due back?"

"Sometime tonight."

"Wes. Listen carefully. I need backup at the Martinez Ranch. Organize a posse to round up Hector Martinez and Skip."

"Who?"

"You heard right. Hector and Skip. And make sure Pilar is safe."

"You mean arrest them?" Wes's voice burst out over the mike.

"That's exactly what I mean."

"I hope you know what you're doing. The sheriff doesn't like speculation."

"Neither do I. Speculation has no place in an arrest."

"What are the charges?"

"Possession of contraband, smuggling, endangerment and maybe accessory to murder."

"Alex," Wes's voice came cracking back, "what's going on? What's your twenty? And what's all the noise?"

"I'll explain everything after I set down in Wickenburg," she said.

"Alex, give it up. Come home. The sheriff will have your head for this. Hector is one of his major campaign contributors. And I don't need to remind you who Skip is."

"Thanks for the warning, Wes. Now get the posse."

"I'd like to help you, but no can do," Wes declared. "I value my head. And this is something I could never explain."

"You won't have to. I'll take full responsibility."

"I don't know...."

"Trust me on this one, Wes. I'll explain everything when I arrive."

"Alex? You okay?"

"That's a ten-four. Thanks, Wes."

"Ten-four," he said. "Over."

For the next few seconds, Alex sat quietly at the controls. Was someone other than Hector trying to kill them? It seemed that way. But why? Did the perp think she and Gage knew enough to expose him? Or was he just trying to stop them before they put it all together? A chill speared its way through her. Okay. It admittedly scared her, but she didn't know the word *defeat*. She would press on to find Ken's murderer.

"Alex!" Gage said. "You okay?"

"Yeah, I'm fine. Gage, who do you think camped across the creek?"

"I'm not sure, but I hope Tucker can account for his time."

"What's that supposed to mean?"

"It doesn't mean anything. Pure speculation. But suppose Tucker killed his own deputy. Maybe Ken suspected Skip's illegal activities."

"Tuck has always been the logical one, sweating out crimes others would give up on, but he's also a gentle man, a man incapable of murder."

"How will he take it?" Gage asked.

"What? The fact that his son is going to be arrested on felony charges?" The last thing in the world Alex wanted to do was to tell anyone that. Least of all Tuck. "You know I don't really get it," Alex said.

"What?"

"I don't completely understand Skip's role in this whole mess."

"Hector used him as an inside track to the sheriff's department. Who could do it better than Skip, whose dad is the substation commander? Skip's young, vulnerable and trying to survive in an exclusive resort town."

"All his bitterness for Tucker—I never realized it was so strong. I knew they weren't close, but I didn't think Skip resented him."

"How did Skip's mother die?"

"Tragically. She was a beautiful, kind woman. Tucker and Libby had tried for years to have a baby. Libby was forty years old when Skip was born. Childbirth left her weak. Complications set in. She was sickly afterwards. Then, about ten years later, she went in for minor surgery. She never came out of the anesthetic. It nearly killed Tucker. Up until then, he'd doted on that boy. Then after they buried Libby, he buried himself in his job. Skip was left pretty much on his own."

"His mother is dead and his dad doesn't have time for him." Gage said. "The groundwork had already been laid when Hector approached him. Deprived, vulnerable and the substation commander's son. Neat and tidy."

"Gage?"

"What?" he murmured. He'd cursed the desert for two days, but now he welcomed the sight of it. From the air, it seemed less frightening.

"If Hector was telling the truth, then who killed Ken?"

He was deliberately dispassionate. And there came silence so prolonged that she wondered if he'd heard her. "The pieces to the puzzle don't fit together," he finally replied.

"What we uncovered at the ranch is only confusing the case." She paused. "But I have a theory. I'm not sure how, but I think the shooter is tied to Hector's smuggling ring. A fence maybe, possibly a customer. His name could be in Hector's house, among his papers. I'll check it out as soon as we track down Digger."

"Track?"

"Well, yeah. He doesn't take to strangers. We'll have to ease in."

"In a chopper?"

"I'm counting on this head wind to swallow the noise. Digger would run from this bird, but he won't run from me." Alex paused to study the expanse of desert below.

"What's to keep this ole coot from shooting us?" Gage's calm expression changed to one of fear.

"Nothing." Alex forced her calmest voice. "I'd better go in first."

"Oh, swell. You'll be the appetizer and I'll be the main course."

The morning sun was pleasantly warm, and the empty desert below looked its loveliest. There was a certain dignity in the many cacti that seemed to reach for heaven. Gage was aware of this with part of his mind, but behind the simple beauty there was an invisible cloud, the lingering menace of the man who was following them. Gage saw nothing, yet he was aware of the danger. And there were moments when that danger seemed close. But such thoughts were foolish. The chopper had given them time and distance.

He was finding Alex's rashness increasingly difficult to deal with. Her determination only added to the burden. But why on earth was he preoccupied with her? She was certainly not his responsibility. He wasn't a bodyguard. But, damn it, he felt responsible for her. Protective of her. And he didn't like the feeling. Not one bit. He'd failed so miserably before. . . .

"You ready to land?" she asked brightly.

"I haven't been ready for any of—"

"We're going down."

"I was afraid of that."

"That's good," she said. "Fear's not all bad. It just might keep us alive." She maneuvered the bird downward until it was sitting precariously on top of a huge, flat boulder.

"Alex, maybe we should rethink this. Cut our losses and head back to Wickenburg."

"Nothing doing. Stay in the chopper if you like, but I'm too close to give up now." She turned off the engine and sighed. "I have to do this."

"Yeah, I know." And he did. He knew he had to look after her, too. "Let's go," he said with a lightness he certainly did not feel.

Gage's first step sent him sliding off the boulder, onto a narrow trail. He felt sure the desert was having a great silent laugh at his expense. He attempted to collect his wits and regain his footing before Alex arrived.

"You okay?" she asked.

"I guess I lost my legs on that ride," he replied. "But they're coming back."

"Can I give you a hand?"

"I can manage very well without your help."

"Spoken like a true desert rat," she said.

Today was like the first day of this trek. Except that instead of growing stiff and sore, Gage grew stiffer and sorer. He had been drawn to Alex first just because of the investigation. He had wanted her as a link between him and her deceased partner. But now, he wanted more. Much more. Now he needed her for personal reasons, even though he hesitated to admit it to himself.

The desert's raw beauty hit him in the face. The boulder's treacherous trail led down over the face of a cliff. It was a test even for the surefooted. At the cliff's base were thick brush and palo verde trees. Alex and Gage stepped delicately, allowing the trail to take them down. Then they slid down a slope of bald rock and into a valley that was about three miles square. The high, red cliffs and clumps of scrub oak at their feet offered the only color in the landscape. Everything else was dull and colorless—sand hills, sand flats, rocks, sagebrush, greasewood and sheep.

It wasn't what Gage saw that made him feel threatened. It was the missing signs of human life. And he wanted some sign. It would have been a relief to see people. Shouts of anger. Anything.

An adobe structure, an outbuilding that belonged to the mine, was two or three hundred yards away. Gage wondered if Digger would be clever, stupid, hostile, friendly or resigned.

They cautiously made their way along, keeping their eyes and ears alert. The desert appeared serene, but that ill feeling nagged at Gage. The wind persisted, kicking up dust balls in every direction. He strained his eyes, searching the area as far as he could see, but there was nothing and no one.

"Look," he began, "I'm not sure it's such a good idea to bust in on Digger."

"I don't intend to bust in on him. He sets traps for animals and humans. I'll spring one to get his attention."

"You might as well know right now, I'm no good at this Jungle Jim stuff."

She studied him thoughtfully for a moment, then broke into a gentle laugh. His sense of humor took over and he laughed in response. When their laughter was finally spent, the pair approached the adobe building and mine entrance. They stopped short and rested behind a thicket of greasewood. Alex's slitted eyes evaluated the situation.

"You're about to meet your maker." The harsh words startled Gage. He thought he felt a gun barrel poke into his back. "Kneel or I'll shoot you where you stand."

"Wait a minute, Digger," Alex said casually. "You've got us at a disadvantage."

"I've got two tenderfeet at my mercy, and I'm not a merciful man."

"We're unarmed," Gage huffed. By now, Gage had dropped to his knees. He was considering the possibility that he was drawing his last breath.

"Missy, is that you?" Digger demanded.

"This is no way to welcome a friend, you sly old fox," Alex said softly.

"Hell, fire and damnation. All you had to do was tell me who you were. I didn't recognize you in those clothes. I nearly took your head off."

"Digger," she said, "this is real uncomfortable. Can my friend stand up?"

"You can," he replied. "That means you, mister." He nudged Gage with the barrel of his 30-30.

"Thanks," Gage said with a little stab of apprehension as he stood and turned around to face Digger. He found Digger more of a disappointment than a surprise. A hard-used man, he was slight in size and big of voice. He had watery eyes and was stoop shouldered. He was also badly in need of a bath. He possessed an anguished look and a dreadful cough. Gage glanced at Digger's calloused hands and at his seamed face. It appeared to be as rough as a cob. The miner's steely, penetrating eyes took in everything.

"It was luck—you finding me at home," Digger said.

"Pure luck," Gage echoed.

"What's the trouble?" the old man asked. "I'm not in the habit of receiving social calls."

Gage took in the old man's gun. The Winchester 30-30 was at least seventy-five years old. "Imagine that," he said. "Dying at the end of a beauty like that."

"Winchester saddle rifle. Finest little weapon ever made," the miner said. A grin lifted his wrinkled face. "My pa built the stock himself from a pepper tree." He gestured toward Gage with the gun. "Go on, stroke her if you like. She's just like a fine woman. You've got to take good care of her."

"She's really a beauty."

"Digger can shoot a fly off a steer's nose from fifty feet," Alex boasted.

Digger just stood there, blushing and agreeing. "Yup. She shoots straight as spit." His hearty laugh suggested boundless energy. "A man's gun is the only thing he can depend on for sure."

"Digger, we don't have a lot of time...." Alex pleaded.

"You're wasting a good piece of it right now," he said.

"The way I see it," she began, "you're a man of honor. I was hoping you might have seen something the night Ken was murdered."

Digger looked at Alex. He lowered his gaze and smiled, but his tone was not altogether friendly. "You might just as well put your hopes in one hand and your spit in the other and see which hand fills up first."

A cop had the opportunity to study human nature, and Gage had been a student of it for a long time. Alex Sinclair was clever. She stood mute, thinking and choosing her words carefully in this delicate but important meeting with a possible witness.

"I didn't think that much went on out here that you didn't know about," she said. "I think Ken witnessed a crime, and that he was silenced by murder."

"You came a long way for nothing," Digger informed her, screwing his face into a tight grimace. "The desert is full of danger. People don't respect it like they should."

The wind carried the faint dissonant sounds of a burro's bray and the far-off barking of dogs. A pang of fear jolted through Gage's body. He thought he heard an engine—a car engine.

"They say Ken pulled off the road to take a nap. They say he acted negligently when he failed to call for backup."

Digger just swung his head back and forth. He wasn't saying yes. He wasn't saying no. He wasn't saying anything. Alex's guilt trip had failed to force his hand.

"I thought you might have been there. But the others—they say you could never have covered so great a distance. . . ."

As they talked, Digger's eyes were constantly taking in his surroundings, watchful for any movement out of the ordinary. He wasn't a man to be caught off guard. Digger was obviously not a man easily persuaded either. But Alex was employing all her wily charm.

"And what do you say?" said Digger.

"I say they're wrong." Alex looked at the miner sympathetically. "They say your age restricts you, but I figure differently."

"I'm fit as a fiddle," Digger promptly informed her. "I can travel anywhere."

"I knew that the minute I laid eyes on you."

Digger cleared his throat, smoothed back his wooly hair, then let his shoulders sag. "I've been around enough to have seen plenty."

Gage felt certain that the miner was adroit in his knowledge of the desert. An impressive performance, Gage thought as Alex smiled sweetly at Digger.

"Even so," she said, "it happened at night. Even with good vision, it would have been hard to see what happened."

Digger's rebuttal came swiftly: "I know every anthill, every rat's nest and every landing strip within a hundred miles of here." He lifted his bushy eyebrows to observe Alex's reaction. "And I'm just buying time. It won't be long before I'll have to pick up and prospect for a new claim. Civilization has a way of closing in on you."

"You're right about one thing. No one knows this desert the way you do," she said.

"It's a damn shame," Digger responded, "what they're doing to this desert. Human cargo shipments from across the border are pushing this far east. Folks help the mesquite farmers truck their crops to illegal landing strips. You wouldn't believe the goings on around this place at night."

He had underestimated Alex, Gage decided. She was lining up the questions, and in a minute, she'd be milking the answers right out of the old coot, with friendly persuasion.

"Sorry we bothered you," she said. "It's time we were getting back to Wickenburg. Come on, Gage."

Shrewd, Gage thought. She'd put the bite on Digger. Now she was going in for the kill.

"Wait just a minute."

"I'm sorry, Digger. It wasn't such a good idea to come here and put you on the spot."

The intensity in his eyes wasn't really from anger, but from vulnerability. "Assuming I had been there," Digger began, feigning indifference, "it ain't hard to count headlights." He narrowed his eyes and pinched his chin.

"Assuming you had been there and assuming your sight is as good as you say, how many sets of headlights would you have counted?"

"Four." He answered without hesitation.

"Four?" Gage echoed. He looked at Digger. Digger was dirty, but he was honest. Gage was convinced that the miner spoke the truth.

"Four?" Alex asked.

"Yup, but it was two against two."

"What?"

"Two cars had stars on their doors. I figured the odds were even between the gringos and the law. And when the gringos left, I figured it was time for me to leave, too. I didn't want any trouble with those deputies."

"Where were the deputies?" Alex asked, baffled.

"Parked on the mine road. They never even saw them two trucks hightailing it across the desert. I heard the shot then, and I knew nothing good was coming from all that late-night traffic. I kept on going."

There was more to this than was meeting the eye, Gage thought. And then, out of nowhere, a bullet suddenly exploded, putting all his senses on alert. "Hit the ground," Gage ordered.

Digger got off a shot before Gage even realized that he had taken aim. There was another pop. It sounded like a bursting tire. In the distance, Gage saw a pickup truck catapult through the air and over an embankment. He couldn't see where it landed, but rising smoke signaled the location.

THEY NEARED THE WRECKAGE. The only sign of movement was the spinning tires of the pickup. Gage was visibly anxious, but obviously fighting to stay calm. His jaw repeatedly flexed in response to his heightened emotions.

Alex screamed, "They're dead!" She pointed to the gully where the truck had landed bottom side up.

"Just like I thought," Digger said. They were nearer now. He pointed at the tire he'd just shot. "She fires straight as spit." He was still gripping the 30-30, his knuckles white. "You can stake your life on this gun."

"Digger, cover me while I check for survivors," Gage said.

"What was that?" Alex asked. She thought she heard a voice moaning. Then it sounded again. A cry of agony. She stood ramrod straight, arms crossed, and watched Gage make his way down the incline to the wreckage.

"One's alive!" he shouted back.

"Who is it?" she asked apprehensively.

"Skip, but he's barely breathing." There was a pause while he checked the others. "Hector's dead. So is the other man. I don't know who he is."

Dead? Alex's mind was in utter turmoil. It was déjà vu. Only this time, it wasn't Ken who was dead. She tried to tell herself that Skip was responsible for what had happened to him. It was no use.

"I'll need some help," Gage called.

"I'm on my way," Alex responded. "Digger, do you have an army blan—"

On the ground, at her feet, the blanket lay. Digger was gone. Alex scrounged around until she found two sturdy mesquite branches. It was crude, but it was all they had. She ripped the corners of the blanket and tied them to the branches, creating a stretcher. She made her way down to the wreckage. Her breathing came rapidly, and her lungs felt as though they were on fire.

"Oh, no. . . ." she mumbled. She knelt in front of Skip.

"Alex!" Gage said. "Snap out of it. I need you. Skip needs you." Gage went to her side, pulled her up and drew her into his arms. He stroked her back in silence.

Another piece of her world had fallen in. The tears that rolled down her cheeks felt hot and tasted salty. But the severity of the situation was forcing her to think clearly. "I'm okay," she said, pulling away. But she wasn't okay. She didn't think she ever would be again.

Gage reached out to smooth her hair. Together, they rolled Skip's limp body onto its side and slipped the stretcher underneath him. It was clear that Skip needed prompt treatment to survive. He had suffered a severe blow to the head. His pupils were unevenly dilated. Alex knew that that might indicate brain injury or skull fracture. "We've got to save him," she said. Alex crept over to the wrecked pickup to peer inside. Her heartbeat accelerated. She audibly gasped. "Oh, no."

"What is it?" Gage asked, shaken by her reaction.

"It's Marvin. . . ."

"The mechanic?" He turned his attention to Alex.

"He must have been the one camped across the wash," she said. Then, in a monotone voice, she added, "Marvin must have killed Ken."

"What are you doing?" Gage asked.

"The only way we can place Marvin at the murder scene is through ballistics. I'm collecting all their weapons," she replied without emotion.

Her no-nonsense tone surprised even her. It felt like suspended animation and she was in the middle of it. Delayed reaction wasn't anything new to her. And it would come— the reaction. Uninvited. When she wasn't expecting it. So.

It had all come down to this. Three locals. Two dead. One guilty of murder.

THE TRIP HOME was nearly over. Back in the chopper, Alex had radioed Wes about events. He would dispatch a team to pick up the bodies before returning to Wickenburg, and he informed her that the Martinez ranch had been secured.

"Marvin killed him," she said after a long silence.

"That's a bit premature," Gage responded.

"He rigged my radiator hose to come off. He figured the Bronco would break down in the desert, giving him a chance to catch up and murder us. Marvin camped across the wash that night."

"It's a moot point," Gage said. The radio interrupted him.

"This is Wickenburg tower, come back Charlie Niner Three Zero Delta."

"Wickenburg tower, I'm requesting clearance for an emergency landing. Over," said Alex.

"Charlie Niner Three Zero Delta, what is the nature of your emergency? Over."

"I need medical backup. We have an emergency aboard," she replied. "Over." Perspiration beaded on her forehead. Alex gripped the stick.

"What is your current position? Over."

"I'm approaching from northwest to avoid traffic. I have just crossed the Wickenburg Inn, ten miles north of town. Over."

"Alex, this is Bob Bradley, over. Maintain your approach and descend to a thousand feet. Your ETA is five minutes. Over."

"Affirmative. Over."

"We've got a complete emergency team on standby," Bob assured her. "Take your time. When you're ready, I'll begin the checklist. Over."

"Ten-four, Bob. Thank you, over and out."

By now, Alex's hands were slick with sweat, and nerves had given her a cotton mouth. Skip remained unconscious. She could hear his shallow breathing, an indication that his condition was steadily deteriorating. She felt Gage put his hand on her shoulder and in a steady voice, he began a calming massage to soothe her soul and spirit.

"We're almost home."

He was offering support. Gage squeezed her shoulder and the gesture swelled her heart. When Bob's voice sounded, Alex broke her visual embrace with Gage.

"Alex, we've got you in sight," Bob said. "Hold steady. Over."

"Ten-four, over," she answered.

"Descend to five hundred feet and hold her steady. Over."

Alex's eyes gravitated to the altimeter. "Five hundred feet. Over."

"Level out, nice and easy and set her down," Bob's calm voice instructed.

"Roger."

Adrenaline pumped through her veins as the landing pad reached up toward the chopper and the two became one.

Within minutes, paramedics converged on the scene and removed Skip's limp body. He was five minutes away from the hospital now. Relief flooded Alex's senses. In the distance, she heard a wailing siren.

"You did it," Gage was saying. "You pulled it off."

"We," she said, trying to steady her rubbery legs. "We did it."

"You've got style. That was real impressive."

"Wanting to stay alive has a way of motivating you," she said.

"Come here," Gage said, throwing a long arm around her neck and embracing her. "You've got a nice touch. Real nice." He pulled away, but not before he savored the scent of her hair. "Here's your lucky penny back," he said, gesturing toward her with the coin.

"You keep it," she said, giving him a thumbs-up signal.

THIS IS SOME KIND of homecoming! I've been worried about you. Where did you get these clothes?"

Same old Wes, Alex thought. Two men dead, Skip unconscious, and all Wes could think of was what she was wearing.

"You look like hell," he continued, assessing the sloppy sweatsuit. It hung on her body in much the same way that clothes hang on coat hangers.

"I didn't have time to be choosy," Alex answered. She stood for a moment on the concrete, inhaling the sweet, warm air. This was the old Alex, the Alex who could draw on her inner strength. And she was going to need to. She still had to deal with Tucker.

Gage was walking away. She felt a sudden sharp longing. For what? A different life? An ordinary life? She wondered. She knew the answer, but she simply refused to think about it. Not now, anyway. Not until this thing was over. But the longing persisted against her wishes. And she could do nothing but wait for it to exhaust itself. In the meantime, Gage was walking out of her life. "Gage, wait a minute," she called after him, ignoring Wes. Suddenly, she broke into a run. He stopped short, allowing her to catch up.

"What?" he asked as he turned toward her.

"You were my rock through this," she said, "and—well—I wanted to thank you."

"This is your stage. I was just along for the ride. And it was the ride of my life. Nice going," he said, smiling down at her.

For a brief moment, her spirit spiraled. Then sickeningly, it descended to a bitter low. The task ahead was haunting her. How was she going to tell a father that his son was a felon, and that he was near death? She didn't get it. Why did the good guys always get hurt? She loved Tucker like a father. He'd never missed a single graduation—not from junior high, high school, college or the academy. She felt a rush of guilt for ever doubting him. "Gage, will you ride with me to Tuck's house?" she asked.

"Are you sure that's what you want?"

"We started this thing together. I think we should finish it that way. What do you say?"

"I'll drive."

Alex moved toward the patrol car with renewed strength. She didn't know how she could tell Tucker about Skip. And she might not know until she stood face-to-face with him. One thing was certain. There was no easy way out of this. She slid into the passenger side.

"Okay," Gage said, staring the engine. "Which way?"

"West on U.S. 60 to Vulture Mine Road. Then turn onto U.S. 89."

"Highway 89? I didn't realize Tucker lived near the murder site."

"It was convenient for Skip."

"That close to home, you'd have thought that Tucker could have kept a better eye on him." Gage paused. "Maybe he did."

"There's nothing to support your contention that Tucker's involved in this." Her emotions seesawed.

"Will you at least listen to my contention?" he asked. She looked at Gage, and he continued on an even bleaker note.

"What if he'd suspected Skip's activities and he'd followed him that night. When he learned the truth—"

"Wait a minute. According to Digger, Hector and Skip left before Ken saw them."

"Let's assume he recognized their trucks and got suspicious. Then Tucker arrived. Ken confronted Tucker. Tuck, fearing exposure and damage to Skip's future, killed Ken. He's a man with a motive. That's what's been wrong with this case all along. It's been a ringer from day one."

"Yeah, but the wrong head's been in the noose, Ken's. You can't hang a man who's already dead." Alex paused. For Alex, Ken's murder had not yet receded from the ranks of tragedy. "Anyway, that's a big if," Alex added.

"Not if Tucker has an alibi."

What Gage was suggesting was no easier to accept than Ken's death. It amounted to a trade-off. She reminded herself that Gage had only come to give Ken's murder a place in a file cabinet of skeletons.

Gage eased the car onto the main highway and turned west. Silence stretched between them. Alex lowered her eyes to glance at her wristwatch. Four-forty-five. Gage made a right onto Vulture Mine Road and then turned onto highway 89. She told him to slow down. "It's the white house set back off the road," she said. "The one with the stand of cottonwood trees around it."

He turned into the driveway and followed it to the front of a neat-looking house. The car bounced across a pothole, then came to an abrupt halt. Alex sucked in a deep breath as though for courage. This was going to be a long day. At the moment, she felt more dead than alive. She regarded the slump block, ranch-style home. She'd watched Skip grow up there. Labeling him a criminal had never been in her plans.

"It's going to be okay," Gage told her in a soft voice.

"No. No, it isn't."

"Let's get this thing over with," Gage said, exiting the car.

They walked up to the front door together. Alex rang the bell. When Tucker pulled open the door, their presence seemed to startle him. Out of uniform and in his bathrobe, he looked vulnerable, like any other father.

"What the hell's wrong?" he demanded in a gruff tone.

"It's Skip, Tuck. He's been hurt in an auto accident," Alex said, her throat constricted.

"Dead or alive? Is he dead or alive?"

"Alive." It was painful watching shock drain the color from Tucker's face. "Get some clothes on," she said. "You can ride with us."

"How bad?" he persisted.

"It's a head injury, I think."

Tuck steadied himself in the doorway.

"There's more," Alex said. "We've got a felony going down."

"A felony?" he echoed.

Wickenburg was a small town. A felony charge wasn't unheard of, but it wasn't an everyday occurrence. Alex hoped to get the lieutenant into the car before she had to tell him the whole story. "Get dressed. We'll talk on the way to the hospital. Hurry."

Welcoming a chance to temporarily escape Tucker, she led the way back to the patrol car. In less than five minutes, Tucker followed.

"Damn it," he blurted out as he climbed in, "are you gonna tell me what this is about?"

"I think we've got the perp—"

"Ken's?" Tuck interrupted.

"Yeah," she hedged.

"Who?"

"Hector Martinez and Marvin Dickerson," Alex said. They're both dead."

Tuck rubbed his head.

"I think Marvin was the shooter," she continued.

"Marvin?"

Something of the pain that Tucker was feeling showed on is face.

"I'm not sure why he did it, but I think Marvin drove to 1e murder sight and killed Ken. We won't know for sure ntil ballistics."

After the hospital, Alex intended to go to the substation nd file an affidavit for a search warrant. She hoped she ould tie Damato to Marvin's telephone bills.

"I can't believe this," Tucker mumbled.

As they sped toward the hospital, Alex wished she were aving her troubles behind. The simple, bittersweet truth rought tears to her eyes. "Tuck—"

"I don't get it," he cut in.

"Tuck, will you just listen for a minute?" she pleaded.

She glanced into the rearview mirror. Gage stared back at er from behind the wheel. She looked over at Tuck, who as seated next to her in the back seat. His hands were lded neatly in his lap. Except for the tear that streaked own his cheek, Alex wouldn't have known anything was niss. She felt like some sort of self-appointed execu-oner.

"I haven't told you everything," she confessed. "There's ore, and it's bad."

Tucker's jowls tightened while he fought for control. He as momentarily speechless.

"Skip is connected to this mess," she blurted out. She ached for Tucker's hand. It was a flopping, lifeless ap-endage. All energy seemed to have been drained from him.

She was watching her old friend have the life crushed out of him.

"Skip?" His implacable expression vanished, wiped away by astonishment. Even though his heart was breaking, he responded quickly. "What the hell's going on here?"

"Martinez has been operating a very sophisticated smuggling ring from his ranch," Alex said.

"Drugs?" Tucker asked.

"No. At least not that I know of. Illegal exporting...rare animals."

"Skip was fencing for Martinez?" Tuck asked, hoping his son was guilty of this lesser offense.

"Not exactly. Martinez was the fence. Skip was the wheel man." She squeezed Tucker's hand. "That's not the worst." Silence stretched between them. How do you tell someone that his son had attempted murder? "Skip, along with Hector and Marvin, tried to kill us at Inspiration Mine."

"Like hell he did." Tucker turned to face her and jerked his hand free. "Who told you that?"

"I was there."

Tucker sat in shocked silence, denial written all over his face. Alex reached over, wrapping warm fingers around his wrist. Tuck declined the gesture. Forcing his eyes away from her, he looked out the window.

"It won't make things easier," she said, "but I'm sorry."

She didn't want to think about this right now. From somewhere, she needed to dredge up faith that she would do the right thing by filing charges against Skip. She was about to take away the only thing in the world Tucker had left to live for.

Chapter Thirteen

While machines breathed life into Skip, Alex was filing charges against him at the substation. Gage went with her to offer support.

"Book Skip on attempted murder," she told Wes.

"Murder?" the lanky deputy echoed.

"Yes," she murmured. "And put a guard on his hospital room."

Shaken, she turned away. Alex's words echoed in Gage's head. Pain or guilt, he wasn't sure which, was building in the pit of his stomach. He wished he could shut out the world for a moment and with it, all his troubles and painful memories. He knew this was the toughest thing Alex would ever have to do. He knitted his brows in a frown.

If Skip woke from his coma, it would be Gage's job to question him until he found out why Ken Forney had been on that deserted road. He was certain Ken hadn't pulled off for a snooze. He'd seen something, all right. And from everything Gage had been able to learn about Ken, he hadn't been a man of great causes, but he had had integrity. Maybe he had been like a spider caught in his own web. The question was why?

"He's your collar, Alex," Wes was saying. "Any other charges?"

"Accessory to murder, reckless endangerment. I'll give you more information on the poaching as soon as I meet with the prosecuting attorney," she answered.

Gage remained silent. She was a fine deputy. A blind man could see that. Lately, he had had the feeling he was losing his touch. He watched Alex bag the weapons confiscated at the scene.

"Make sure these are on the morning shuttle out of here to the Phoenix crime lab," she said to Wes.

"You got it. Want me to do the labels?" he asked, seemingly aware of Alex's shaking hands.

"Thanks."

There was still one important thing to figure out, Gage thought. Why hadn't Ken radioed and given his location for a backup? Breaking contact wasn't logical. But who was talking about logical? How could Gage match wits with a dead man? He turned his attention back to Alex.

"You okay?" Gage asked, slipping a protective arm around her shoulders.

"Yeah," she replied. "I'm fine. I'm waiting for the judge to issue a search warrant."

"Marvin's house?" he asked.

She nodded.

"I'll go with you." *I'll take care of you,* he wanted to add.

"Looks like you two got lucky," Wes said. His cheery attitude seemed intolerable and out of place.

"What?" Alex asked.

"I thought we'd have to give this one up to the wild blue yonder. No kidding—"

"Stop it, Wes," Alex said. "We're talking about Tucker's son, his life. Just stop it."

"Take it easy, Alex," Wes said. "I didn't mean anything personal."

Alex looked as though she had been struck. Color drained from her face, her hands dropped to her sides. *No. You're too insensitive to get personal,* Gage thought. He exhaled, hoping when he spoke, the hard edge in his voice would be gone. "Steady," Gage said to Alex. "You're a professional."

"I'm about to ruin two lives, three, when I tell Ken's wife who murdered her husband and why."

Gage drew in a breath and held it. It didn't help. He slapped his breast pocket. That didn't help, either. The cigarettes were still gone. "Damn it," he said adamantly to no one in particular. Then, to Alex, he said, "Come on, let's get out of here. I'll give you a ride home."

"Thanks," she replied, obviously grateful for the opportunity to leave the substation. "Call me at home, Wes, when the judge rules on my affidavit for the warrant."

"Sure thing, Alex."

Outside she said, "Gage, Ken would have appreciated what you've done for him."

The way she stated it, as if it really mattered what he'd done, created a huge swell of emotion in Gage's chest.

GAGE POINTED HIS CAR toward the highway that hugged the Hassayampa River, then turned east toward Alex's apartment. The river, lined on both sides by towering cottonwood trees, looked like a green ribbon. It extended across the brown foothills of Wickenburg. Just beyond, the peaks of the Vulture Mountains jabbed at the blue afternoon sky. Alex had always loved the river. It stood out in stark contrast to the arid desert terrain.

Wait a minute, she thought. *The tapes.* She felt like she was in a dark room and the lights had come on. This ugly affair was almost over and she still hadn't heard them.

"Gage," she began, "I want to listen to the tapes."

"You're asking me to do something unethical. I don't work that way. My report will be filed in a few days. Then, and only then, will I release the tapes."

"But you don't understand—"

"No, Alex. The answer is no."

He was a man of principle. That didn't make her feel any better. Defeat sapped her energy.

Gage turned on the radio. The music provided a welcome break from the silence. It relaxed Alex. She leaned her head against the window, feeling a sense of relief. In spite of all the obstacles, Ken's murderer was identified and accounted for.

The tune ended and a deep-voiced announcer began the news broadcast by mentioning Ken Forney's name. Alex stiffened. She turned her full attention to the radio.

"As authorities wind up their investigation, the Maricopa County Sheriff's Department released the tapes of the slain deputy's last radio transmission this morning. Sheriff's officials report an unexplained time lapse on the recording. No explanation has been offered by the sheriff. *The Pat McMahon Show* will air the tapes tomorrow beginning at one o'clock."

The words rocked around inside Alex's skull. Had Gage released the tapes? But when could he have done that? He leaned forward and turned off the radio. The silence was screaming in her ears. She looked accusingly at him, her eyes blazing. "Unethical?" she snarled. Her voice dripped menace. But inside, she felt betrayed. She felt as though she were dissolving in despair.

"Alex, you've got to believe me," Gage pleaded. He sounded like a desperate, misunderstood man. "I don't know who released those tapes to the media, but it wasn't me. I wouldn't do that."

Her lips turned white from the taut line she drew them into. "You've been using me," she said. "And the worst part is that I believed you."

"I was honest with you then and I am now," Gage insisted. "I don't know who released those tapes."

"Maybe not, but you could go on record supporting Ken's integrity and put a stop to the rumors."

"By compromising my own?" Gage said.

"They're calling Ken a coward. His widow and child have to live with that."

"I can't do anything about rumors or the people who start them."

"Where do you think those people got their rumors? From the sheriff," she said caustically, answering her own question. "The Sheriff's Department made a premature judgment. Then the department sent you, the man with integrity and principles, to corroborate its verdict."

Gage looked away from Alex. He pulled into the parking lot outside her apartment, turned off the engine and pushed his head back against the headrest. In a display of trustworthiness, he reached over and touched her hand.

"If you're suggesting that I don't feel for Ken Forney's widow and child, you're wrong. But those feelings don't alter my responsibilities."

Alex tightened at his touch. She couldn't help but recoil instinctively in order to protect herself. She withdrew her hand.

"And what exactly is your job?" she asked.

"To sift out the truth and, hopefully, spare another deputy's life should similar circumstances occur. I don't want to hurt anyone, but if it comes down to that, I'd rather live with hurt than death."

"It's duty above all else, Lieutenant?" Alex felt anger color her face. "You're the man who draws the line."

"You know as well as I do that in this business, you have to be flexible. Hardly a day goes by that I don't move that line."

"I guess whether or not you move it depends on whether it's working for you or against you."

"You've been pretty anxious to move it to your advantage," he snapped back.

"This isn't about me. Offering your help was just your devious way of getting inside my head for your own purposes."

"I wasn't pretending, not about anything. Don't pull any guilt trips on me, Alex. I rejected the ideas that concerned your partner's integrity."

Alex heaved a sigh. "Why did you lie to me?" she asked. "Do you think I'm a fool?"

"No," he said. "Of course not. I've done everything in my power to make this easy on you."

"Short of lying?"

"I haven't lied to you."

"Enough has been said for one day. You'll understand if I don't ask you in?"

Gage countered her remark with silence.

"Always the professional," she said. She reached for the door handle.

Gage grabbed her arm. "Wait a minute."

The suddenness of his act stopped her cold.

"It doesn't have to be like this," he said.

"No? You're the man who keeps slamming the door in my face."

"That's not fair."

"Every time I trust you, you betray me," she said, trying to keep her voice level.

"Do you think I enjoy seeing you hurt?" he asked.

"I don't know what I think anymore."

"Alex, I care about you."

"If you didn't care about me, I'd be patrolling right now. What's more, I'd probably have answers concerning Ken's radio breach."

"I did you a favor when I pulled you out of that patrol car. Tucker agreed that it was the right thing to do. And the sooner you come to terms with that, the sooner you'll be back on active duty."

"Is that it?" she asked. "You'll dangle my job over my head every time you want something from me?" Her anger was very close at hand. "A little dispassionate passion?"

Gage stared unbelievingly at Alex. Close to losing control, his voice was cold and deliberate. "It's been a long time since I've cared enough about anything or anyone to get this mad. Are you suggesting what I think you are? I'll tell you one thing, if we're ever together it won't be a compromise. You'll want to make love as much as I will," he declared. He pushed her car door open.

Without looking back, without so much as a goodbye, she exited the car and walked the short distance to her apartment.

"DAMN," GAGE MUTTERED. He had done it again. Why hadn't he been more subtle? More understanding? He admitted to himself that he'd overreacted. He admitted to haste. And he admitted that Alex was getting under his skin. By the time he pulled into the parking lot at the Rancho Grande Hotel, his anger had subsided by a degree or two, but his spirit still sagged.

He reached for his briefcase, then opened the car door. The tapes were inside his briefcase. He had listened to them over and over. Each time he heard them, he came to the same conclusion. Ken was guilty of dereliction of duty. But everything he had learned about Ken contradicted that theory. And so did the things he'd heard from Hector and Skip.

When Gage reached the door to his room, he heard the phone ringing. He hurried with the lock. "Hello," Gage said.

"Hello. I've tried to reach you all afternoon," Sheriff Wainwright said.

The familiar voice quickly put Gage's anxieties to rest. "Why," Gage demanded, "did you release those tapes to the media?"

"I'm not above anything that will keep the press from dragging the reputation of the Sheriff's Department through the mud."

"Your self-serving attitude is touching," Gage grumbled.

"And your insolence is something I can do without," the sheriff warned. "Those tapes are public record."

"No matter who it destroys?" Gage implored.

"Did I get him killed?" the sheriff snarled. "This isn't my fault. A deputy became complacent. That got him murdered."

"You've hurt his family along with other innocent people," Gage said. "And worse, you've made public what should have been private—the final moments of a man's life. I don't think you even know what you've done."

"I do know!" the sheriff said. "My job is on the line. I'm up to my waist in bad press." He lowered his voice to a civil tone. "I've got a family, too. So don't tell me I don't know what those people are feeling. There's no room for your self-righteousness in this investigation. Get rid of it and get me a report."

"Why did you call?" Gage asked.

"To congratulate you on an excellent job. Tucker tells me you've identified the shooter."

"Ballistics will make the final determination."

"I'll read about it in your report."

"I haven't written the report yet," Gage said.

"When you do, I expect you to clear it with my office before submitting it to your own," he said.

"Exactly who's writing it?" Gage demanded.

"This is a team effort, I'll remind you."

"This is one member of the team who can't be pushed around."

"Don't get personally involved in this, Gage. It could get painful," the sheriff warned.

"Come off it," Gage demanded.

"Just get me something in writing."

"Let's get something straight," Gage said. "I don't punch a time clock. What I do is work until the job is done."

"All right. How long do you need?"

"It depends," Gage informed him, then sucked in a deep breath. He puffed his cheeks, then exhaled.

"Depends on what?" the sheriff asked. "This isn't pleasure, Gage. It's your job. I see a conflict of interest here."

"You're out of line with that remark."

"Just get me the report."

Gage heard a loud click. Guilt surged through his heart because he was feeling way too much for Alexis Sinclair. He had thought he'd put love behind him after he'd buried his wife.

He had taken this job in Internal Affairs to fulfill a promise to Laura. No more waltzing around with a concealed gun and a hidden badge acting like Sonny Crockett on *Miami Vice*. But Laura was dead, and his undercover work was the reason. It should have been him.

She had lingered for three days in intensive care. Before she'd died, she had made him promise not to seek revenge. He had vowed to hang up his career in law enforcement, but

Sheriff Wainwright had persuaded him to try a position in Internal Affairs where he'd have fixed hours. It was supposed to be a clean slice of law enforcement, black-and-white with no gray areas.

ALEX UNLOCKED HER DOOR and slipped inside the safety of home. The air was cool, but stuffy and still. She walked into the kitchen and paused. She listened to the room for some sign of life because, right now, she felt dead. She heard the hum of the fridge, the churning of new ice in the freezer, but no human sounds.

Despair rolled through her, squashing her hopes. The madness of it all exploded somewhere deep inside her. A wild laugh pushed up inside her throat like steam rising. She clamped her mouth shut and pressed her face against her hands. After a moment, she walked to the sink and splashed cool water onto her face. The cold was numbing, but it revived her. She dried her face and lifted her hair to press a damp paper towel to her neck.

She dropped onto the sofa and covered her face with her hands. Now, fury almost choked her. She told herself that she'd left the world behind. It didn't help. Angry tears filled her eyes and spilled onto her cheeks. Choked by disappointment and regret, she wondered why Gage had deceived her about the tapes. What a fool she had been. He'd sold out after all. She ordered herself to think. She couldn't give up now.

The telephone rang and the shrill peal pried her from her thoughts. "Hello."

"Alex?" Jill's tone conveyed urgency.

"Hi," Alex said, taking more comfort from the sound of her roommate's voice than she had expected.

"I've been trying to reach you for a couple of days. You okay?" Jill asked.

"I'm fine," Alex said. "Where are you?"

"Still in Mexico. I wanted to know how you were.... How's it going?"

Alex had dreaded this moment from the instant she answered the phone. "Jill, I've got bad news."

"Oh, no. What is it?"

"It's a long story. We may have identified Ken's murderer."

"Who?" Jill asked incredulously.

"Marvin Dickerson."

"Little Marvin? The mechanic?"

"This is even more shocking—he's dead, along with Hector Martinez. And Skip is in a coma at the hospital."

"The lieutenant's son? Oh, Alex, no. I don't get it."

"I'll know more when we get ballistics on Marvin's weapon."

"Are you holding up?" Jill asked.

"I'll get through it."

"I never doubted that for a minute. And I'm right behind you, just in case you fall. Keep it in mind. When you're down, I'm down."

"The biggest disappointment is that Ken's reputation is still on the line," Alex said. "Oh, Jill, what on earth kept him from calling in his location for a backup?"

"I've thought about that." Jill paused for a moment. "Were you able to find out anything from those involved?"

"Not much."

"Anything from the transmission tapes?"

"I haven't been privy to them."

"Maybe the crime started before he reached that deserted road. You've got to listen to those tapes."

"The whole world will hear them tomorrow. They've been turned over to the press. Anyway, if there was anything on them, I suppose it would have been checked out already."

"Maybe not. If the Sheriff's Department has been negligent in their observations, it's just possible they missed some minute detail."

There was a roaring in Alex's head. Jill was right. There was one tiny ray of light still shining from the case. Alex hoped it would be enough to turn the situation around. She would tackle one problem at a time. But there were so many and there was so little time. There were only seven days left.

IT WAS FIVE in the morning, but she'd barely been able to close her eyes. The hospital came into sight and she turned into the east parking lot. Inside the building, she found Tuck. He was hunched over on a sofa in the tiny lounge. He tilted his head back to focus on her. What disturbed Alex most was that she wasn't through dealing him misery. She cared about the old salt and was not without a sense of fairness.

He stood suddenly and reached out to hug her. When he released her, the gray wisps of hair around his ears stood on end. Alex reached out tenderly and smoothed them back. His tears seemed out of character, incongruent with his thick, robust, fatherly body.

"Have you seen Skip?" she asked.

"Briefly."

"How is he?"

Tucker shrugged. His thin smile communicated everything. "The same. No change."

"Tuck, I have to tell you—"

"No, kiddo. I have to tell you something. You did a damn fine job. And that's because you're a fine deputy sheriff. You did what you had to do. I understand that. And that's enough said."

He meant it, and she knew that. "You okay?" she asked.

"I'm a tough bird," he said. "How else could a person have lasted around that place for twenty years?"

After having some coffee and breakfast with Tuck in the hospital cafeteria, Alex prepared to leave. Maybe she could sleep now that things were all right between Tuck and herself. Or, if she couldn't sleep, maybe she could visit Gage Morgan. It was nearly seven o'clock. As she reached the hospital door, she looked back and saw Tucker behind her. His eyes were kind. She knew that look. It meant that everything would be okay. Still, Alex knew better. Things would never be the same again.

She walked out to the parking lot and unlocked her rental car. She slid behind the wheel and rolled down the window. She backed out of the parking space, then saw the lieutenant. He was on the entrance steps, waiting. She eased up beside him.

"Telephone," Tucker said.

"Who is it?"

"Gage Morgan."

"Tell him I'm on my way over right now."

Tucker nodded acknowledgement and turned to go back inside.

Alex pulled out of the parking lot and hooked a left onto the road. Perfect timing, she thought. She had to know if Skip's statement was going to influence the outcome of Gage's report. And she wanted to hear the tapes. The Rancho Grande was already in sight. She zipped along like an overzealous teenager. At an intersection, she raced through a yellow light then swung wide to turn right. Dust flew as she drove into the hotel parking lot. She eased into the first parking space and jumped out without locking up. A brisk walk led her directly to Room 17. She knocked enthusiastically. When Gage opened the door, he looked startled.

"I've called everywhere for you."

"Can I come in?" Alex asked. She forced her voice to sound light.

Her heart was pounding. In the morning light, the sky was turning the color of bruised plums. Rain? Maybe, Alex thought.

"Of course," Gage said, stepping aside.

Inside, they regarded each other across the few feet that separated them. Something leapt between them, charging the air, electrifying it, and its power frightened Alex a little. She felt anxious, the way she had the night in the desert when he had held her. They had crossed a boundary then, and they were about to cross another now. She wasn't sure that she wanted to.

"I thought you would still be upset," he said.

"I got over it. Acting out your anger becomes tedious."

"Look, I'm glad you came, but I was just on my way out the door. Can we continue this later?"

"Is this the brush-off?"

"No. Nothing like that. I have an appointment, that's all. Can I call you tonight?"

"Tonight?" she echoed, knowing that she had absolutely nothing planned, and that she desperately needed some sleep. "Why don't you just drop by?"

"About seven?"

"Fine."

"I'll bring dinner." Gage was quiet for a moment. "You do want me to come?" he asked.

The disappointment in his voice made her smile. She knew she was feeling way too much for him. "Yes, I want you to come," she said, and turned to leave.

Chapter Fourteen

It seemed like only minutes later. The phone was ringing in Alex's ear again, only now, it was midnight. She had waited. Gage had stood her up. She had made herself vulnerable again.

"Alex." Gage's voice sounded urgent. "I know it's late, but I have to talk to you."

"What is it?" Alex demanded in a flat tone. "Just say it, Gage. You had your chance. I waited for you, remember?"

"I'm sorry about that. Something came up." He paused. "Alex, I want you to hear the tapes."

"The tapes?" she asked. She raised up and sat on the edge of the bed, hugging her knees to her with her free arm. "Why now?" She could barely get the words out. "Why after the news has played them for the world to hear?"

"Did you listen?"

"No."

"I want you to hear them because I don't condone what the sheriff did," Gage said. "He turned the tapes over to the media."

"You wasted your time calling me, you—"

"Would you just listen to what I'm saying?" Gage interrupted. "It's not the tapes I'm talking about, it's us."

"Us?" It was an ordinary word, but it possessed power. "Is that what we're talking about?"

"This entire thing is about us," he said.

Alex knew what he was saying. Some part of her seemed to have known it since the beginning. The next question, the necessary question, was the one she didn't really want to ask. "Have you already listened to them?"

"Over and over, and—"

"And now you think you can lure me with them." She stood. Her movements were as slow, languid and controlled as a cat's.

"No," he said. "But we have to talk. The sooner the better. Tonight." Silence hung like an unwanted guest. "It won't be fatal."

"I don't know, Gage," she said. "I'd have to think about it."

"How long do you need?"

"Longer than five minutes," she said.

"All right, then. I'll pick you up in fifteen minutes." He paused. "Alex? Did you hear me?"

She knew the other meaning in the question. "It's late. The impropriety..." she said.

"To hell with impropriety. I need some answers."

What did that mean? she wondered. Did Ken's reputation still have a chance to survive this ugly mess? "What kind of answers?"

"The kind only a partner can give me. How about it? Fifteen minutes?"

"Thirty."

"I take it that's a yes?" he asked.

"It's a yes, but let's talk on neutral ground."

"Thirty minutes," Gage said. There was silence, a click, and then the dial tone buzzed in her ear. Alex felt scared because she was already feeling so much for Gage Morgan, and scared because of what she might hear on the tapes. But she had to listen. She was desperate and time was running out. . . .

THE RIVER WAS a different place at night, with the moon rising over the water, cool and luminous and nearly full. They walked along the bank, she and Gage, their feet bare, the sand cool against their soles. Alex hadn't intended to come here with him tonight. But she had agreed. Part of her wanted to know which man was the true Gage Morgan—the cool investigator from Internal Affairs or the warm, caring man who professed sincere concern for her and her murdered partner. So far, the true Gage remained hidden. Alex knew that camouflage was a professional necessity for both of them. Gage wasn't asking for details about Ken, and she wasn't offering them.

"I can never get over the cold in Arizona," she said. "I got used to the heat, but the cold, it's—"

"Primitive," Gage said, as though only half listening to her.

Alex had made her position clear tonight and Gage was respecting it. He reached for her hand and held it. "You are cold," he said, drawing her hand up to his lips and kissing the back of it.

Alex felt herself shiver. In the moonlight, his eyes were the color of melting ice, cool and seductive. His thumb stroked the back of her hand and moved slowly down the knuckles, then up again. *He's going to kiss me,* she thought. But he didn't. Not then.

"I have to tell you something," Gage uttered in a low voice.

"Go ahead," she whispered.

"It's just that—when I'm with you, you make me feel good. And I don't want anything to get in our way. Not tonight, anyway. Deal?"

She gazed at him in the darkness. The answer was in her eyes. Slowly, he moved his head toward hers. His lips grazed hers briefly, then retreated, then touched again. It was longer this time. And while his mouth lingered on hers, he slid his arms around her waist and cradled her body to his, gently at first. His touch sent blood through her veins, and her head careened as she felt his arms crushing her to him.

Gage traced the shape of her mouth with his own. Abandoning inhibition, her breath grew shallow and swift as she drowned in his kiss. There were no singing birds at this late hour. No ringing bells. Just Alex and Gage falling a little bit in love.

It was too soon, but the kiss eventually broke. They remained locked together, hanging on for life. Alex felt the heat from his uneven breathing warming her ear.

"I've been wanting to do that ever since we flew out of the desert," he confessed.

"I'm glad you did."

"Come on," he whispered. "I'll take you home."

They rode in silence. Thoughts exploded in her mind like lightning from a summer storm. Would it be too forward to ask him in? She couldn't decide. They pulled into the parking lot and Gage eased into a space outside her apartment. After turning off the engine, he sat quietly for a moment. Without warning, Alex opened the door and then turned back to speak. "Come in with me."

He simply nodded consent and slid his six-foot-plus frame out into the cool night air. They didn't converse until they were inside her apartment.

"Make yourself comfortable. I'll put on a pot of coffee."

Alex went through the motions of making the coffee without thinking about what she was doing. She *did* want to hear those tapes. And as soon as the coffee was done, she'd march back in there and tell Gage Morgan. She reached back into the cabinet. The imported cookies would add a nice touch, she thought, readying a tray. She picked it up and headed back into the living room.

"I thought you might enjoy these—"

She didn't finish. Gage had pulled off his shoes. He had made a pillow out of his coat. And he was stretched out on the sofa, sleeping soundly. She pulled an afghan over him and went to bed herself. It was not exactly how she'd expected this night to end.

CONSCIOUSNESS CAME IN gradual stages the next morning. It had been a long time since she'd awakened with a man in the house. Not that there had been that many. Alex considered herself an old-fashioned, straitlaced lady. Yet she wasn't feeling guilty. Uneasy maybe, but not guilty.

She wanted to ease out of bed and make coffee before he woke. It would be a lot easier to face him with her clothes on, too. She got up and slipped on a pair of jeans and T-shirt. In the bathroom, she brushed her teeth and splashed cold water on her face. She padded through the living room, where Gage still slept on the couch, on her way to the kitchen.

He was lying on his back, face toward her, sleeping like a baby. The emotion Gage had drawn from her last night still surprised her. She had been certain that her misery wouldn't surrender to any other feeling. But then, she admitted, nothing was certain these days. Especially when it came to Gage Morgan. She was drawn to him in a way she'd never been drawn to any man before. Alex staunchly refused to submit to allegations in her mind and heart that said she was falling in love with Gage Morgan.

In the kitchen, the scent of just-brewed coffee drifted up from the pot, filling her senses. Alex prepared a tray and headed back to the living room and Gage. She found him still sleeping soundly. "Good morning, sleepyhead."

Alex's words penetrated Gage's dream and he bolted up from the couch. "What time is it?" he asked, bleary-eyed.

"It's after seven. I'm sorry," she soothed while she set the tray of coffee down. "I didn't mean to startle you. When can I hear the tapes?" She hoped her anxiety wasn't too obvious.

"Right now," he answered.

Alex felt a flicker of alarm as she studied Gage's face. His expression grew serious. "What's wrong?" she asked.

"I'm always like this until that first cup of coffee."

She handed him a cup and he accepted it gratefully. Alex lifted her own cup and swallowed a sip, eyeing him over the brim. "There's a recorder on the end table. And I brought your briefcase in."

Gage looked at her with tender appraisal. "Alex, are you ready for this?"

"I don't know for sure," she answered softly, "but I have to hear them."

"No, you don't. I have a transcript you can read."

Alex gasped. "No. That's just words. I have to listen."

The tenderness in Gage's voice had sent a new surge of anxiety coiling through her body. She was about to hear the words that Ken had spoken at the end of his life. Had he known he was about to die? Had he been afraid? Had he made a mistake that night? The only thing she knew was that none of this could have been his fault.

Gage raised the cup to his lips and took another sip of coffee. Alex studied his eyes. After a moment, he sat the coffee down and proceeded to slip the first tape into the small tape deck. Alex set her cup down and stood. She crossed her arms for comfort and went to the window to gaze outside. Unsure of how she was going to react, she sucked in a breath of air and held it briefly, as though it might strengthen her courage.

With his finger, Gage clicked on the tape recorder and heaved a huge sigh. The tape began, and with it, the sound of Ken's voice.

To Alex, it was as if he were standing right there next to her. With her mind's eye, she could almost see Ken in the patrol car, smiling down at her. A sob rose in her throat. Gage stood, went to her and pressed a tissue into her hand. She wiped the tears from her face and continued to listen.

Straining to distinguish the words from the static, a familiar calm embraced Alex. Ken sounded confident. A smile parted her lips. Her partner, her friend, engaged in a brief conversation with the dispatcher. "...ten-twenty... uh...north on...uh...89. Ten-four."

His uneventful departure from the substation hinted at nothing unusual. No yawns from a fatigued deputy. Why would there be? Alex's muscles tensed with apprehension, but she heard nothing at all unusual in Ken's tone. A sense of normalcy was the only pertinent thing the tape was revealing. Misery twisted her heart. She realized that the end of the tape was nearing and that Ken's transmission was breaking up. "Ten-four...913 here...my...twenty...milepost mark...258...89...nor...chas...roa...ru—"

Alex struggled to put sense to Ken's last words, but they were garbled, mixed up. And there was nothing else to be heard. Nothing else to say. Tears streamed down her face. Suddenly, she was sobbing, not only for the loss of Ken, but or all the losses she'd suffered over the past few weeks. For he loss of her job and her confidence. And for her guilt, oo. Deep down inside she had wondered, just like everybody else, if Ken had gotten complacent that night. She drew a quick, jagged breath and spoke in a rush of words. "The tape doesn't change a thing, does it?"

"It's okay," Gage was saying. "It's okay." He put his arms around Alex's shoulders.

"No, it's not okay," she said. "I should have been there."

That was a foolish idea and it destroyed Gage's control. "Damn it, Alex! Thank God you're alive. Had you been here, you'd probably be dead right now, too."

"I didn't expect you to understand," she said while pulling away from him.

"I do understand. I *was* there for my wife, to protect her...." He paused. "She was shot in front of me. All I could do was stand there."

Alex gasped.

"You're among the living," he continued, "and until you et rid of this guilt, you won't get rid of your fear."

"I know it's crazy, but I still can't shake this feeling that f I'd been there, Ken might not have made any mistakes. He vas used to working with me. We were a team. Maybe I ould have prevented—" She couldn't finish. Instead, she it her lower lip. But it was too late. The words were out. And from the look on Gage's face, he hadn't missed the nessage.

"You've had me fooled," Gage said, "I've thought you vere fighting everyone else's conclusions. But you've been ighting your own. You're more certain than I am that your artner made a mistake."

"No. That isn't what I meant."

"I thought you were blaming yourself, but you've been blaming Ken. You're convinced he made a mistake and you're scared—scared you'll make one, too!"

"No! You're wrong. You have no right to make those judgments. I want you to leave."

Gage stepped toward her, arms outstretched, but she backed away. "Alex, you've got to face it before you can deal with it. It won't go away."

"I was wrong about you."

"No. You weren't wrong. My report will still reflect the facts, no matter who it hurts." He paused. "So you see, I'm what you thought me to be all along. But I'm proud that I'm the kind of Internal Affairs investigator who no one can influence. Not you, not the sheriff—"

"You don't have to defend your position to me. Nothing will bring Ken back," she mumbled.

"No, it won't, but doing my job right might save you from dying with him."

She shook his words away. Unconsciously, she chewed on her lower lip.

"It's time you stopped embracing your grief. Stop blaming yourself, and stop blaming Ken."

Choked by guilt and regret, Alex knew Gage was right. And she had to face the possibility that Ken might have made a mistake. Gloom claimed her, stripping away her capacity for any further argument. This conversation had violated her emotional boundaries.

"If you really want to support your partner," Gage persisted, "stand by him in death by accepting his weaknesses as well as his strengths. Ken Forney wasn't just a deputy sheriff. He was a human being, too, and human beings mak mistakes. You can't allow your loyalty to veil the truth. He might have made a mistake, a fatal mistake.''

Alex felt a painful admission showing in her eyes. The dull expression in Gage's eyes told her that she had lost him for good. And in five more days everything else would be lost too. She allowed her gaze to wander away from Gage.

Gage was standing ramrod straight, facing her. "You've got to stop running.'' Without another word, Gage turned and left her apartment.

Chapter Fifteen

The words hung there like the smell of rotten food. Gage
had read and reread the report until he couldn't keep the
words from running together. Either way, it came out the
same: dereliction of duty. He shrugged. Solid evidence
stacked up against Ken Forney. There would be no evading
the issue. The case was airtight. And Gage had a thing about
airtight cases. They made him nervous.

He rocked back in the vinyl chair and studied his tiny cubicle at the substation. The room beyond the cubicle smelled
of stale smoke, wet coffee grounds and the pine cleaner the
janitor used to mop the floor. A plant sitting in the win-
dowsill was turning brown. Gage wondered how anything
could survive in this environment. He stood and walked over
to open the window. Fresh air sounded good. The window
was stuck. "Forget it," he muttered, and sat back down.
The words in front of him seemed to merge. He placed the
report in a brown envelope.

The days had passed with no word from Alex. Two of
them. The silence told him much more than he cared to admit. Thoughts of her had invaded his mind and body with
driving persistence. Before her, his private moods had been
reserved for his wife Laura. Not now. The situation served
to reinforce what he had believed all along, that emotiona

involvements meant trouble. Why was it so hard to admit? He loved Alex. But some people just weren't destined for love, he thought.

Duty above all else, right? he asked himself. He had never compromised his position with his personal feelings. He wouldn't now. He refused to carry this misery over the outcome of his investigation, and what it would do to Alex. It wasn't his cross to bear. Alex was slipping through his fingers once and for all. Maybe it was better that way.

He slapped his hand to his breast pocket. Old habit. He eyed the cigarettes lying on the opposite desk. "What the hell," he muttered, and reached across for one. The cigarette hung in his mouth for a moment while he searched for matches. He clawed and probed recklessly for anything to light the beast hanging from his mouth. His addiction had beaten him. "Doesn't anybody have a match?" He pulled out the thin center desk drawer. One stick match. He scratched it with his fingernail. Nothing. "Great," he grumbled. Again, he struck it, and still nothing. The third attempt ignited the match and he set fire to the cigarette. His eyes narrowed against the smoke he exhaled. Suddenly he sputtered and coughed.

He remembered why he'd quit and ground out the smoldering stick of tobacco. His head spun. He felt weak. He rested his elbows on the desk and closed his eyes. It was no good. He just kept seeing Alex's face.

He opened his eyes and looked down at the brown envelope. He opened it and pulled out the report. The words were the same. So was his opinion. Nothing in his findings could sway him. And changing the report would take some swaying because his mind was made up. In his opinion, based on the facts and the tape, Ken had made a grave error, indeed. An error that cost him his life. He had failed to radio for a backup. But why did his whole profile contradict that mistake? Why hadn't he radioed his location? A twenty-year veteran should have known better.

Gage pushed other distressing thoughts out of his mind. Oh, Ken's wife would get the insurance and the pension. Still, she would have to live with the conclusions Gage was about to make public, that Ken, a veteran deputy sheriff, circumvented procedure and paid the high price of death for his judgment error. Gage settled back to reread his report for the last time.

ONE MORE DAY and Gage would file the report that would cast Ken's lack of integrity in stone. A search of Marvin's house had turned up zilch. The crime lab was still working on ballistics. And Skip's condition remained the same. Everything remained the same.

Emotion clogged Alex's throat as she followed the winding path to Ken's front door. She'd put off this meeting with Ken's wife until the last glimmer of hope was gone. Her previous resolutions to salvage Ken's good name were only roadside skeletons now. Some friend and partner she'd turned out to be. "Follow every lead. Check out every detail before you draw a conclusion," Ken had always told her. But that's what she had done from day one. And it hadn't changed a thing. She knocked on the front door and waited.

"Alex? Is that you?" Sandy asked. She was petite and attractive for her age.

For Alex, the words didn't come. Silence lingered between Sandy and herself. Alex fumbled with her car keys and dropped her gaze to the floor. "I thought it was time," she finally managed to say.

"Come in," Sandy said, pulling the distraught deputy sheriff into her arms.

"I've come to comfort *you*," Alex said in a shaky voice.

"Whatever the reason, I'm glad you're here." Sandy's voice was husky and full of emotion.

The two women embraced. At last when the emotion subsided, they sat down at the kitchen table. Sandy poured coffee.

"Thanks," Alex said. "I would have called sooner." She paused, giving herself a moment to think. "Sandy, it doesn't look good for Ken. I've done all I can...."

"Yes, I know you have," Sandy said, setting down her coffee cup with a resolute sigh. "You simply can't feel responsible, Alex. In my heart, I know there had to have been a reason for Ken's actions. But what's the point in searching for answers where there are none? The investigation is nearing a close?" she asked.

Alex blinked back the mist in her eyes, then said, "That's why I'm here. I wanted you to hear it from me first."

"I appreciate that."

"Sandy, we think Marvin murdered Ken."

"Marvin?"

"Hector Martinez was using Marvin, as well as Skip, to help run his very sophisticated smuggling operation."

"Drugs?"

"No. Exotic animals—among other things. But that's over now." Alex paused. "Hector and Marvin were killed when their truck crashed in the desert. Skip's in a coma."

Sandy sat back in her chair and stared blankly at nothing in particular. Finally, she returned her gaze to face Alex.

"Hector had been operating a smuggling ring. Ken happened along at the wrong time and the wrong place. He scared Hector and Skip. They drove off before Marvin arrived."

"Then that would explain why Ken didn't radio for backup!"

"No," Alex replied. "Ken would have seen only Marvin's headlights. And this is the part I really don't understand. Ken was trapped and outnumbered."

Sandy shook her head. "It looks bad, huh?"

Alex nodded. She had never experienced such total defeat.

"How's Tucker handling this?"

"He got past the denial and now he's holding his own. It's been tough."

"My heart goes out to him," Sandy said. "At times the burden has been more than I can stand. In all the second guessing I've done, I never suspected—never dreamed—that it would turn out to be one of the family. I expected a stranger. Someone who would have meant nothing to me. That would have been easier."

"I know," Alex said.

"Tucker called once," Sandy said, "but he was so emotionally broken up, he couldn't talk. I tried to reassure him. We must have sounded pitiful. Oh, Alex. Why?"

"I wish I understood."

"How have you been holding up?" Sandy asked.

"I'm all right," Alex lied. "How's Paul doing?"

"He's been my rock. I couldn't have gotten through this without his strength and support. Just like his dad..." Sandy's words trailed off.

Alex cleared her throat. "I'd better be going."

"Of course. Thanks for coming. It means a great deal to me. Ken thought so much of you. You know that, don't you?"

"I do."

The next pause that passed between them seemed to last forever. Alex tried desperately to find the right thing to say. When the words left her lips, she felt a burden lift from her shoulders and her soul. She had faced a formidable challenge and had gotten through it. "Goodbye, Sandy."

"No, not good-bye. Ken's gone, but we can still be friends."

They embraced again, and Alex walked out the door. She felt she had failed. Minimizing the impact of Gage Morgan's report had been her goal, but she had failed miserably.

AT THE SUBSTATION Gage was typing Ken Forney's seventy-two-hour profile. The phone rang. He lifted the receiver, if for no other reason than to silence it. "Hello?"

"Gage?" The sheriff's familiar voice drawled through the receiver.

"Yeah," Gage answered in a flat monotone.

"Where's my report?" the sheriff demanded. "What are you dragging your feet for?"

"These things take time," Gage assured him. "You know that." Why didn't he just tell the sheriff that it would be filed in the morning?

"Especially when you use the department as your own private detective agency."

"What's that supposed to mean?" Gage asked.

"Do you think I haven't known what's been going on? You violated procedure with the Sinclair woman."

"Procedure?" Gage echoed. "I've covered for you more times than I care to admit. Where do you get off suggesting that?"

"You promised me a report days ago," the sheriff reminded him.

"And I try to fulfill my promises," Gage said. "But I'm calling the shots on this investigation. When the profile is complete, you'll get your report." The report was finished. Why was he lying?

"Investigate all you want," the sheriff said. "It won't change the outcome of things. Turn in the report and get it over with. I'll expect it in the morning."

"I'll live with the outcome the rest of my life. When I submit my report, there won't be any doubts in my mind. Assumptions have no place in my work." Gage clenched his fist into a ball and pounded it on the desk. "I'll tell you something else. I'm good at what I do. Very good."

"Have it your way," the sheriff said. "But I'm marking time while I wait for that report."

Gage hung up the phone. He began to type again, but another familiar voice startled him.

"When are you going home?" Wes asked.

"*You* ever heard of knocking?" Gage replied.

"You nervous or what?" Wes asked with a chuckle in his tone. Gage answered with silence. "It's almost seven o'clock," Wes continued, looking down to glimpse at Gage's papers. "When will you be finished?"

"Soon," Gage answered. He felt that Wes was waiting for him to say something. When he didn't, Wes picked up the slack.

"Have you had something to eat?"

"Yeah," Gage answered.

"When?"

"Yesterday."

"You look awful."

"Thanks," Gage said.

"Want a pizza?"

"No."

"Go home, my friend," Wes advised him. "You can look at that stuff all you want, but the words are not going to change. Do you know that, Gage? If you don't get some rest, you're liable to die."

"The answer is in here somewhere," Gage said.

"It always is, and it'll be there tomorrow."

"Then let's get that pizza," Gage said.

"I hate pizza," Wes grumbled. "Let's get drunk."

Ten minutes later, they slid onto bar stools at the Bar Seven. Entering the restaurant was like taking a trip back in time. Classic adobe construction using native designs created the character of the Wild West. Sculptured walls provided an ideal backdrop for the artifacts displayed. A multicolored Navaho rug covered every glass-topped table. Gage tilted his head back and admired the carved corbels and coved ceilings. The only thing missing was a dozen or so horses tethered just outside the door. A beehive fireplace in one corner of the dining room added to the informal atmosphere.

"What do you want to eat?" Wes asked. "Hey, Gage, what do you want?"

Gage looked up and saw a waitress flit past. She slammed down two cups of coffee. Wes had apparently nixed the idea of getting drunk. To Gage, the coffee tasted weak and it was barely warm. Willie Nelson was singing "Blue Eyes Crying in the Rain" on the jukebox.

"Sorry," Gage said. "I'll have anything you're going to have."

"Food. I'm having food. What we have here is a restaurant. They bring you food here."

"I don't know what I'm doing anymore," Gage said. "Do you know what I mean?"

"You're just playing a game," Wes replied.

"So that's why I've spent two years as an IA man?"

"The ground rules keep changing," Wes informed him. "The bad guys have a stronger team right now. You like to suffer, Lieutenant. You wear suffering like a fine pair of boots."

"You want to match ulcers?" Gage asked.

"They got a spicy chili burger here that'll either burn them out or kill you," Wes said.

"You're on."

Wes ordered for them, and Gage pressed on about the investigation. If he could somehow minimize the inconsistencies, it could influence the outcome of his report.

"You knew Ken Forney?" Gage asked.

"Everybody knew Ken."

"How did the man and the deputy mix?"

"Ken would have rather died then corrupt his position with the Sheriff's Department," Wes said. "He had a strong mind, a powerful will, and he didn't know the word *temptation*."

"Sounds like the man had integrity."

"The way I see it," Wes said, "it was no accident that Ken was out there that night."

"Let me see if I get this," Gage said. "You don't believe it was a bizarre coincidence that Ken drove onto that deserted road?"

"For a while, I did. I kept wondering if he'd followed someone out there."

"No good," Gage said. "In a remote area, a tail is a dead giveaway. I checked. We had a full moon the night Ken was slain."

"And that being the case," Wes added, "he could have picked up light reflecting off a car from the road."

Gage's implacable expression vanished, wiped away by astonishment. He answered quickly over his choking, beating heart. "That's what I've missed."

Thoughts spun in his head while he worked to untangle the web. Gage knew finding the way through a maze meant starting at the beginning. Why not revisit the murder scene one last time?

"You're a fine investigator," Wes was saying. "I owe you an apology. I underestimated you." The remark gave their newly found friendship a different edge. "But I've got to tell you, you're everything a cop doesn't like about an Internal Affairs investigator. You're tough, intelligent, direct and unapologetic."

"I'm not sure, but I think I just received a compliment," Gage admitted.

"You haven't eaten," Wes said. "What are you doing?"

"Something I've got to do."

"What?"

"I need to visit the crime scene again."

Wes was too startled to offer any objection. "Okay, I'll drive you," the lanky deputy suggested.

"No," Gage said. "I have to do this alone." If he was going to have to live with his report for the rest of his life, he didn't want anyone else to blame for it.

Chapter Sixteen

Alex wondered what had gotten into her. Gage had far too much integrity to compromise his job. She admired that about him. Why couldn't she admit to him that he was right? That even she blamed Ken, in part, for his own murder.

She paced in her living room, torn between right and wrong. It was clear Gage had given up on her. And why shouldn't he? She deserved it. The important thing now was to get on with her life, to get back on the active-duty roster and begin working again. But the only way she could do that was to call Gage. It had been Tuck's decision finally, but Gage had requested the desk-duty assignment. It was up to him to get her back on patrol. She'd proven herself, hadn't she? All she had to do was call him and ask.

The pain she'd seen in Gage's eyes that night in the desert still haunted her. He had loved his wife deeply. Now, Alex was at an impasse. She would have to overcome it before she could deal with anything else. She was in love with Gage Morgan, and that feeling was bursting forth inside her.

She flopped down on the couch and hugged a pillow to her. He wasn't going to call. It was over and she wasn't going to hear from Gage Morgan again. She turned her face into the pillow, wondering how she would deal with that. All day, she'd been filled with a need to see him, touch him or to at least hear his voice. Suddenly, she threw the pillow down.

She owed Gage an apology. Her misery had forced her to manufacture conclusions—the wrong conclusions. She wanted no illusions between them, even if their affection for each other was over. But she didn't want it to be over! And, she thought as long as one breath remained in her lungs, it wouldn't be over.

"BULLNECK," ALEX SAID. "Where's Gage?"

"Dunno," the desk sergeant mumbled. He seemed irritated that she had interrupted him. He was reading the newspaper.

"Wes's truck is outside. Where is he?"

"Lifting weights in the basement." Bullneck paused. "No, I think he went into the showers."

"Thanks," she called over her shoulder.

"Hey! Where you goin'?"

"To the locker room. I need to talk to him."

She strode into the musty-smelling area and called out to Wes. "Hey in there."

"Hold down a bench," Wes called back. "I'll be out in a minute."

She'd looked in Ken's locker a thousand times, and a thousand times she'd seen the same thing—nothing. At least nothing unusual. Notepads, a box of ammo, felt-tip pens. Felt-tip pens. Ken used felt-tip pens. No wonder there were no impressions for the lab to pick up from his notepad. If he had written a report, it could have been ripped off and destroyed, leaving no trace on the blank pages of the pad.

"Pitch me a towel from my locker," Wes's voice echoed from the shower room.

"Okay."

A minute later, he appeared.

"What are you doing here?"

"Looking for Gage Morgan. Have you seen him?"

"Yeah. Around seven he said he was headed out to revisit the crime scene. Should be back by now. Did you try his room?"

"He's not there." She looked at her watch. Nine o'clock. Her heart plunged. "I'm going after him."

"Alex, wait—"

"What is it?"

"I hope you two get together...."

"Thanks, Wes."

"But be careful. The desert's dangerous. Ken just happened to be at the wrong place at the wrong time. A few minutes later, and he might have followed Marvin in."

"Yeah. Right. I gotta go." Alex grabbed her purse, feeling driven, and burst through the rear door, heading to her car. Determined to find Gage, she headed out Highway 89 to the desolate spot where Ken had been murdered. Fears and insecurities were left behind. Her confidence repossessed her. She was a deputy sheriff again. And a good one. *But what if Gage isn't out there?* a small voice argued inside her. This was dangerous and foolhardy. But what was new?

Tucker's driveway was just ahead. Alex decided to turn off and inquire about Skip's progress. She slowed the car and turned in. A glance at the windows revealed no signs of life. The house was unusually black, except for the reflections of the moon. A hospital visit would have been a better idea. But the department's Blazer was there. She rubbed the heel of her hand against her temple. What was nagging her about the vehicles?

She shut off the ignition and got out of the rental car. A faint breeze skipped over her, stirring her hair. The dissonant sounds of frogs and buzzing insects rose up from the grounds. A dim porch light lit the stoop enough for her to see the doorbell. She rang it. Nothing. She tried the door. Locked. If Tuck was sleeping, he needed the rest. She decided to leave.

Thank goodness for the full moon. Before she even turned off the highway, she saw a reflection of light in her rearview mirror. A car? Maybe. She took her gun off the dash, unholstered it and laid it on the seat beside her. The car's windows were rolled down and the wind rushed by, smacking her in the face. She was wide awake and alert. She kept one eye on the rearview.

It wasn't unusual for traffic to be on the roads at this time of night, but once past the Aguila turnoff, U.S. 89 turned into a desolate stretch of highway. It climbed up Yarnell Hill to a treacherous stretch of winding, hairpin turns leading to Prescott. This was the scenic route that tourists drove during the day. So who did the headlights behind her belong to?

She sucked in air when her chest constricted, and she felt the back of her neck tighten into knots. She knew that if she glanced around, she would draw attention. Instead, she sped up and cut her headlights. Then, without warning, Tucker's voice bounced over the shortwave channel Alex was monitoring. She nearly ran off the road.

"Will the nine-seventeen with the nine-eighteen come back, please?"

Tucker had just called her a crazy woman with a gun. Normally, she would have found humor in the remark. Right now her hand was shaking, so she barely managed to pick up a mike and respond. "Tuck, I just left your house."

"Pull . . . the . . . I want to . . . you."

"Come back?" she said.

"Pull . . ."

There was only silence. Her car radio had gone dead. And now, Tuck was tailgating her. The Inspiration Mine turnoff jumped in front of her and she slammed on the brakes to make the turn. The Blazer almost rear-ended her. She made the turn. The car barely sat down between bumps as she sped down the road.

"I can't believe it!" Alex yelled. "Why is Tucker doing this?"

She drew quick, short breaths. Her heartbeat thundered in her ears. With only the moon to light her way, she didn' see the other car in time to stop. She slammed on the brakes, then fishtailed, spinning off the road. She had narrowly missed Gage's car.

Gage ran quickly over to her. "What the hell were you trying to do?" he demanded. When he recognized Alex, fury yielded to shock. "Alex? Are you crazy coming ou here alone like this?"

"I—I was worried about you."

"Are you hurt?" he asked, pulling her door open.

"Just shaken," she assured him. "Gage, Tuck followed me out here. I don't know what came over me. I got scared. We were talking on the radio. Our connection just broke up."

"You're primed for paranoia," he told her.

"No," she said. She looked around in time to see head lights. "Here he is. Take my gun," she said. She shoved the .38 into Gage's hand.

"Wait a minute. There's another car. I think—it's Wes!" Gage said.

Wes eased his patrol car in behind the Blazer. He got out at the same time that Tucker did. The two men walked toward Alex and Gage.

Alex's gaze connected momentarily with first Tuck's, then Wes's. Then she went on the attack.

"Why wouldn't you answer your door?" she demanded of Tuck.

"I was on the phone with Wes. He called, worried about you. He wanted me to follow you out here. I had to get my clothes on."

"You nearly scared—"

"Just hold on," Tuck cut in. "I've got some news for you."

Alex stiffened.

"Ballistics confirmed Marvin's gun as the murder weapon."

Alex hadn't realized she'd been holding her breath. She released it. Her body sagged. It was over. But she still had a score to settle with Wes. "Why did you follow me out here?" she asked him. Did he think her incompetent? Of course. That had to be it. Well, she would tell him a thing or two. "Now, you listen to me, Wes Davenport. I'm a deputy sheriff, too. I wear a badge and a gun just like you. I can outshoot you, outrun you and outfox you any day of the week. Are you going to tell me why you followed me out here?"

"I've been trying," he said in an even tone. "You haven't stopped talking."

Alex felt his eyes burning a hole through her.

"I was worried about you coming out here alone in the middle of the night," he said. "I'd have been worried about any deputy pulling a stunt like this. Actually, I've always kind of liked the idea you were a woman," he added. Wes didn't seem to recognize the chauvinism in his own remark.

"I'm sorry, Wes," Alex admitted.

"Me, too," Gage conceded. "But it's a good thing someone happened along. I've been stuck for nearly two hours."

"Why didn't you radio for help?" Wes asked.

"I tried, but my radio went dead."

His radio went dead, too? Coincidence? Alex doubted it

"I don't think this isolated little valley allows radio waves in or out of it," Alex mumbled. She looked up toward the transmitter tower on Yarnell Hill.

"What?" Tuck asked.

"When Ken drove onto this road, he drove into a radio dead zone. Don't you see," she pleaded, "he couldn't have called for backup if he'd wanted to. He never had a chance."

"Probably not," Gage said, shaking his head slowly. "I suppose from there it's history."

"You need assistance getting clear?" Wes asked.

"No, thanks," Gage said. "The Blazer will do fine."

"I'm out of here, then," Wes said. "See you all back at the station." When he reached his patrol car, he wheeled around. "I never thought I'd say this, but I'm glad you two are— I'm relieved that the two of you— What I'm trying to say is that you two belong together," he muttered. "Tuck could pull you over these sand dunes all the way back to Wickenburg with that roadrunner." Wes waved and continued walking toward his car.

Roadrunner? Roadrunner...roadrunner. While the word spun in her head, Alex pressed her temples. Oh, no! That's what Ken was trying to say that night. He'd spotted the Blazer. Wes was nearly to it now.

"Wes!" Alex called out. "Wait a minute."

The lanky deputy wheeled around slowly, his gun drawn.

"Drop your weapons," he ordered Gage and Tucker.

"Take your best shot," Gage challenged, "I'm gambling I can drop you first, and if I don't, Tucker will."

"The first bullet belongs to Alex," Wes warned. He aimed for her head.

Tucker reluctantly obeyed. His gun thudded onto the sand. But Gage stood his ground.

"You nearly pulled it off," Alex whispered. "You came o close."

"I had a hunch, but ballistics—" Tucker began.

"He switched the guns," Alex cut in. "Didn't you? You emoved Marvin's .38 that night and replaced it with the one ou used."

"You've always been bright," Wes jeered.

"You were driving the Blazer that night," Alex continued. "You and Marvin. But it was Ken who arrived here irst."

"A clever guess."

"No. I became suspicious at the substation when you said verything would have turned out differently if Ken had arived after Marvin. How could you have known who arived first? But that missing detail explained the lack of car racks. All you had to do was offer backup."

"What about the animal blood?" Gage asked.

"That's the reason it all came down to this," Wes said. "Ken drove by the garage to see if Marvin wanted to ride vith him. Marvin said no, but figured Ken was headed in the vrong direction. Who could have known he'd come out this vay on U.S. 89? We seldom patrol here at night."

"Maybe something caught his interest," Alex said.

"He must have spotted Hector and Skip and followed hem. By the time Marvin and I arrived, clouds covered the ull moon. We didn't see Ken."

"But the animal blood?" Alex pressed.

"I hit a dog driving out here and stopped. Marvin got out o see about it. He had blood on his hands and his concience. He must have transferred it to the car when he ooked in after I shot Ken."

Alex cringed. "But why'd you kill him, Wes?"

"I've been competing with him for a long time. You and I could have been friends, if you'd given it a chance. He always got what I wanted."

"So you took his gun after you shot him," Alex said, "to make him look like a coward."

"You're grabbing it real good," Wes said. "I applied for the detective slot. Tucker had his mind set on promoting Ken." He paused. "When I learned that Skip had taken the Damato file, I began paying attention to him—something his dad never did."

"So you decided to blackmail Hector. But how did you know he'd be out there with Skip?"

"Not much gets by you, gal. The kid told Marvin everything. We had a load of birds in the Blazer. Marvin had just smuggled them across the border. Your partner put it all together real fast."

Still shaken from the turn of events, Alex wondered why the process had narrowed down the good guys instead of the bad.

"You can't kill all of us," Gage said.

"No, but a tidy accident could, while you drive up Yarnel Hill to examine the transmission tower. A distraught father at the wheel—" He paused. "Alex, I didn't want it to end this way, but I'm relieved it's finally over."

"Not quite over," she responded. "If you check, you'll find I unloaded your gun while you showered at the substation. Call it intuition or call it good police work. I'm a cop, Wes. Don't you ever forget that."

"Shrewd, but it won't work," Wes said.

Alex wheeled around to face Gage and Tuck.

"Cuff him," she said.

Gage helped Tuck handcuff Wes and load him into the Blazer. Then the lieutenant walked over to speak to Alex.

"Nice police work, kiddo. A good cop never loses sight of the objective."

"Yeah? Well this cop is shaking like a leaf."

"Then that makes two of us," Tuck said, and wheeled round to leave.

"Three," Gage chimed in.

"Alex can pull you out," Tuck said, gesturing to Gage's car.

"We'll ride back together," she said. "We can send a tow truck for his car."

"Alex," Gage said. "How did you—"

"I owe you an apology, Gage," she said, cutting in.

"Wait a minute," he said. "I have something I have to tell you."

This is it, she thought. *He's filing his report, and then he's leaving.* That's what he came to do, she knew that. He owed her nothing.

Gage stood there quietly for a moment, as though lost in thought. "It's peaceful out here," he finally said.

She nodded, realizing he was chattering, making idle conversation, but the longer they talked, the longer she could put off the inevitable. He turned to face her square on. A look of frustration fitted his features.

"I'm a man who can admit he's wrong. And I've been wrong," he began. The words poured out, bumping into one another. "From the first day, this case looked hopeless, pointless, just an exercise in procedure. But I was wrong about you. You're a fine cop, Alex."

"What made you do this? I mean coming out here again?" she asked. Looking into his eyes, she thought about how desperately she needed him. "The evidence was damning."

"I didn't care what the evidence said," he told her abruptly. "Ken Forney's profile said he wasn't the type of deputy who went on a midnight run to the middle of nowhere, not without a reason or a backup. And that was the confusing part of the mystery." Gage fixed his glance on

Alex, with kindness in his calm gray eyes. "I never doubted what you were telling me. I just couldn't prove it. Until now. We got lucky. I'll be honest with you, I thought it highly unlikely that I could clear Ken in my report."

"Oh, Ken . . . Ken . . ." Alex said, her voice breaking. Ken had nearly been trapped by the system. Rage diluted her sorrow. It was such an injustice, and it threatened to choke her. How could the whole thing have been prevented? She folded her arms defensively across her stomach, as if to say, Don't hurt me any more.

"That's right," Gage said with heartfelt conviction. "Go ahead and let it out. I'm here for you. Lean on me."

She leaned into him. His arms felt so strong around her, so dependable and so loving. The truth about Ken's murder had been found, and the pain she'd felt all along reared its head like an ugly serpent. She'd waited a long time to tell her partner goodbye. It seemed appropriate now that she bid him this final farewell out here where he had paid the ultimate price, where he had surrendered his life. Alex spoke in a shaky voice. "You were right all along about everything." Her head reclined, and her eyes held tears. "And I was wrong about a lot of things. About why you came here and about what you do, what you stand for. Can you forgive me?" *I love you, Gage Morgan,* she thought. His face twitched as if he'd heard the thought.

"I've told you before," he said. "It's impossible to draw the line without moving it. Alex, you can't let this thing drag you backwards. Let go of it. Forgive and forget. Ken's cleared."

So why didn't she feel better? Perhaps because this was an empty victory. It couldn't bring Ken back. She looked up at Gage. "Thank you."

"For what?"

"For keeping this investigation open, for saving his reputation against all hope, and maybe for saving another deputy's life in similar circumstances. Anyone else would have given up the effort long ago and gone with the obvious. And the obvious truth might have killed someone else."

"Don't make it sound as though I've made such a difference," he said. "I held off on submitting a report because I had to. It was my job."

Alex had tired of hearing that last statement until now. She forced her eyes open wide. "I suppose we're finished here," she said, hoping the moonlight wouldn't reveal the sadness in her eyes.

"It's over," Gage said.

That sounded so final. His words stung. He was speaking again, prying her out of her denial.

"Alex, there's something else."

Goodbyes. He was going to tell her goodbye, she decided. His timing was appropriate enough. But that wasn't making it any easier for her. She could be strong about this. She would simply walk away.

"Looks like you've got a vacancy to fill," Gage said, his voice intruding on the silence. "You'll be needing a new partner."

No, she thought miserably. *It can't be over, not like this.* "Are you saying goodbye?"

"Alex, listen to me." Gage tried to pull her closer to him, but she recoiled.

"Don't touch me," she said. How could she just walk away from him? She loved him.

"Alex, will you just listen to me!"

"No! I—I don't want to hear goodbye," she said.

"Look at me," he coaxed, turning her chin up toward him. "You'll never hear goodbye from me. The truth is, I've been miserable these past few days. I don't want to be without you, Alex. I have to work out some very important things. It won't be easy, but if you'll have me, you do need a new partner."

Partner? Had she heard him right? "Are you volunteering?"

"Alex, I've made a decision. I'm turning in my resignation as soon as I file my report. And it just so happens that I'm looking for a partner, too, for my new business venture. I received my PI license from the Department of Public Safety in the mail today. It'll be tough going for a while, but—"

"Sorry, but I already have my life mapped out," she informed him.

Gage stared dumbfounded.

"I'm resigning from the Sheriff's Department, too. There's this man I'm crazy about. We're going to get married, have a few kids and hang out a private-eye shingle."

"Come here," Gage said, even though she was already wrapped in his arms. "You're about as subtle as a plane crash."

Alex stood in his arms, smiling, like she'd belonged there all her life. She hooked her arms tightly around his neck. Moonlight varnished the surface of his eyes and they twinkled. Her new-found strength was shaken by his touch.

"We've got a report to file," she whispered.

"Just how many kids did you have in mind?" he asked in a lazy, sexy voice.

"Oh, an even dozen or so."

"I love you, Alexis Sinclair."

"I know," she whispered, and with soul-deep honesty, she added, "and I love you."

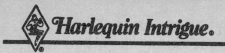

It looks like a charming old building near the Baltimore waterfront, but inside 43 Light Street lurks danger ... and romance.

Labeled a "true master of intrigue" by *Rave Reviews*, bestselling Rebecca York continues her exciting series with #179 SKIN DEEP, coming to you in February 1992.

Dr. Kathryn Martin, a 43 Light Street occupant, suddenly finds herself caught up in the glamorous world of a posh Georgetown beauty salon when her sister is found dead. Not even former love Mac Mackenzie can believe the diabolic schemes Katie uncovers....

Watch for #179 SKIN DEEP, in February 1992, and all the upcoming 43 Light Street titles for top-notch suspense and romance.

HARLEQUIN

Romance®

This September, travel to England
with Harlequin Romance
FIRST CLASS title #3149,
ROSES HAVE THORNS
by Betty Neels

It was Radolf Nauta's fault that Sarah lost her job at the hospital and was forced to look elsewhere for a living. So she wasn't
particulary pleased to meet him again in a totally different environment. Not that he seemed disposed to be gracious to her:
arrogant, opinionated and entirely too sure of himself, Radolf
was just the sort of man Sarah disliked most. And yet, the
more she saw of him, the more she found herself wondering
what he really thought about her—which was stupid, because
he was the last man on earth she could ever love....

Coming Soon

Fashion A Whole New You
in classic romantic style
with a trip for two to Paris
via American Airlines®, a
brand-new Mercury Sable
LS and a $2,000 Fashion
Allowance.

Plus, romantic free gifts* are yours to
Fashion A Whole New You.

From September through November, you can take part in
this exciting opportunity from Harlequin.

Watch for details in September.

* with proofs-of-purchase, plus postage and handling

Harlequin Intrigue®

COMING NEXT MONTH

#169 PAST SINS by Alice Harron Orr

A suicide at the family's upstate New York manor
brought heiress Gretchen Wulfert home. But her life
in posh European watering holes hadn't prepared her
for her sinister legacy of darkness and danger... or
for handyman Boyd Emery. Suddenly she found
herself relying body and soul on a man well versed in
the art of deception.

#170 FUGITIVE HEART by Carly Bishop

Once, Bree Gregory and Michael Tallent had been
friends—and all too briefly, lovers. Now, Michael
turned up in the small Colorado town to which Bree
had fled. She'd taken on a new identity, to hide the
tragic secrets of her past and to protect her son—
Michael's son. Then she found herself the target of
an unknown killer. Thrust once more into Michael's
arms, could she trust him again?

Speak no evil...

Alone on the desert's moonlit sands, Alexis
Sinclair's partner became a murder victim in forty-
five very silent minutes. Internal Affairs
investigator Gage Morgan had uncovered no clues,
no leads and no answers to the most disturbing
aspect of the crime.

Why hadn't a veteran cop called for backup? Alexis
had a hunch—one that led her deep into the stark
Arizona desert.

Snakes, scorpions and rock slides were standard
fare for a homegirl like Alexis. In fact, she thought
she knew all the dangers of the vast arid landscape.
But her education was just beginning...and Gage
was proving a fine teacher.

ISBN 0-373-22168-1

22168

0 65373 00275 4

PRINTED IN U.S.A.